DARKEST MATE
REJECTED FATE BOOK ONE

ALEXIS CALDER

This book is a work of fiction. The names, characters and events in this book are the products of the author's imagination or are used fictitiously. Any similarity to real persons living or dead is coincidental and not intended by the author.

Copyright © 2021 by Alexis Calder
All rights reserved.

No part of this book may be reproduced in any form or by any electronic or mechanical means, including information storage and retrieval systems, without written permission from the author, except for the use of brief quotations in a book review.

Cover Artwork by Melody Simmons
Editing by Court of Spice

Also by Alexis Calder

Moon Cursed Series

Wolf Marked

Wolf Untamed

Wolf Chosen

Royal Mates Series

Shifter Claimed

Shifter Fated

Shifter Rising

Academy of Elites Series

Academy of Elites: Untamed Magic

Academy of Elites: Broken Magic

Academy of Elites: Fated Magic

Academy of Elites: Unbound Magic

Brimstone Academy Series

Brimstone Academy: Semester One

Brimstone Academy: Semester Two

Bloodfire Academy Series

Bloodfire Academy: Cursed Magic

Romcom books published under Lexi Calder:

In Hate With My Boss

Love to Hate You

CHAPTER ONE

THE SMELL of sweat and cheap beer permeated the air, the scent sour and familiar. The soles of my shoes stuck to the floor as I walked, creating a squelching sound. I glanced down, making the mistake of seeing the floor in the daylight. It was dim in here, but the sticky residue of spilled drinks and dark spots that were probably blood weren't hidden yet. In a few hours, it would be too dark to notice. I hated this place in the day. It reminded me of how awful it really was but it was the best paying job I could land.

The Night Howler was a dark and dingy bar with a dozen tables, a long bar with stools, and a scuffed-up dance floor. The windows were caked in grime, letting in little light. By sunset, the bare bulbs hanging from the exposed ceiling would cast long shadows on the already sketchy patrons.

Howler was the only bar in the Fringes, so it was the

hottest place to be after a day of doing whatever it was the members of my pack did. I learned from a young age not to ask too many questions. Life in the Shadow Pack was different from other packs. We were misfits, rejects, and criminals. Shifters cast out from society, or as in my case, abandoned, with nowhere else to go. If you thought too long on any of it, you started to feel guilty. Or at least I did, but I couldn't say the same for the rest of my pack.

Ahead, I saw the band on the wobbly stage setting up. They plugged in guitars and microphones, stopping every few seconds to take long swigs from their beers. I knew Holden didn't pay the bands he booked to play here, but they got free booze all night long. Some of the bands even tipped well when we dropped their orders. I paused, trying to discern which group it was tonight. My shoulders slumped. Blake Shreave's band didn't tip. And after a few drinks, Blake got grabby. I was going to have to steer clear of the stage tonight.

"Hey, gorgeous," Blake called. "How about meeting me in the bathroom between sets tonight."

I rolled my eyes. "You know it's never going to happen, Blake."

"Why not, sweetheart? You're good at taking orders. Just let me take the lead. You might like it," he said.

"You couldn't handle me," I said.

"Is that a challenge?" He raised his brows.

"Go back to your band, Blake," I said.

"Later it is." He raised his beer bottle in the air, then

took a swig. "You'll be begging for my cock sooner or later."

"Sure, you keep telling yourself that while you give your right hand a workout," I said as I tied my apron around my waist.

Blake's bandmates laughed. "She's got your number," one of them called.

I grinned, enjoying the angry look on Blake's face. Asshole had spent years hitting on me but never once tipped. I'm not saying I'd jump into bed with him if he paid me, but after watching couples on dates, I could confidently say the guys who tipped were the better choice. The ones who stiffed me were always the assholes. Not that I needed to see his tipping habits to know Blake was an asshole. We'd gone to high school together, and I knew far too much about how awful he was.

I crossed the empty dance floor. A couple of regular patrons were already scattered around in booths or at the bar. Kayla, who was behind the bar tonight, lifted her chin by way of greeting before returning to stirring the bucket of margarita mix. We'd go through the entire five-gallon tub tonight, as usual.

I stopped in front of the bar. "Hey, Kayla. How was your night off?"

"Eh, you know. Partied till dawn, hooked up with a hottie, robbed a bank."

I chuckled. "So Netflix marathon in sweat pants?"

"You know it." She smiled.

"Who else is on tonight?" I asked.

Kayla shrugged. "Louis will be back here with me in an hour."

"Please tell me I'm not working the floor solo again tonight." My boss had been cutting shifts lately, and I'd worked on my own a lot. Sure, I made bank those nights, but there was a reason the only thing any of us had the energy for on a night off was Netflix. "I don't think I can handle Friday crowds on my own."

"I thought it was Darleen and Kennedy, but they should have been here already." Kayla pulled the spoon out of the margarita mix and popped a lid on it.

"Well, we'll make the best of it, I suppose." If they didn't show, I'd get my ass kicked, but I'd probably make enough for my entire rent tonight. That would give me extra to throw at my debt to the pack.

"Hey, careful when you check in with the boss. He's in a mood today," she warned.

"Thanks." I gave her a little wave and turned toward the kitchen. The small staff of cooks was busy prepping along the back counter. None of them noticed me when I walked inside.

We only sold a few menu items, but shifters ate as much as they drank. It wasn't unusual for a male to order a couple of burgers and a plate of nachos for himself. Some of the ladies ate that much, too. The more often we shifted, the higher our metabolisms. I had yet to experience it for myself, though. I wasn't in a hurry for my first shift, but I knew it would come soon. When you weren't invited to the parties or midnight runs, the thought of shifting was a little sad. I knew once I had my first shift, I'd need to run in the woods on occasion, but doing it alone felt pathetic. I was hoping I could pay off my debt before my first shift, but it wasn't likely.

I walked past the deep fryer. The dark oil was already steaming and the scent of yesterday's French fries seemed to hang in the air like a cloud. At least the floor wasn't sticky back here. While they might not ever clean the front, the head cook kept the stainless steel and tile surfaces of the kitchen spotless. It was one of the few places I was willing to eat at in the Fringes.

The office door was closed. I could see my boss, Holden Baker, hunched over his small desk through the window. I knocked on the glass and put on my best fake smile. I really fucking hated this job. Holden was one of the worst parts about it, but there was no way I'd be on the path to paying off my debt with any other legitimate job.

Holden motioned for me to enter, so I opened the door and stepped inside. The room was more like a closet than an actual office and I was grateful I didn't have to spend much time in here. There was a small desk at the back of the room, covered in papers. His chair was the only one in the office. Behind him was a framed print of dogs playing poker. Everyone knew it covered the wall safe, but Holden seemed to think it was cleverly hidden.

A second door led to a space where Holden stored all the liquor. It was better protected than the cash in the safe. Four separate deadbolts on the door made it a pain the ass to restock mid-shift, but I didn't blame him for protecting his product. Our sales were driven by alcohol and while Holden had the market cornered in terms of bars in the Fringes, he was smart enough to sell the good stuff. People were willing to pay premium prices. His profits went up, and my tips reflected it.

"Tell me Darleen and Kennedy are out there," Holden said.

"Nice to see you, too, boss," I said.

He glared at me. "We have onions that need used."

"Push onion rings. You got it." I hated my job so much. Quickly, I reminded myself that I had three more years of this, then I would be free of my debt. It felt like an eternity, but I'd already survived two years. I could make it a few more.

"Anything else?" I asked.

"Keep an eye on Dax and his friends. Kid might be the next alpha, but I don't want him tearing up my place cause he can't handle his booze," Holden said.

"Got it." Internally, I was hoping that Dax and his friends wouldn't show tonight. He and his friends had been making my life a living hell for as long as I could remember. Their trips home to the Fringes were growing less frequent, and I hoped that trend continued. The only perk of me not being allowed to attend college was that I got a break from them.

Holden went back to the papers on his desk, so I walked to the door. Just as I pulled it open, he cleared his throat. I resisted letting out a dramatic sigh before turning back to him. "Was there something else?"

"You see Darleen, you send her in."

"Sure." I made my exit quickly before he could summon me back.

It was odd that Darleen wasn't here yet. She was a few years older than me and despite the fact that we'd worked together a while; I didn't know her well. She kept to herself and didn't talk much. On weekends, she worked in the bar's basement for half the night, leaving the whole bar for Kennedy and I to run. No matter how many times I'd asked, she never let me in on what went on down there.

Kennedy, on the other hand, was often late. She'd probably show up, eventually. She was good at her job even if she struggled with time management. Kennedy was the closest thing I had to a friend in this shit hole, but we'd never spent time together outside of work. I got the sense that none of us enjoyed being here. We all had something that made the Howler our last resort.

When I exited the kitchen, the band was in full swing and most of the tables were already full. I'd been gone only a few minutes, but Friday night was kicking off.

Pulling a notepad out of my apron, I got to work making the rounds at the tables. All too soon, I was navigating around patrons, carrying drinks and food to tables, and grabbing the dirty dishes to drop in the back. The night was flying by in a rush of activity, keeping me too busy to think.

That was the one perk of this job. When we had a rush,

I couldn't let my mind wander. It took all of my focus to keep up with orders and tables.

As tables cleared out and new customers arrived, I greeted familiar faces and dropped food. It was repetitive and while my face hurt from fake smiling; I had to admit the tips tonight were hot.

I backed into the swinging door to the kitchen, a load of plates in my hands. After I dumped them by the dishwasher, I glanced over at the cooks, who were busy frying and grilling and slicing. I hadn't had a chance to say hello to them yet. "Having a good night back here?"

Anton, the head cook, looked up. "We're nearly through those moldy onions."

I wrinkled my nose. "Moldy?"

"Don't order anything with onion tonight," he said. "Calling them moldy is a kindness."

Sounded like Holden. Cutting corners.

"I'll let Kayla know," I said.

"Ask her for her phone number, too," Anton said.

"Ask her yourself," I called as I headed back to the doors.

A new group of people were waiting at the farthest table and I weaved around shifters who were badly dancing to Blake's band. As I approached, my heart sank. I wasn't in the mood for Dax and his friends. Why couldn't they just stay in the city and go to bars near their school?

I paused and glanced around for Kennedy, hoping she'd shown up. I could guilt her for being late and pass them off to her. Unfortunately, it was still just me and Kayla. With a groan, I walked toward the table.

Dax Carver and his friends were the definition of bad seeds. Growing up, they'd tortured and bullied me for fun. The worst part was that as the next alpha of the Shadow Wolves, Dax was able to get everyone else on board. I spent most of my childhood and teen years nursing black eyes and broken ribs. It wasn't until they left for college that I was able to stop looking over my shoulder every five minutes.

"Well, well, well, if it's not my favorite flower," Dax drolled.

"School finally kick you and your minions out?" While I wouldn't want them back in town, it would make me feel a little better to see them get thrown out.

He smirked. "It's winter break. Lucky for you, we get an entire month away."

Fuck. I forgot about that. They'd all stayed over the summer and I rarely saw them. It had been a wonderful few months. I wasn't looking forward to them staying in town for a while. You'd think they'd want to take advantage of not being stuck in our shitty town.

As Shadow Wolves, we were forbidden to leave the Fringes. The only exception was to attend college in the city, a luxury that only applied to a select few members of our pack. They said it was based on grades and abilities, but we all knew it was determined by status.

"We're having a reunion tonight out by the lake. The whole gang will be there. You should come," Dax said.

"I'm not interested in attending as a piñata. Hard pass," I said.

Stacey, Dax's on-again-off-again girlfriend, giggled, then grabbed Dax's arm possessively. As if she'd ever have to pry him away from me. No, thanks.

I picked up my notebook, ready to move on from them. "Can I recommend the onion rings?"

"Four pitchers of beer, four nachos, and what the hell, add a couple of onion rings," Dax said.

"You got it." I hoped they all got food poisoning and died from the moldy onions.

I turned and walked away from the table, and headed to the bar to get the beer. Kennedy nearly collided with me. She was breathless and her cheeks were pink. Her usually perfectly styled dark hair was in a frizzy mess on top of her head.

"What's wrong, Kennedy?" I asked.

"You don't know?" Her brow was furrowed, and she looked terrified. Kennedy was a tough shifter. On more than one occasion, she'd tossed a rowdy customer from the bar. Like most shifters, she was strong and tall. I was the odd one out at barely over five feet.

"Spill," I demanded.

"It's Darleen. I just heard."

"What about her?" I pushed.

"She stole a car with her boyfriend and tried to sell it to a buyer," she said.

I blinked, waiting for the punchline. That wasn't

anything unusual out here. There had to be something special about the car. "Was it the alpha's car?"

Kennedy shook her head. "The buyer was in Umbra territory. But I heard it was a set-up. They didn't even give them a warning before they ripped out their throats. Two of our pack, just gone."

I sucked in a breath, and my heart raced. Darleen was dead? And by the Umbra Wolves? Everyone knew not to cross into their territory. "Why would she do that?"

"We all get desperate sometimes," Kennedy whispered.

"That doesn't sound like her. She was careful." It didn't seem real. We weren't close, but it still felt like a punch in the gut. She'd been here last night working with me.

"I can't believe the Umbra wolves would lure someone in like that. Darleen was smart. I can't believe she's gone," Kennedy said. "She could be a real bitch, but I never wanted her dead."

We'd all lost friends. It was part of growing up in the Shadows. Most of us learned long ago not to cry. But this felt different. The Umbra Wolves were awful, but I'd never heard of them setting a trap to lure us into their territory.

"She must have really needed the funds." I could relate to that. There were times I was tempted to take the easy way out to earn more cash, but everything had a price.

"I might hate this place, but I guess there are worse options," Kennedy said. "We'll need a new server."

"Yeah," I agreed.

"Boss wants to see you." Kennedy's expression changed. She lifted her chin and all the sorrow was gone from her eyes.

That was how it was here. No weakness. No attachment. Strength at all times. I wasn't the best at that, and had worn my emotions on my sleeves as a kid. It was probably why I'd been targeted by Dax and his gang. I'd gotten better over the years. Harder. I took a deep breath. "Can you put in the order for table eleven?"

Kennedy glanced behind her. "Ugh. Dax and company."

"If it makes you feel better, the onions are moldy." I handed her the paper I'd written their order on.

She grinned. "Maybe I'll send over an extra order or two. On the house."

"I'll throw in some of my tips to help cover that," I said.

She laughed. "You got it."

"Good luck," I said.

"Oh, I don't need any luck. You might with the boss, though. He's fuming mad that Darleen isn't here," she said.

I nodded and turned toward the kitchen. Of course, that would be Holden's reaction. If any of us died, he'd be pissed about the inconvenience it caused him.

Holden was pacing in his tiny office when I arrived. I knocked on the glass. "You wanted to see me?"

He opened the door. "Darleen is dead."

"I heard," I said, keeping my emotions to myself.

"She was supposed to work the event in the basement. Now, I don't have anyone."

"Okay. I'm sorry?" I wasn't sure what he wanted me to say.

"I need you in the basement tonight," he said with a growl.

My brow furrowed. For the last two years, I'd seen shifters take the back stairs to private, very loud, gatherings in the basement. Somehow, he'd managed to keep exactly what went on down there a secret from me. Not even my regular customers would spill. I'd given up on figuring it out. "You serious?"

"I've got a big event tonight and nobody to staff it. So I'm going to trust you with this." He moved closer so he was standing in front of me, looking down at me.

"This is inner circle shit. You can't breathe a word about what you see down there. Do not cross me," he warned.

I lifted my chin, trying to look tough. It was harder while he was standing at his full six feet. Sure, Holden was out of shape and soft around the middle, but he was still a huge male. I'd seen his wolf before, too. I knew enough not to cross him, but if I was getting involved with something illegal, it had to be worth it. "What's the pay?"

He lifted an amused brow. "Are you questioning me?"

"I asked a simple question," I said.

"You want to keep your job, you'll do this," he said.

"You need me. You said so yourself. Make it worth my time," I said.

Holden made an amused sound. "You're going to want to keep that fire about you tonight in the basement."

"There are things I won't do," I clarified.

"Relax. It's the same job you do upstairs," he said. "Tips are better, though."

"Tips aren't a guarantee," I said.

"Standard rate is a thousand dollars if you do well," he said. "Plus tips."

My eyes widened. A thousand dollars on top of tips? That was more than I usually made in two weeks. "I'm in."

"Take the back stairs. Joe will show you where to go when you get down there." Holden crossed his arms over his chest. "And Ivy, for once in your life, play the part of the sweet girl I know is buried deep down."

I quirked a brow. "You sure about that?"

"Trust me on this. Think of it like acting. You play the role, they'll shove cash in your tip jar," he said.

I wasn't sure I liked where this was going, but I knew he had these basement events often. If I could rake in extra every month on top of my regular income, I had a shot at paying off my debt so much faster. Maybe even before my first shift.

My heart raced, and pure elation radiated through me. Once my debt was paid, I could finally have some level of protection and I'd gain my freedom. Until I paid off the debt the pack assigned for raising me as a foundling, I wasn't a full member. I was restricted from what I could and couldn't do. This could change everything.

CHAPTER TWO

As I made my way to the basement staircase, I wondered what I'd find. Gambling came to mind as the most likely possibility. Betting and deals were a big part of pack life, though they were rarely conducted in private. In fact, there wasn't a whole lot that was discouraged in the Fringes. What could be going on down there that had to be hidden away?

As I descended the steps, I could hear the sounds of voices. They cheered and hollered in unison, getting louder with each step I took. When I emerged into the expansive basement, I was hit with the overwhelming scent of sweat mingling with the copper scent of blood. Above the din of people cheering, I could hear the unmistakable sound of fists against flesh. The sounds hit me before I got a glimpse of the men beating the shit out of each other. I craned my neck to get a peek at the spectacle just as a roar of approval reverberated inside the dimly lit space.

The basement was unfinished. Cement floors, exposed beams for walls, and unfinished ceilings were illuminated by bare bulbs. It wasn't much less refined than the upper level, but it added to the feeling of hiding the activities taking place.

A huge, elevated square stood at the center of the gathered crowds. Ropes surrounded it, keeping the viewers apart from the entertainment. Two figures circled, seemingly unperturbed by their black eyes and blood smeared across their faces.

The males were both shirtless and attacked each other by any means necessary. From what I could see in my few moments of watching, there likely weren't rules in this fight. One of the fighters landed a kick to the head of the other, knocking him to the ground. I lost sight of the fight for a moment as I navigated through the throng of onlookers.

When I looked up, I was able to identify the fighters. Melvin Stone, one of my former classmates, was on the floor, his cries muted by the din. Stuart McKenzie, beta of our pack, was holding Melvin down. Melvin screamed as Stuart held the injured man under his foot. Melvin's right arm was bent in an unnatural position and he tried to move to cradle the injured limb. Stuart was faster, and he grabbed the fallen man's arm, pulling upward.

I winced as the sound of cracking bones cut through the yells of the crowd. Melvin howled, an agonizing sound that caused some onlookers to hold their breath, while others intensified their cheers. His body went limp as he succumbed to the pain. Stuart kicked him in the side. "Do you submit?"

Melvin turned just enough to spit blood on the mat. "I surrender," Melvin wheezed. "I submit."

Stuart let go of the other shifter's arm, and rose to his full, impressive height. Arms raised in victory, he grinned at his adoring fans.

I turned away, repressing the urge to throw up. So this was what they were doing down here. Cash changed hands as bets were paid. I still wasn't sure why this was taking place in hiding, but I was glad it wasn't something worse. I could handle getting drinks while a group of shifters watched their friends beat the shit out of each other.

"Ivy?" Someone was tugging on my shirt and I turned to see a small male in glasses who yelled my name.

"Joe?"

The man nodded, causing his glasses to slip down his nose. He pressed them up with his index finger, then locked his gray eyes on me. "This way. I'll show you how we run things down here."

I nodded, trying to hide my surprise at his appearance. From what I knew of Holden, he ran with the big guys. He wasn't a favorite of the alpha, but his friends were other large shifters with questionable businesses.

It's funny, all this time, I thought I was working for a legit company. Turned out, most of Holden's business probably came from the fights. It didn't make sense that this would be hidden, though. I could see an event like this bringing in the whole pack. He was missing out on a lot of paying customers.

Joe stopped in front of a bar in the back corner, manned by two bartenders. The one on the right had an average build and had light brown hair and amber eyes. The other was tall and blonde with bright blue eyes. He was traditionally handsome, but old enough to be my father. I'd never seen either of these shifters around, but both were males who were probably at least twenty years my senior.

"This is Ivy. She's filling in for Darleen," Joe announced.

"So glad you're here. We can't keep up," the blonde bartender said. "I'm Evan, he's Randy."

"Nice to meet you," I said reflexively.

They ran through the details for working the crowd, covered the pricing tiers, and handed me a tray. They stuck a glass on top and Evan shoved a five-dollar bill in the glass. "So they know where to put the tips."

"Thanks," I said.

"Don't fuck it up," Joe called. "These are VIPs. Watch your sass."

"Apparently my reputation precedes me," I said.

"I'm serious. Holden won't tolerate any disrespect with these clients," Joe said.

"I got it. I have been dealing with drunks upstairs for the last two years. I think I can handle it," I said.

Joe didn't look convinced, but I wasn't about to wait around. There were worse ways to earn a thousand dollars. Getting drinks for drunk assholes was what I did.

It didn't take long before I'd made several rounds back and forth between the gathered group and the bar. I was surprised how many shifters I recognized, and how many I didn't. Some of the people in the audience didn't look like they belonged in the Fringes. They were dressed far too nice and carried themselves in a way that stood out. I pushed it from my mind; I wasn't here to judge. I was here to get drunks to part with their cash.

I dropped another round of empty glasses at the bar. "Two gin and tonics, three bourbons straight, and a vodka martini."

Evan got to work pouring the drinks while Randy made some drinks for a group of women who'd walked up to the bar. All of them were dripping in jewelry and even I could tell their shoes and bags were expensive. You couldn't get stuff like that in the Fringes unless you stole it. And if you had it, you'd likely fence it to someone else. There wasn't much reason to dress to impress around here.

The ladies were all laugher and gossip as they walked away. I leaned in close to Randy. "Where are they from?"

He smirked. "Those are Umbra shifters."

"You're shitting me." We weren't allowed to cross into their territory, but in exchange, they stayed out of ours. My jaw dropped open. "So that's why this is so on the down low."

"It's a good gig, kid. Trust me. It's worth keeping your mouth shut," he said.

Evan set the drinks on my tray. "They slum it here for a few hours a week and we get paid."

"So they can come into our territory…" Anger bubbled inside me as I thought about Darleen. She was dead because of members of that pack. They didn't care about hurting us, yet they came here to gamble and watch shifters fight?

"Don't overthink it or it'll make you crazy. Just try to remember you're getting a lot of money from them," Evan said.

I frowned. How was I supposed to fake it around these people?

"Less chatting, more selling," Joe called.

I hadn't even seen him approach, but I didn't want him to know what we'd been discussing, so I grabbed my tray and made my way back to the crowd. Every time I dropped off a drink, the shifters shoved cash in the cup on my tray. It wasn't the usual dollar bills I got upstairs. Most of them gave me twenties. There were even a few hundreds in there. How much money did these people have?

I had just reached the bar again when a voice carried over speakers, filling the whole space with sound. "Attention please." The crowd quieted.

I set the tray down while the bartenders made the next round of drinks and carefully shoved most of my tips into my apron. Then I turned to look at Joe standing in the center of the ring. "We've seen some great fights tonight but we all know what we're really here for."

The audience responded with cheers of approval.

Joe was grinning wide, loving every moment in the spotlight. "Our defending champion. The undefeated Dark Wolf against one of our own, Dax Carver."

I raised a surprised brow. Dax was going to fight someone? I'd been at the receiving end of blows from him, but I'd never seen him in an actual fight. Dax climbed into the ring, bare chested and pumping his fists in the air. I rolled my eyes. He sure knew how to look the part of a cocky asshole.

In the two years since we'd last spent time together, Dax had changed a little. He'd always been handsome, but he'd filled out for the better. His chest was firm and muscular. His shoulders and biceps were strong and well defined. In the booth upstairs, I hadn't noticed how much more mature he looked.

Fuck. When had Dax gone from attractive to insanely hot? Why was it always the assholes who got the good looks?

A second shifter entered the ring. He was in a dark hoodie and had his back to me, but I could tell he was a big guy. Dax looked like he was similar in size, but I couldn't really tell from my place at the bar.

"Ready," Randy said.

I turned back to the bar and picked up my tray. "How long has Dax been coming down here?"

"First time I've seen him," Randy said.

Cash was trading hands and bookies were furiously writing down bets in notebooks as I entered the mass of people. Everyone had pushed in closer to the ring and it was harder to navigate back to my customers.

Several times, I had to back up to avoid having someone walk right into me. The chatter and energy leading up to the fight was palpable. There had been at least six other fights since I'd arrived, and none of them got the crowd this riled up.

I glanced over at the ring, hoping to catch a glimpse of the undefeated Dark Wolf. He had removed his hoodie, revealing a muscular back, strong shoulders and short dark hair. I couldn't even see his face, but I was frozen in place, looking at him wide eyed. There was something about him that pulled me in, forcing me to stare.

He rolled his shoulders, then tilted his head from side to side slowly. As I watched the muscles in his back ripple and his arms flex and relax, my breath hitched. Warmth radiated from my center, and the unmistakable sensation of longing rushed through me.

What the fuck was wrong with me?

I shook my head, trying to break the spell he had over me. Something was very wrong with me. I'd seen shirtless men more times than I could count. It was part of being a shifter. We didn't get freaked out by nudity. But that man wasn't just a normal shirtless male, he was a work of fucking art.

Forcing myself to tear my gaze away, I went back to delivering drinks. It was harder to find the customers who'd placed the orders since everyone had moved closer to the ring.

I was down to my last two drinks when the crowd pushed forward again. I moved with them, managing to maintain control of my tray. I was up by the front of the ring now and Joe had just stepped toward the middle again.

"Last call to place bets," Joe said.

I knew once the fight started, it would be impossible to find the shifters who ordered these drinks. With a sigh, I wondered if I should cut my losses and get out of here before the bell rang.

With a look over my shoulder, I checked on the status of the fighters. That's when I saw his face for the first time.

The Dark Wolf's eyes met mine, and I felt like I'd been punched in the gut. All air left my lungs, and I felt like I was falling. He was captivating in a way I couldn't explain. His dark eyes pulled me in and weren't ever going to let me go.

I couldn't breathe, I couldn't think. The only thing I wanted to do was drag my fingers down his bare chest and get him out of his pants. It was as if I'd lost all control of myself. There was something there between us, a connection that didn't make sense. I felt like I was being pulled into something bigger than myself. It was terrifying and exhilarating at the same time.

"To your corners," Joe called.

The Dark Wolf tore his gaze from me and I stumbled back, as if I'd been released from an invisible hold that had kept me in place. My foot landed on someone else's and I turned too fast, causing the remaining drinks to fall from my tray. They went all over one of the women I'd seen at the bar earlier.

She screamed, and the tray clattered to the ground. I quickly reached down to pick it up. "I'm so sorry."

"You clumsy bitch. This dress is worth more than your life."

"I said I was sorry." I carefully picked up the broken glass, setting the pieces on the tray.

A shadow passed over me and I looked up to see a really pissed off male. He glared down at me. "You ruined my girlfriend's dress."

"It was an accident." I went back to picking up the pieces of glass.

Suddenly, a fist hit my face and I was knocked to the ground. The angry man kicked me right in the gut. I curled up, trying to protect myself as blow after blow hit me.

I heard a collective gasp, followed by the sound of a fist making contact. It took a moment for me to realize I wasn't the one being attacked.

Cautiously, I looked up and saw the Dark Wolf land a punch right in the jaw of my assailant.

CHAPTER THREE

I rolled away to gain some distance between the brawling males. When I pushed myself to standing, the man who attacked me was on his knees. The Dark Wolf glared down at him.

"You touch her again, and I'll kill you myself," he said through gritted teeth.

Panting, I watched the exchange. Who was this guy and why did he care what happened to me? I'd been thrown around a lot and never once had anyone stand up for me.

"Yeah, you got it," the kneeling man said.

"Apologize." The Dark Wolf growled.

"Sorry." The word came out quickly, and he looked up at me with a terrified expression.

I wasn't sure what to do. None of this made sense. I glanced around and noticed that the crowd had backed up, creating a space around us. Everyone was staring.

"Well, do you accept his apology?" The woman I'd spilled on asked.

"Um, sure," I said.

The Dark Wolf grunted, then turned and walked away. I followed him and reached for his arm to get his attention. When I touched him, my fingertips felt like they'd been burned. I pulled my hand away. He stopped and looked over his shoulder at me. "What?"

A rush of heat fueled by desire flooded through me, making me momentarily mute. After a few shaky breaths, I found my voice. "What was all that about?"

"He could have killed you. A thank you is enough."

I arched a brow. "I didn't need you to do that. I can handle myself."

The corner of his lips lifted in an amused smirk. "Sure you can, Sugar."

I narrowed my eyes. "Don't call me that."

He scoffed. "Sugar? You're probably right. You don't seem sweet enough for that name. I am still waiting on my thank you, after all."

"Don't count on it. I told you, I could have handled it," I said.

"If you say so." He walked away, then climbed back into the ring. "We doing this?"

I looked up and caught Dax staring at me, his jaw open in disbelief. Our eyes met, and he closed his mouth, then turned away. He seemed just as surprised as I was that a random stranger had intervened on my behalf.

With my head down to prevent any more attention, I

made my way back to where I'd dropped my tray. To my surprise, the man who had attacked me was holding it and it was full of the broken glass. Even the cash I'd dropped was with the pieces.

"Here's your tray," he said.

I took it from him. "Thanks."

"Look, can we forget that happened?" he asked.

I caught the eye of his girlfriend. She was chewing on her lower lip as if she was nervous. What the fuck was going on here?

"I didn't know you were involved with the Dark Wolf," he added.

I wasn't, even if his words sent a thrill straight to my center. *Fuck.* What was it about that male that made me want to go straight to getting naked with him?

The male and his girlfriend were still waiting for a response, and I was smart enough not to reveal that the whole thing was a big misunderstanding. "Hey, I'm fine. No worries."

They both let out a sigh of relief and I forced a smile on my face as I walked away. I knew the Dark Wolf wasn't a member of my pack. If I'd seen him around town before, I'd have remembered. He was either an Umbra wolf or from one of the neighboring packs, if this was an open event. It was likely I'd only see him again if he came here to fight. My heart raced at the possibility.

Don't be stupid. Even if I was interested in him, pack law forbade us from partnering with outsiders without being full pack members. Even a full Shadow Wolf had to get approval from the alpha to have a relationship outside our pack. Until my debt was paid, I belonged to the Shadow Pack. I had no freedom. The things that were allowed for others were off limits for me.

"Let's get this party started!" Joe called.

The whispers and mummers of the audience turned to cheers as everyone soon forgot about me and got back into position to watch the fight.

Relieved that I wasn't the center of attention, I returned to the bar and set my tray full of broken glass and soggy cash on the counter.

"What was that all about?" Evan asked.

"I have no idea," I admitted.

"That Dark Wolf is dangerous," Evan warned.

"I've seen him take down males twice his size," Randy added.

I lifted a skeptical brow. It was hard to imagine a shifter twice as large as he was. When I'd seen him from a distance, I thought he was similar in build to Dax, but after our encounter, I realized I'd been wrong. He was huge. Probably close to two feet taller than me and solid muscle. I wouldn't want to cross him.

"Okay, fine," Randy seemed to read my expression, "maybe not larger shifters, but he's broken a lot of bones."

"There's a reason he's undefeated," Evan said. "I don't think anyone has a chance against him."

"So you're saying Dax is about to get the shit beat out of him?" I couldn't mask the excitement in my tone.

"You can count on it," Evan said. "If his dad knew he was down here, we'd be shut down."

That caught my attention. "The alpha doesn't know about this?" Our beta had been in the ring when I arrived.

"He's not exactly keen on mixing the packs for anything," Evan said.

That made more sense. We had strict rules on borders. But I was surprised that he hadn't found out yet. "How do they keep it secret? I mean, Dax found out about it."

"Alpha came once," Randy explained. "They set up a night where there were no other packs. Just Shadows. He thinks that's all it is and he can't get in the ring. If someone beats him, he'll lose his place as alpha. Him coming down here puts him at risk of a challenge. You know the alpha can't turn down a fight."

"I didn't realize it applied to a non-challenge fight." Everyone knew you could challenge for the position of alpha. I'd even seen a couple of over-zealous wolves challenge our alpha. They'd all lost spectacularly.

"All fights with an alpha are a challenge," Evan said.

"You might as well wait back here. Nobody's going to order a drink during this fight," Randy said. "We usually clean up since it's the last fight of the night."

"Sounds good." I wanted to watch the Dark Wolf fight Dax, but I didn't want to be rude. I pulled off my apron and set it on the counter so I could count my cash. "What's the tip share down here?"

"No need," Randy replied. "We get a standard rate."

"How much does Holden make off of these fights?" I

asked, knowing that he'd had promised me a huge bonus for doing this.

"They get a cut of all the betting. Plus a fee at the door," Randy explained.

"I'm guessing those aren't little bets." I shoved the cash from my tray into my apron, then walked to a trash can to dump in the shattered glass.

"There's a reason he's willing to risk getting caught. Nobody in the Fringes has the kind of money the Umbra wolves do," Randy said.

Randy, Evan, and I got to work wiping down bottles, washing glasses, and cleaning trays. I stole as many glimpses of the fight as I could. Every time the crowd reacted, I paused what I was doing, my heart racing. Each time I checked, Dax was reeling from an attack, and I breathed a sigh of relief. For some reason, the idea of the Dark Wolf getting injured freaked me out. Who knew I was so easily swayed by a super sexy shifter?

"Go watch," Evan said.

"What? No, I'm helping." I realized I'd been wiping the same tray for ten minutes.

"I know that look. We all know you can't touch, but there's no harm in looking," Evan teased.

I was about to object when a collective groan came from the crowd. I turned to see the Dark Wolf against the ropes. Dax landed a punch on the other shifter's jaw. I gasped and my eyes widened in fear. Without thinking, I set the tray down and took a few steps forward.

Dax punched the Dark Wolf again. His head turned

with the impact and bright red blood ran from his nose. My chest tightened. I wanted to run to him and save him the way he'd saved me.

Suddenly, the Dark Wolf looked over and our eyes met. He winked. I tensed. There was meaning in that expression. Then I realized he was playing.

Dax punched him again, but the Dark Wolf caught his fist with his huge hand, then pulled Dax's arm down. With a movement so fast I nearly missed it, the Dark Wolf turned the tables and Dax was on the ground.

With his knee on Dax's back, the Dark Wolf leaned in. I could tell he was saying something, but I wasn't close enough to hear. Though the cheers and calls from the crowd likely prevented anyone from hearing.

Dax squirmed, trying to break the hold, but he was pinned well. I held my breath, waiting to see if Dax was going to submit. He wasn't alpha yet, but he would be eventually. Losing had to be a blow to his ego.

Suddenly, the lights went out. Everyone gasped and a few people screamed. Emergency lights along the floor flickered to life. I hadn't noticed those, and I was honestly surprised they were there.

"What's going on?" I asked, returning to the bartenders.

"Evacuation," Randy said.

My eyes had adjusted to the dim light and I could now see that the crowd was following the lights to another set of stairs to exit the basement. Dax was still on the ground in the ring, but the Dark Wolf was gone.

The lights flickered back on and I saw the unmistakable form of Preston Carver, our alpha, walking toward the ring. Some of the wolves had remained behind, but now I knew the members of other packs must have fled.

I risked moving closer to the ring. Preston stopped in front of it, his expression dark as he stared at his son. Dax was standing in the center of the ring, bruises already showing on his face, and blood running from his nose and mouth.

"I told you never to come down here," Preston said with a growl.

"I'm not a child anymore, Dad," Dax said.

"You are the future alpha. If you lose, you make me look bad and you weaken your status," he said.

"I didn't lose," he said.

"Who did you fight?" he asked. "Where's your opponent?"

Dax glanced around, then pointed at me. "Ivy."

"What?" I didn't want to be involved in this.

Preston glared at me. "You challenged your future alpha?"

Fuck. I hated Dax, but there was no way I wanted to be even more on his bad side than I already was for simply existing. "We used to fight all the time in high school and I missed the practice."

"You let a foundling beat the shit out of you?" Preston no longer looked angry. Instead, he looked amused.

"She's got to practice somehow," Dax said.

"He went easy on me," I added. I knew I was going to

get hell from Dax if his dad thought I'd beat him up. I knew I likely had signs of a black eye from my earlier encounter, but I didn't look nearly as bad as Dax.

Preston grunted. "That's good, son. A pack is only as strong as its weakest member."

What the fuck was going on here? I knew enough to keep my mouth shut, but I felt like I was living in an alternate universe.

Preston walked over to me. "Did you leave the ring because you thought I wouldn't approve?"

I looked over at Dax, who was nodding at me. I turned back to Preston. "Yeah."

"Well, don't let me stop you, go finish." Preston gestured to the ring.

My stomach tightened. Was he serious? He wanted me to fight Dax right now? I shook my head. "We were done. I tapped out."

"Don't lie. Look how many blows you got in. Go finish." It was a command, and I had no choice but to follow. You didn't disobey the alpha.

I swallowed hard against a lump in my throat as I walked toward the ring. It had been two years since I'd been in a fight to defend myself. Sure, I'd stayed in shape and made regular use of the punching bag in my apartment. But that wasn't the same. And it wasn't Dax.

My whole body was shaking as I climbed under the ropes.

"Should we finish this?" Dax asked, stepping into the role with ease. It was as if we really had been fighting. I got the sense that he was going to try to impress his dad, which meant I was in for some serious pain if I didn't defend myself.

I blew out a breath. The only way I had a shot at surviving this was if I didn't hold back. It wasn't like this was the first time I'd be throwing a punch at him. For once, it was just the two of us. None of his friends could join in or take over. Maybe I could get a few hits in before he knocked me out.

"Go on," Preston called. "Fight."

CHAPTER FOUR

Everyone who grew up in the Shadows knew how to fight. It was taught in school and I wasn't the only kid who was jumped for no reason. Granted, I was pretty sure I got beat up more than most, but in this moment I was a little grateful.

I could hold my own. The question was, could I do it against Dax as he was now? He looked bigger than he had in high school. Stronger. Possibly faster. He'd probably been training his wolf since I knew he'd shifted last summer, and I knew he practiced fighting. All I did was get out my stress on a punching bag. I didn't even have the extra shifter strength since my wolf had been a no-show so far. Not that I was worried. I had a few years before I'd be considered a late bloomer, but it was another way I was at a disadvantage.

Fuck. This was turning into one of the worst days of my life.

I glanced at the crowd and caught sight of money changing hands. People were actually betting on this? There was no way anyone thought I was going to win.

"You all know the drill," Joe was in the center of the ring now. I hadn't even noticed him join us. "No rules. Fight till someone submits or they're unconscious."

Wonderful. This wasn't going to suck at all. Something roared to life inside me. It was as if another part of me was fighting to get out. I could feel the rage and anger burning in my chest. A desperate desire to fight and win.

I had yet to shift, but I'd heard about how sometimes wolves came from life or death situations. It could help force the shift. Since most of us didn't shift until we were in our twenties, I hadn't worried too much. But this was new. Something that was part of me, but wasn't me.

Deep down, I knew it was my wolf. And she was hungry for a fight. We'd been taught to lean into our wolf side, but the whole thing caught me off guard.

I vaguely registered the sound of a bell, and Dax advanced. *Shit.* I'd been distracted, and the fight had started.

Internally, I wanted to flee, to get away from him. Why would I purposefully go into a fight? That new part of me seemed to tug at me, moving me toward my opponent. She was angry, and she wanted to brawl.

I put my fists up, more to defend myself than anything else, but the movement sent a rush of adrenaline that spiked my confidence. Dax closed in on me, his fist aiming for my face. I managed to move just in time, but his next blow landed in my stomach.

With a grunt, I doubled over, but my instincts sent me right back into attack position and without thinking, I landed a kick in his side. Dax growled and jumped back, out of my range. I'd been in enough fights to know what to do, but I'd forgotten what I was capable of. Seeing Dax take a step back reminded me that I had some power here. Sure, he was going to kick my ass, but I could do some damage in the meantime.

With a smirk, I moved closer to him. I wasn't going to go down easy. Dax grinned and I could tell he was impressed that I was putting effort into this. He lunged forward and grabbed me, pulling me into a tight hold. I struggled, twisting and turning to break it, but he squeezed tighter.

"You've never been a great fighter," he said. "All those times we fought, you always went down so quickly."

"If I remember correctly, you always had help." I lifted my arms fast, breaking free of his hold. Then I turned and managed to clip his jaw with my fist. I winced as pain shot through my knuckles into my wrist. I forgot how much it hurt to punch someone.

Dax hit me back, and we went back and forth a few rounds, dodging, blocking, and hitting each other. I had to admit; I was getting a rush from the fight. The sensation I'd felt at the beginning was growing, fueling my movements, and encouraging me. I'd never felt so powerful or so strong in my life.

Joe stepped in to separate us, telling us we'd completed a round. I wasn't sure how the rounds worked, but I wasn't going to argue with a minute to catch my breath.

Sweat rolled down my cheek, and I quickly wiped it away. Sucking in air, I studied my opponent. Dax grinned and winked from across the ring. His dark wavy hair was slicked back and sweat glistened over his broad shoulders and rock-hard abs. He cracked his knuckles and rolled his shoulders before locking his deep brown eyes on me. Dax was definitely at his best when he was in a fight.

When I got to my corner, Randy handed me a glass of water. "You're killing it, girl."

"Thanks." Everything hurt, but the restless part of me that had been awoken was enjoying the hell out of this.

My whole body ached. My right eye was swelling and I could taste blood in my mouth. It didn't matter. I'd made it this far. What if I could make it longer? For the first time, I started to wonder if I could beat him. It didn't hurt to try.

The bell rang, and Dax stepped toward the center of the ring, waiting for me. I moved my head toward each shoulder, my neck cracking. Then I stepped forward, hoping the glare I was throwing his way made me look intimidating.

"You could tap out now, darling," Dax said.

"No way," I hissed.

He charged forward, ducking down so his shoulder made contact with my stomach. His arms wrapped around me and he threw me to the mat. The air left my lungs, but I rallied quickly, wrapping my legs around him and shoving his shoulders off.

I was able to twist enough to get out of his grasp, but before I was fully standing, he pulled me back down. My chin hit the mat and stars danced in my eyes.

Dax's lips brushed against my ear. "Submit."

"No," I growled.

He grasped my arm, twisting it behind my back. I tried to break the hold, but he held me firm. This was it. He had me pinned. I'd lasted this long, but I was coming to the end without getting in a final blow. *Dammit.* I'd been so close. I really had started to think I could win.

Suddenly, Dax eased his grip just enough that I could squirm away. I stood, then turned on him, sweeping my leg under his feet. He went down on his back, his expression startled. It took everything I had not to gloat. I'd caught him by surprise.

I shoved my knee into his chest and held his arms down, using everything I had to keep him pinned.

He smirked. "You're better than you were in high school."

"Like I said, we never fought one on one." The thing deep in my chest roared, as if pissed that I was denying it the credit. I wasn't even sure of what exactly it was yet.

"I kinda like being under you. Maybe we can meet up later and do this naked." He kissed the air.

My nose wrinkled. "Never going to happen."

"I saw the way you looked at me in high school. You've always wanted me," he said.

"Don't flatter yourself," I said.

I was so close to winning this thing. I just needed to keep him down. I could almost taste victory.

With dizzying speed, Dax reversed the hold, and suddenly, I was the one on the mat. Dax straddled my hips. Leaning forward, he stretched my arms out behind my head, holding them to the mat. "You got cocky, started counting the victory before you had it."

"Asshole," I spat.

"Don't be that way, darling, I'm sure you're enjoying me being on top."

I squirmed and fought his hold, but he had me held tight. I kicked up my legs and lifted my hips. Dax was easily double my weight, and he was a whole foot taller than me. When he decided he wanted to keep me down, there wasn't much I could do to get away.

"Do you submit?" Joe was right in my face.

I glared up at Dax. "You let me pin you, didn't you?"

He grinned. "I didn't want you to lose too quickly. But you did have a good hold on me before you got distracted."

I should have known he was playing me. I never actually had a chance. "Fine. I submit."

I was so pissed I'd let my guard down. He was right; I thought I had it in the bag. "Fuck."

Dax leaned down. "Is that an invitation for later?"

"Don't count on it," I snapped. I was fuming. I'd gone into this thinking I'd lose, but once I tasted the possibilities of winning, I wanted it.

"Such a sore loser," he said as he released his grip. He stood, then offered his hand.

I glared at him.

"Come on, Ivy," he said. "Everyone's watching."

I knew he meant that his dad was watching.

"Get up," he said. "Fun's over."

I caught the hint of a threat in his tone. For a few minutes during the fight, it felt like we were equals. But that wasn't the case. This changed nothing.

I cursed him internally while accepting his hand.

He pulled me up with ease, once again reminding me of how much stronger he was. "We should do that again sometime."

"Hard pass," I said.

The roar of the audience hit me like a wave crashing down on me. During the fight, I'd blocked them out and now that we were finished, it was overwhelming. Preston climbed into the ring, a look of pride on his face.

"No weakness," Preston said as he clapped his son on the back. Then he turned to me. "You've come a long way since that day you were dropped at the foundling home. I have to say I'm impressed. I look forward to seeing what you can do after you finally shift."

"Thanks," I said.

Preston put his arm around his son's shoulders and the two of them walked away, deep in conversation.

I stood rooted in place for a moment, unsure of what I should do. Finally, I realized nobody was even looking at me. They were all waiting to congratulate Dax for beating me up. Sometimes I really hated my pack.

When I waked to the edge of the ring, I was surprised to find Evan and Randy waiting for me.

"I can't believe how well you took that," Randy said.

"I didn't really have a choice," I said.

"You did good, kid," Evan said.

"Come on, I'll show you to the locker room. They have ice back there. You could use some." Evan set his hand on my back and guided me away from the ring. "Have you had your first shift yet?"

"No," I said.

"Damn. You're going to be feeling those injuries for a few days. Usually they don't let anyone pre-shift up there," he said.

"Hopefully, nobody will force me up there again," I said. "Next time, I'm saying no."

"I don't understand why Dax did that. Are you two fooling around?" Evan asked.

I laughed, then winced from the pain the action caused. Even talking hurt, but I wasn't about to let them think I was fucking Dax. "We've never gotten along."

"When the Dark Wolf punched that guy out for hurting you, I swear Dax looked like he was going to rip him to pieces. I've never seen jealously like that," Evan said.

"You must have misunderstood. He was probably pissed that he wasn't the center of attention."

"I don't think so," Evan replied.

I thought back to the moment when the stranger had jumped in to defend me. A shiver ran down my spine. I had no idea who the Dark Wolf was, but he had been the most alluring male I'd ever seen. I wasn't a one-night stand kind of woman, but I'd make an exception for him. "Who is he?"

"The Dark Wolf?" Evan asked.

"Nobody knows," Randy said quickly. "Besides, even if we did, we wouldn't be allowed to say."

"Why do I get the sense that you're hiding something from me?" I asked.

We stopped walking, and Evan lowered his hand from my back. "We'll let Holden know you did good tonight."

I could tell the conversation was over. They weren't going to spill, even if they did know more. We did just meet tonight. Maybe with time, I could gain their trust.

We were standing in front of a doorway, the two bartenders looking at me as if I might drop dead any second. I hated how fragile I felt. I'd held my own okay against Dax, but finding out that he'd let me pin him was a blow to my ego. In a real fight, if he'd actually wanted to harm me, I wasn't sure I'd have any chance. I wondered how that might change after I shifted. Not that it mattered. What kind of fighting skills did I need as a waitress?

"Why don't you clean up? We'll wait here," Randy said. "Holden always comes down to check everything out before he pays us. You have a few minutes."

I peered into the doorway and saw the row of sinks.

Washing the blood off my face would be nice, though I wasn't sure I wanted to see how I looked.

Cautiously, I stepped through the doorway and found myself in a locker room. Benches stood along one wall and a few actual lockers against another. To my right were three sinks and beyond them was a single stall and a urinal.

Dax was zipping up his fly as he turned to face me. "Well, well, well. You and me, alone in here. My night just keeps getting better."

CHAPTER
FIVE

"Don't flatter yourself, Dax," I said. "You owe me, and you know it."

He shrugged. "Maybe. I think you might have liked it. Center of attention; me and you so close."

I gestured to my aching face. "Nobody likes getting the shit beat out of them."

"You held your own better than I would have thought," he said.

"You're a sadist. And an asshole," I said.

He strolled toward me, and I wrinkled my nose. "Aren't you going to wash your hands?"

With a laugh, he changed direction and headed to one of the sinks. "Since you asked so nicely."

I moved to a free sink and caught a glimpse of myself in the mirror. I looked even worse than I thought. My eye was swollen shut and my other eye was bloodshot. My blonde hair had started the evening in a ponytail, but now it looked like I'd had the same hair tie in for days without washing or brushing. It was a chaotic mess. My lips were caked in dry blood and now that I was starting to pay attention to my injuries, I realized it hurt every time I took a breath.

"I can't believe you made me get in there with you," I hissed as I turned on the faucet. As I went through the motions of cleaning up, my mind wandered to Dax's original challenger. Who was the Dark Wolf? Dax owed me after what I did. Maybe he'd tell me.

After I was done washing my hands and splashing water on my face, I gently dried off with a paper towel. I tossed the towel in the trash can and turned to Dax. "Who was that male you were fighting?"

"He calls himself the Dark Wolf. Stupid name, if you ask me," he grumbled.

"Who is he, really?" I asked. "He's not a Shadow."

"No, he's not," Dax agreed. "He's far worse."

"So, he's Umbra?" I pressed.

"He's none of your business is what he is. But he did seem to be interested in you. I didn't realize it was mutual," he said.

"It's not," I lied.

"Why exactly did he rush to your side like some kind of knight in shining armor?" Dax asked.

"Why would I know? I never saw him before tonight," I replied.

"Well, you won't be seeing him again. I won't have

those outsiders here after I'm alpha," Dax said, a threat in his tone.

My stomach tightened in fear at the thought of never seeing the Dark Wolf again. I pushed the idea from my mind. That was insane. Why should I care about some shifter from another pack?

Dax took a step closer to me. "I never really noticed you before tonight. I see that now."

I lifted my brows. "If that were true, I wouldn't have spent spring break in eighth grade recovering from broken ribs thanks to you."

"Childhood pranks." He waved his hand.

"The way you treated me wasn't childhood pranks. You hurt me. More than once. More than just tonight."

"And tonight you demonstrated the payoff of all that hard work. All those years of me pushing you. You haven't even had your first shift, and you did good. I can't imagine how strong you'll be when your wolf arrives," he said.

"Is this supposed to be making me feel better? I'm going to be in pain for days from this," I said.

He moved closer until there were only a few inches between us. I sucked in a breath and forced myself to hold my ground. Was this some kind of bizarre test? Was he trying to see if I'd flinch? My whole life I'd stood up to Dax, and it had always cost me, but I wasn't about to bow to him now. Once he was alpha, I wasn't going to have a choice. But he wasn't alpha yet.

"What do you want from me, Dax?" I asked. "Your

friends aren't around to see you show off and you've already gotten your blows in. What more could you need?"

He was fast, his hand moving behind my head and his lips pressing against mine before I realized what was happening. My eyes widened, and I shoved him, breaking the contact before I stepped away.

"What the fuck are you doing?" I took another step back, but I was already prepared to kick him in the crotch if he came near me.

"Don't you feel it? The heat between us? I've never seen a woman fight like you did tonight. So much fire, so much passion. Shit, that stranger saw it in you before I saw it myself," he said.

My brow furrowed. "The Dark Wolf? He saw me cowering in a ball on the ground. You saw me trying to defend myself. There was no passion in anything I did tonight. It was pure survival."

"Think about it, Ivy. We'd be great together. You're feisty, smart, and sexy as hell. I'll admit, you were always the hottest girl in school, you just didn't have the status. But I'm going to be alpha. I'll have more than enough status for both of us. Plus, I'd have the authority to wipe your debts. You'd be free," he said. "Think about it. We could do great things together."

It felt like I'd just been dunked into ice water. Was he saying what I thought he was saying? Sure, Dax was attractive. And he was going to be the most powerful shifter in the Shadows. More importantly, being with him would clear my debts to the pack. I could finally be a full member.

The problem was, I'd be trading in one type of debt for another. If I was with Dax, I would be his. I still wouldn't have the freedom I craved. Besides, even if I wanted to be with him, which I didn't, there was no way his dad would support it.

"Dax Carver, you promised me you wouldn't be down here all night," a whiny female voice echoed around the locker room.

I didn't need to turn around to know that Stacey had joined us.

"What's *she* doing here?" Stacey said.

"Good night, Dax." I turned around and Stacey glared at me. I walked past her and out of the locker room without a backward glance.

Randy and Evan were true to their word. Both males were waiting for me outside. "Holden here yet?"

"He's by the bar," Evan said.

We walked back to where we'd started the evening. I'd only been down here a few hours, but it felt like it was going to be one of those nights that stayed with you. If Holden made good on the pay, I'd probably do it again, but I'd have to see about getting Joe to institute a rule that waiters can't fight.

"Did you hook up with the baby alpha in the locker room?" Randy asked.

"Nope," I said. "Not my type."

"You were in there a long time," Evan added.

"Nothing happened." The words came out more defensively than I wanted, but it wasn't my fault Dax had tried to kiss me. And I sure as hell didn't kiss him back.

Holden's hands were on his hips, and his face was as red as a tomato. I half expected to see steam coming out of his ears. "You had one job."

I glanced over at the bartenders next to me before looking back at Holden. "Are you serious? You can't possibly be mad at me for getting in the ring. The alpha made me."

"I don't give a damn about that. That was a good show. People will remember that. I'm pissed that you dropped a tray on a VIP's dress," Holden said.

"That's what you're mad about?" I asked. "It was an accident. We got it all worked out."

"Don't let it happen again." He dropped his arms to his side.

"Okay," I said. "I won't."

"Fine." He pulled an envelope out of his pocket. "I had to deduct for the broken glasses and the dry-cleaning bill."

I resisted the urge to roll my eyes. Honestly, I would work this event again just for the tips. Anything in that envelope was just icing on the cake. I reached for it and Holden set it in my hand. Then he turned and gave envelopes to Evan and Randy.

"You think she can handle it down here?" Holden asked them.

"She did good, boss," Evan said.

"Yeah, nicer than Darleen, too," Randy added.

Holden turned to me. "Alright, kid. We've got to lay low for a week or two, but we'll have another event soon. I guess you're in if you want it."

I couldn't believe my luck. This was going to get me to my goal so much faster. It didn't matter if it was slightly illegal. I wasn't breaking any rules. I was simply taking drinks to people who ordered them. Plus, maybe I'd get to see the Dark Wolf again. The thought made my heart race. "I'm ready when you are."

"Good. Go on home. Kennedy can handle the rest of the night upstairs," Holden said.

"You sure?" I didn't want to go back up to the main bar, but I hated the idea of leaving Kennedy there alone.

"You're opening tomorrow to make up for it," he said.

My shoulders slumped. That meant I was working a double shift instead of sleeping late. "Alright. Home it is."

"Want me to walk you out?" Evan offered as he handed me my apron from on top of the counter.

"I'm good, thanks," I said.

"You saw her in the ring," Randy said. "I feel bad for anyone who tries anything."

I wasn't so sure about that. Especially with how sore I was from the fight. Going home was the best possible thing that could happen. I was going to soak in a bathtub full of ice water, then sleep till morning.

After stashing my cash in my socks just in case, I took the back set of stairs from the basement. None of the emergency lights were lit now, but I was curious to see where all the shifters from other packs had gone.

To my surprise, the stairway led me up to the alley behind the Night Howler. It was a dark and lined with a few dumpsters. I wondered if this was the route those shifters took to attend the fights as well.

I walked carefully, avoiding the questionable puddles and trash, as I made my way to the main road. A few cars passed by and a couple of patrons were standing outside the front entrance of the Howler, smoking cigarettes. Based on the limited pedestrians, it was probably later than I realized. Time seemed to move differently in that basement. I'd been so busy, I hadn't stopped to look.

My breath came out in clouds and I shoved my hands into my jean pockets. It had been warm enough when I arrived to skip the jacket, but now I was regretting that decision. I turned and walked the block to the public parking lot. The streetlights weren't lit as usual, making it darker tonight. Sometimes one light might go out, but as I got closer to the lot, I noticed that both the lights were out. It looked much creepier out here without the lighting. I didn't have the night vision of most of the residents around here yet. Another perk of completing that first shift one of these days. I shivered. The sooner I got home, the better.

The lot was about half full, a sign that things were winding down for the evening. A few figures lingered in the parking lot, shifters walking toward their vehicles to head home after a night out. As I got a little closer, the figures started to come together, and they began to walk toward me. I recognized the shadowy figure leading the group.

"What do you want, Stacey?" I asked, not hiding the exasperation in my voice.

"Nothing much," she said as she moved closer. "We're just here to teach you a little lesson."

Out of the corner of my eye, I noticed other figures closing in on me from either side. I was surrounded. Stacey and all her friends. The same group who had spent their childhoods bullying me, minus Dax. I suppose he already got his blows in tonight.

"Enough," I snapped. "Just let me go home. We're not in high school anymore. You don't have to push the foundling around. You won. You're off in college, and I'm stuck here. Isn't that punishment enough?"

"If only it was that easy," she said. "But you aren't satisfied with what you have. So you have to move in on other people's boyfriends."

"That's what this is about?" I started laughing. "Please, you can keep him."

That's when Stacey punched me in the face. "Who's laughing now, bitch?"

CHAPTER
SIX

Doubled over, I sucked in a quick breath, ignoring the pain as best I could. Before I stood, I glanced around to see what I was in for. It was one thing to fight back when I had a chance. It was another to be jumped and outnumbered. Especially while still recovering from my last round of blows.

Someone kicked the back of my legs and I went down, my elbows hitting the asphalt to break my fall. I cried out as bolts of agony shot up and down my arms. Another kick in my side knocked me over, and I quickly shielded my head. I wasn't going to be able to get out of this one. I knew well enough that there were times to fight and times to hide. I needed to protect myself and not engage. They'd get bored and stop, but if I ran, I risked bringing out the hunter inside those who'd already shifted. Worse, I could encourage a shift and I was not in the position to defend myself against a wolf.

More kicks to my stomach and back. I cried as quietly as I could, trying to hold the hurt inside. I didn't want to encourage them. Suddenly, the torment stopped, and I peeked through my arms.

Stacey was crouched in front of me. "You go near him again and next time we'll kill you. Nobody would even notice you missing. It's like that other waitress. She's gone and nobody cares. She won't get a funeral. Nobody will mourn her. People like you don't matter. You're not even pack."

I glared at her. "I told you, I don't have any interest in your boyfriend. But beating up every imaginary threat isn't going to keep him loyal to you and you know it."

She growled and raked her fingernails across my cheek.

I winced and pressed my palm against my stinging flesh.

"I'm going to be the alpha's mate. You're another piece of trash males like him slum it with and then never call." Stacey stood, then kicked me in the gut again.

I grunted but didn't speak. She was unhinged, and there wasn't any way to convince someone like her. Dax and Stacey belonged together. They could make each other miserable.

Laugher and footsteps told me the attack was over and I cautiously pushed myself to sitting. I was lucky; it wasn't as bad as it could have been. Everything hurt. I had no idea which pain was from the new attack or from my earlier fight. It didn't matter. I was grateful to be alive at the moment.

Limping to my car, I thought about Stacey's comments about Darleen. She wasn't wrong. Darleen had been full pack, but her status wasn't high. As much as I hated the thought, there wouldn't be any mourning of her passing. Her parents were dead, and while she wasn't a foundling like me, she had been alone. Her boyfriend was probably all she had, and he'd died with her.

I unlocked my car and gingerly sat down, my body protesting every movement. Was that what was in store for me? Was I going to disappear like Darleen, with nobody to cry at my funeral?

It was a bleak outlook, and one that wasn't all that unusual in the Shadows. Few wolves rose to any level of importance here. Unless you were in the alpha's inner circle, you lived your life, finding joy when you could, then you died. It was far too depressing to consider tonight.

My whole plan for years had been to gain status as a full member of the pack, but then what? Would it even matter or change anything?

Most of the kids I went to high school with were never going to see me as anything other than a foundling. It wasn't like I had a choice. There wasn't anywhere else to go. Shadow wolves weren't welcome in the other packs, so the only other option would be to go feral. Without any pack, even further from society than the Fringes. I shuddered as an icy chill spread down my spine. That was every shifter's worst fear. We took in the outcasts from other packs, but if the Shadow Wolves kicked you out, there was nowhere else to go.

When I pulled up to my apartment building, I noticed my roommate's car was in her spot. I was a little surprised she wasn't out on a date or doing something more interesting than being home. Unlike me, Kate had a far more exciting and interesting life. On occasion, we did things together, but I was almost always working.

Kate was my only true friend. We'd met when we were young, and as the daughter of a respected member of the pack, she didn't get crap for being nice to me. It cost her party invitations, but she never seemed to worry about those too much.

Kate was an artist and did a variety of things around town to pay her rent. She created graphics for events and businesses, created sculptures or paintings on commission, and just about anything else creative she could find. She stayed busy, and she made a good living from doing what she loved. I envied her passion. One of these days, I might let myself explore what I loved, but I'd never taken the time to figure it out. I always knew college wasn't an option, and that I was stuck here. It kind of took the thrill away from hobbies and other interests.

I grabbed my jacket and climbed out of my car. My muscles were stiff and achy from the short time sitting. I was in for a rough couple of days of recovery.

Kate was on the couch, her legs dangling over the armrest. She bolted up when she saw me and locked her green eyes on me. "What happened?"

"Can you at least let me close the door behind me?" I appreciated that she cared, but now that I was home, I didn't really want to think about the events of the evening anymore.

"Seriously, Ivy, who did this to you?" she demanded.

"It's a long story," I said.

She pulled her long dark hair into a bun, then walked to the kitchen. "It's been a while since I had to get you an ice pack. Years." She returned with a bag of frozen peas. "Explain."

I sighed and accepted the bag, then pressed it against the side of my face. There were lots of places hurting, but I'd learned years ago it was best to reduce the injuries on my face. The other parts I could cover up and hide. Bruises were a sign of weakness around here. They singled me out as an easy target when I was younger. I wasn't sure what it would do for me at work since I hadn't had to deal with this since school.

"Did Holden do this? Because I know a guy who can make him disappear. It might cost me a few inappropriate paintings, but you're worth it," she said.

I chuckled, then winced. Note to self, laughter makes it worse. "It wasn't Holden." I walked over to the couch and sat down. Kate took the space next to me, then quickly turned off the TV. She stared at me, waiting for my explanation.

I knew I wasn't going to be able to ignore her, so I quickly explained about the fight and how I got dragged into the ring. I left out the details about the Dark Wolf coming to my rescue and the parking lot tussle with Stacey. No reason to concern her about things she couldn't change.

"Those fights are at Holden's bar? I'd heard about fights happening, but never knew details. I can't believe you ended up in the ring with Dax." She shook her head. "He could have killed you. You haven't even had your first shift yet."

"I know. I think he went easy on me, and I still got my ass kicked," I said.

Kate was a full member of the pack and she'd had her first shift a couple months ago. She didn't talk about it much, but I knew she enjoyed all the hunts and runs with rest of the pack in her wolf form. There was a part of me that longed for my first shift, but I wouldn't be welcome at the events until I paid my debt, so there wasn't much rush.

"So he's fine with breaking the rules, even with his dad in charge. That's very interesting," Kate said. "And Holden is in on it. What do you think that means?"

I hadn't thought about it too much. "They said it was the first time Dax came to fight. Do you think he's known for a while? I mean, even he'd get in trouble for letting in outsiders, right?"

"I'm sure not as much as the rest of us, but if he's participating, I wonder what that means for his rule. Things were bad when the Umbras had a hold over our pack. I've heard the stories. It took years of bloodshed to gain our independence and carve out this territory," Kate said.

I knew the history, same as any other kid raised in the Shadows. While our pack was seen as the outcasts, we had a lot fewer rules and structure than the Umbra pack had. We lived in a shifter only community, magically enchanted to keep humans out. The Umbra pack was embedded into a human city. They ran most everything without the humans catching on. It made for a lot more secrecy, but also led to more corruption, violence, and control. The Umbras kept track of every shifter within their borders and dictated every choice. You couldn't apply for a new job or date someone without their permission. Sure, I would need permission to date an outsider here, but that was about as far as our restrictions went. Well, at least for full pack members.

There were a few more restrictions on me, but once I paid my debt, I'd have my freedom. I knew things weren't perfect here, but there were choices and we didn't have to hide. I didn't have any urge to visit the human city the Umbras ruled. Hiding who and what I was sounded awful. Who would want to live life that way?

"You're not saying you think Dax would let the Umbras back in?" I lowered the bag of frozen peas. "He can't be that stupid, right?"

She shrugged, then reached over and lifted my hand, guiding the bag of peas back to my face. "Leave it on a bit longer. I'll make you some tea."

I wrinkled my nose. "Not your grandma's recipe."

"Yes, my grandma's recipe." She stood. "You're going

to drink it and you're going to like it." She had her hands on her hips and was trying not to crack a smile.

"Fine," I conceded. I wasn't sure if the mixture of herbs that was Kate's go-to for everything from a skinned-knee to a hangover would help me with this, but it wouldn't hurt. It tasted terrible, but Kate's grandmother was a witch and she knew her shit. That was how Kate's family ended up here. Her dad married a half-witch, half-wolf shifter. They weren't welcome in most packs. Here, the weirder the better.

The shop next door to the Night Howler was an apothecary that sold every kind of herb you could dream of. You could also choose from a variety of crystals and talismans. When I was younger, I thought all towns were like ours. Sure, I'd never been anywhere else to know better, but I'd heard enough stories from shifters like Kate's parents to understand how lucky I was to be here.

A dark cloud settled around me as I realized that despite the mix of shifters and openness, I was still an outcast. It wasn't my fault my parents abandoned me. Their action of dropping me at the foundling center set me up for a life as an outsider. It was hard to swallow sometimes.

"Drink it before it gets cold," Kate ordered as she returned with a steaming mug of the herbal concoction.

I could smell it already. Earthy and slightly sweet, it was like eating mushrooms mixed with dirt and a dash of honey. There were very few redeeming qualities about the tea. In the off chance it would help, and because it seemed to please Kate, I set down the peas and accepted the mug.

With any luck, most of my visible wounds would be healed by morning. If the tea didn't help, which I suspected it wouldn't, I had a drawer full of makeup I saved for such special occasions.

I lifted the mug. "Cheers."

CHAPTER SEVEN

My face was covered in purple bruises when I woke. All my muscles ached and breathing hurt. I didn't think I had a broken rib, but they were pretty bruised. I moved slowly, taking care to not injure myself more. It was going to be a tough week as I recovered. Waiting tables wasn't exactly a job where I could sit and rest.

The smell of coffee made me finally toss the covers aside and crawl out of the warmth. I wanted to stay here, wrapped in blankets all day, but I had to get to work for the lunch shift.

At least there was coffee to look forward to. Hissing in pain, I carefully tugged the oversized tee I'd slept in over my head. I blew out a breath as I examined the injuries along my ribcage. As gently as possible, I ran my fingers over my ribs, feeling for their placement. While the marks from last night's fight were obvious, they weren't the worst injury I'd recovered from. The thought was supposed to make me feel better, but it was depressing.

I thought I'd left this behind when I left school. Maybe Stacey would settle down once she and Dax got married. It was a matter of time before he went sniffing around for someone who would buckle to his status and hop into bed with him. Then Stacey would have a new target. Aside from her feeling threatened by me, there wasn't any other reason for her to come after me.

It was harder than I thought to pull on a pair of jeans and a black long-sleeved tee. At least the uniform for the Night Howler would cover most of me. Makeup was going to have to do the trick for the marks on my face.

The tile floor of the kitchen was freezing under my bare feet. I stopped in front of the fridge to read the note on the whiteboard. Kate had already left for a job, but she left a bottle of Tylenol, a sachet of her grandmother's herbal mix, and a pot of coffee. Most of my life wasn't great, but at least I had her. Kate made the tough parts easier to get through.

I padded over to the coffeepot and poured myself a cup, breathing in the comforting scent. I sipped it while I glared at the packet of herbs. I wasn't keen on ruining perfectly good coffee, but I knew Kate wanted me to try it.

With a sigh, I grabbed a tea strainer and added a small pinch of the herbs. Frowning, I dunked the strainer ball into the coffee. Hopefully, it wouldn't change the taste too much.

I grabbed a yogurt and carried it and my coffee to the

couch. It was already ten, so there wasn't enough time to do much before I had to be at work. I forced down the herb-spiked coffee and ate the yogurt. Feeling a little better, I headed back to the kitchen and refilled my coffee cup before heading to start the process of layering on makeup.

Normally, I was a mascara and lip gloss girl. I'd had a fair amount of practice painting on the other layers to hide injuries in my youth. I opened up the foundation and discovered it had dried up. *Fuck*. There wasn't time to run to the store. I did my best with some powder and whatever else I could find. The bruises were still visible, but not as obvious as they had been.

When I arrived at the parking lot near work, I found a spot closest to the main road. The sooner I could get into my car tonight after work, the better. The sun was bright and warm and any lingering reminders of snow earlier in the week were long gone. The only sign that it was winter at all were the decorations on shop windows.

I walked past Marcele's coffee shop. He went all out every holiday, painting snowy scenes and pine trees on his windows. It nearly blocked out the view of the crowd inside. Most shifters weren't morning people, which meant many of the business didn't open until later. Marcele's was one of the exceptions. He opened at eight and would have a steady stream of customers until he closed at six.

The door to the apothecary was propped open, and I caught the scent of herbs and spices as I passed. Dangling crystals shimmered in the windows. I wondered how many shifters around here had some witch heritage. The apothecary wasn't busy yet, but it would be later.

I continued on until I reached the Night Howler. The lunch shift was usually slower, but at least it gave me something to do.

The front door was locked at the Howler and I pounded on it, hoping someone would actually hear me. I didn't work lunch shifts often, but I had waited out here for a long time more than once. With the music the cooks blared, they couldn't hear anyone knocking.

The door opened, and Kayla peeked out. "I didn't know you were working lunch today."

"It's my lucky day." I stepped through the door. "I'm covering for Darleen."

Kayla frowned. "That whole thing sucks. I'm going to miss seeing her scowling face."

"Yeah, she was always good at keeping the drunks in order," I said.

Kayla closed the door behind me and relocked it. We didn't officially open for another hour but there was always something to prep.

"What happened to your face?" she asked casually.

"Oh, nothing," I said.

"By evening nobody's going to see it, but your makeup isn't doing its job."

"I ran out of foundation," I mumbled.

"There's some in my purse in the back. I think it'll be a close enough match. Go take care of it or you're going to be a walking target for any daytime drunk." I gave her a grateful smile and headed to the tiny closet in the kitchen where employees stashed their bags. I kept my car keys in my pocket and didn't bring anything else into work with me. After growing up in the foundling house, I didn't trust leaving my belongings out anywhere. Anything not on you or very well hidden didn't stay yours for long.

I stood in the dark closet, using a tiny mirror I found in Kayla's bag to apply the makeup as best I could. Muffled conversation drifted toward me and I froze. I didn't want anyone to see me in the act of covering up my injuries. The tone of the voice sounded familiar, but I couldn't quite place it. Another voice cut in, the familiar baritone of my boss, Holden.

The closet door was ajar, letting in a crack of light. I peeked through, curious who Holden was speaking with. An intense feeling of longing rushed through me as soon as I caught sight of the familiar profile. No wonder I recognized the voice. It belonged to the Dark Wolf. But what was he doing here? And why was he talking to Holden?

"That's not good enough," he said.

"It's as good as it's going to get. I'm telling you, it's not the right time," Holden said.

"We need to act now. We can't put this off," the Dark Wolf replied.

My whole body tensed and I held my breath as the voices came closer. I knew I shouldn't be hearing this. Not that I could make out what they were discussing, but there was nefarious intent in their tones. Were they talking about the fights? Or something else? Neither would surprise me. Though I was surprised that the Dark Wolf would risk being in our territory during the day. Maybe he wasn't Umbra after all.

"The pieces aren't in place," Holden said. "We need more time."

"Then fucking get them in order or I'm out." The Dark Wolf's tone was threatening.

They stopped in front of the closet, and I tensed. The Dark Wolf was standing with his back to me. I could make out Holden's frustrated expression. Wonderful. He was going to be pissed the rest of the day after this.

"It's not the time. We were almost busted last night," Holden said.

They had to be talking about the fight, right? Was Holden giving the Dark Wolf a cut or something? He was the star of the show.

"I took care of the problem," Holden said. "Dead shifters can't howl."

"How can you be sure you eliminated all the problems? What if she told her friends?" the Dark Wolf asked.

"She's gone, the boyfriend's gone. She didn't have anyone else," Holden said.

I covered my mouth with my hand, and I tried to melt into the wall behind me. *Holy fuck.* They were talking about Darleen. And if Holden didn't kill her himself, he'd had a hand in her demise.

What was going on between them? What had Darleen heard or seen? My heart raced. If they found me here, would they determine I'd heard too much, too? I didn't have my wolf yet. Even if I tried to fight them off, I wouldn't stand a chance. All they had to do was shift, and they'd be able to tear me to unrecognizable pieces. I swallowed against a lump in my throat. Was that what happened to Darleen? Had they set her up in Umbra territory, or had they just used that as the excuse?

"Figure it out, Holden. If you want my support, get it done now." The Dark Wolf walked away, leaving Holden standing with his back to the closet.

His shoulders slumped, and he raked a hand through his hair. I stopped breathing, worried that he'd hear me now that he was alone. After what felt like an eternity, he walked away.

I stood in the closet for a few more minutes before I cautiously peeked out. The coast was clear. Without hesitation, I bolted from the kitchen back to the dining room. I didn't want anyone to know I'd even been back there at all.

The rest of my shift was a blur as I considered what I'd heard. The Dark Wolf and Holden were working on something big. It could be anything. Everything was a hustle here once you dug deep enough. What could possibly be so big that it got Darleen killed?

During the lull after lunch, I headed to the kitchen to grab some food. Jamie, one of the cooks, hooked me up with a grilled cheese and tomato sandwich. It was on a hamburger bun, but it was a nice break from the usual burger or nachos.

I stood at a counter taking hurried bites, knowing that Kayla was the only one out there to handle customers. There weren't any tables when I headed back, but that could change quickly.

Holden's office door opened, and a jolt ran through me. I reminded myself to be cool, to act normal. But being my usual defiant self felt a little more dangerous now.

"Can you cover Darleen's shifts for a few more days?" Holden asked. "I haven't found a replacement yet."

I swallowed the food in my mouth. "Sure, boss."

"What's with the instant compliance?" He lifted a skeptical brow.

"I get to keep the basement shifts, right?" I asked, quickly coming up with a reason why I wasn't complaining about losing my days off.

He grinned. "Yeah, it's yours as long as you stay in line. You really can be calmed down with some cash, can't you?"

"I'm sorry, what?" I couldn't help myself. "That's not an across the board kind of thing. It was an easy gig, doing the same job I already do, but paid better."

Holden chuckled. "Sure. That's all it was."

I rolled my eyes and took a big bite of my sandwich to keep myself from saying anything else.

"We ordered too much merlot," Holden said. "Try to push glasses or bottles tonight."

I nodded and gave a thumbs up while I took my time chewing.

He walked away, and I felt some tension ease. How

was I going to keep working here when I knew he was responsible for Darleen's death? I ran through the other options in my head of places I could work, but any of my other choices were either dangerous or paid half of what I made here.

I took my last bite, then carried my plate over to the dishwasher. If I wanted that debt gone, staying here was my best option. Did it matter that Holden was a murderer? Well, yes, it did. It changed the way I thought about him, but there probably weren't a lot of employers in the Fringes who didn't have blood on their hands.

The Shadow Pack was super fucked up. I often wondered who my parents had been and if they were still around. Did they sneak into our territory and dump me here or were they walking around town passing me in the street without concern?

Since I was dropped as a bundle at the door to the foundling house, I'd never know. My life would've been so different if I'd been dropped with another pack. But that wasn't my lot. This was my life, and I didn't have much choice other than making the best of it. Which meant that for now, I was stuck here. Even if my boss was a killer.

CHAPTER
EIGHT

THE EVENING SHIFT WAS SLAMMED. I got into a flow, grateful for the busy tempo of customers. It took my mind off the conversation I'd overheard and didn't give me time to wonder if my makeup had faded.

Kayla and I ran the whole place all night. She poured the drinks and kept the people sitting at the bar happy while I took all the tables. A few times I had to jump behind the bar and help her mix drinks. The two of us got into an easy rhythm. We worked together well, and it was almost better than when we had another server to divide the tables with.

It helped that most of the customers were lingering tonight. They stayed for hours and I topped off drinks with ease. If they'd turned over faster, I'd have been in trouble.

Sometime around eleven, it started to slow down enough to shove some food in my mouth and take five minutes to breathe in the kitchen. After I washed up, I headed back out and walked over to Kayla. "They made you some food back there. Go eat. I'll cover."

She topped off her customers, then ran to the back. I made sure everyone was all set at the bar, then I did a round checking on my tables. The little bell above the door jingled, and I turned to let the newcomers know they'd have to wait for a table.

My heart stopped. It was Stacey and her friends. I recognized many of them as the same people who had jumped me in the parking lot. In the light of the bar, surrounded by witnesses, I knew they wouldn't try anything. I was essentially Holden's property while I was here and he was already down a server. He might not like me, but I knew he'd kick her out if she tried anything. The thought made my lips curl into a smile. I'd like to see her try.

"I'm sorry, we don't have any open tables," I said. "You'll need to wait."

She narrowed her eyes. "You'd make me, your future alpha queen, wait?"

"You're not anything important yet," I said. "And if you were, I'd still make you wait. There aren't any tables."

She set her hands on her hips. "You wouldn't make Dax wait, I'm sure."

"I'd definitely make him wait," I said.

She rolled her eyes. "I'll tell Holden you treated us like dirt."

"Go ahead." I gestured toward the kitchen. "He's in the back."

She tossed her hair over her shoulders and spun around. With a huff, she exited the bar, her friends following her like baby ducklings.

"What was that all about?" Kayla asked.

"I guess she thought I could magically make an empty table appear just because she's sleeping with the future alpha," I said.

"What, like that's anything special? I think half the town has slept with Dax," Kayla said.

I wrinkled my nose. "Ew. Don't make me lose my dinner."

"I heard about you two the other night. Where I come from, that's foreplay," she teased.

"Never going to happen," I assured her.

She shrugged, then walked back to the bar. I returned to my tables.

The next two weeks passed by quickly. I worked doubles most days and only had one day off. Covering both my shifts and Darleen's meant I was rarely home and when I was, I only slept. I was too tired and too busy to do much other than work, sleep, and eat. It was brutal, but I was getting closer to my goal.

The cash under my mattress was increasing. Last time I'd done the math, I had years left to reach my goal. Between the fight night and the extra shifts, I'd already cut off a couple of months.

While I was grateful for the extra income, I was

exhausted. Thankfully, Stacey and her crew hadn't approached me again and nothing exceptional had happened. It was back to my usual boring life. Even Dax had been absent from the Howler. While I was still wary of Holden, it was getting easier to pretend I hadn't heard anything unusual, which was probably the best thing I could do in terms of self-preservation.

Tonight would be different, though. It was the night before the full moon, which meant my customers would be on edge. Once we had our first shift, we could shift at will with practice. However, the full moon made shifting easier, and most wolf shifters felt compelled to shift on those nights.

In the Shadows, every full moon meant a party for the full pack members. I'd never been, but I'd heard stories. Bonfire, running in the woods, lots of meaningless sex. Basically, it was a giant party that I wasn't able to attend.

When I was a teenager, I'd longed to participate. It seemed like this amazing experience that would help me fit in better. As I got older, I realized I didn't like most of the people I grew up with and a night of nakedness and drinking with them sounded like the opposite of a good time.

Still, it meant for a night off tomorrow. The Night Howler closed on full moon days and so did most of town. Kate would be at the party, only her second time attending since her first shift, so I had the whole place to myself. I had big plans. I was going to sleep late, drink coffee on my balcony, and stay in my pajamas all day. It was going to be a day of absolute bliss. I might even use some of that extra cash to splurge on a steak I could fry up for dinner. I could feel the relaxation already.

My good mood didn't last long. The door opened and Stacey walked in, followed by a few of her friends. Wasn't winter break over yet? Why were they still hanging around town?

She glanced around, then beelined it for the largest booth. I was already annoyed by her presence and I hadn't even talked to her yet. I waited until the group of five was settled before I started walking toward them. Stacey snuggled up next to the male on her side and he threw his arm around her, pulling her closer. My brow furrowed. Interesting. While many shifters weren't loyal to their partners, most had enough respect for who they were with to conduct their affairs in private. Not that anything stayed secret around here for long.

Knowing Stacey, though, she wouldn't risk her position as Dax's girlfriend. Which meant they were in another phase where they weren't together. In high school, I could never keep up with when they were broken up or not.

"Hi there." I plastered on a fake smile. "What can I get you today?"

"Oh, hi, Ivy," Stacey said, her tone oddly dreamy.

My brow furrowed. That wasn't her usual behavior. Come to think of it, even her body language was off. Rather than her being the possessive bitch she was, the tables were turned. The new male was the one holding her like she might escape. I didn't know him, but I'd seen him around town. He was probably five years older than us.

"Who's your new friend?" I hated that concern had seeped into me. This was Stacey, after all. But if she was in distress, I'd at least say something to Holden. I might hate her, but I didn't want to see another woman in trouble.

"This is Colton," she purred, then stroked his cheek like he was a puppy.

Okay, maybe he was the one in distress. "Nice to meet you, Colton." I glanced around at her friends. They all looked a little annoyed, but none of them looked upset. I supposed this was just the new boyfriend.

"He's my true mate," Stacey said. "Imagine that? All those years I chased Dax for what? Nothing could compare to how Colton makes me feel."

Colton leaned in and devoured Stacey's mouth in a way that belonged somewhere far more private than here. I looked away, feeling a little nauseous. "I'm happy for you."

She giggled. "Colton, wait till after."

"Drinks?" I asked.

"Three pitchers of beer," Colton said.

"You got it." I hurried away without waiting to see if they wanted food. I never enjoyed seeing Stacey and Dax together, but that was a whole new level of disturbing.

Thankfully, the newly mated couple kept their hands mostly to themselves whenever I stopped by. Tables filled up, our second bartender and Kennedy arrived, and the four of us managed the chaos and crowds till the shift ended.

Louis and Kennedy had left for the night, and Kayla was in the kitchen washing the parts for the margarita machine. I held down the front, wiping empty tables and imagining how good a bath might feel. The bell jingled. "We're closed. Come back after the full moon."

"I didn't come for a drink," a growly male voice said.

I looked up and saw Dax standing in the doorway. "If you're looking for your girlfriend, she's not here."

"I'm looking for you," he said.

"I don't have anything to say to you." That two weeks of him ignoring me had gone by way too quickly. I wanted nothing more than to return to that. Or for him to return to school. Either way, I was fine if I didn't have to deal with him.

He crossed the room and stopped inches from me. "You're going to be my date tomorrow night at the full moon party."

"Um, no, I'm not," I said. Even if I might be a tiny bit curious about the parties, I was really looking forward to my night off. And I really didn't want to spend more time with all the assholes I got drinks for every other day of the month. This was my night.

"You don't have a choice," he said.

"I do have a choice. And besides, I've never shifted and I'm not a full member," I reminded him. "I'm not welcome, anyway."

"That's why you're coming. You're the only one left in

our graduating class who hasn't shifted yet. My dad thinks the party might force it out of you. He thinks you've held back your wolf. It won't do for a shifter to not shift," he said. "It makes the whole pack look weak."

"Good thing I'm not officially pack," I said.

"If you don't shift soon, you might be facing exile before you even pay off that pathetic debt of yours," he said.

My jaw dropped, and I quickly caught myself and closed it. "You have no authority to do that."

"That's not coming from me," he said. "That's coming from my dad. But as soon as I'm alpha, I get to call the shots. You sure you want to test me?"

"I won't be your date," I said.

He reached up, grabbed my throat, and roughly pushed me against the wall. I dropped the rag and grabbed for his hand. He held tight, making it hard to breathe. My vision blurred, and I gasped, clawing at his arms.

"You will not disrespect me." Dax released my throat, then caged me in, an arm on either side of my head. "Do you understand?"

"Why are you doing this?" I whispered, my voice hoarse.

"I told you. I want you. Right now, I'm giving you a choice, but once I'm alpha, I can force you. I'd rather you accept this on your own." He dropped his hands. "I'll pick you up at sunset."

As he walked away, I reached for my neck and tried to

shake the feeling of his grip from me. I hadn't even seen Dax since that night at the fight, and prior to that, he'd never had any romantic interest in me. Why now?

"You almost done?" Kayla called as she walked out of the kitchen. She was carrying margarita machine parts, which blocked her view. "Want to walk out together?"

I was grateful she hadn't seen me up against the wall. I picked up the discarded towel and tossed it into the laundry basket. There was more I could do, but fuck that. I needed to get out of here. "Yeah, let's go."

My mind replayed the conversation with Dax over and over. I had to think of a way out of it. Dax seemed focused on hooking up with me, no matter what. Was it a conquest thing? Fuck the girl he tormented in high school for some kind of sick notch on his bedpost? Or was there something else going on?

I needed to figure out a way to end this, and I wasn't coming up with anything that wouldn't result in me getting screwed. As much as there was wrong with this pack, I needed them. By the time I arrived home, the only thing I could think of was to go with Dax and be the world's most boring date. It had to be a random fixation. Something that came as a result of Stacey's mating bond. He was probably on the rebound and I was an easy, throw away target. Once he got to know me better, and saw how little we had in common, he would stop, right?

It was the only way I got myself to sleep that night. That little lie that he'd get over this fixation and I could get away unscathed.

CHAPTER NINE

Restless didn't even begin to explain the waves of emotions rolling through me as I waited for the sun to set. Night was coming far too quickly. Damn these short winter days.

I paced around my living room, wishing I had been able to fulfill my fantasy of a quiet day of doing nothing. Instead, the anticipation and dread of what was coming tonight prevented me from even enjoying my coffee while it was still warm. I'd zoned out a few times, wondering what games Dax might be playing. Meanwhile, my coffee was ice cold.

What was he up to? First, he kissed me the night we fought, then he practically vanished for two weeks. Now, he wants to take me to the full moon party. None of it made sense.

I stopped walking as icy cold fear slithered down my

spine. What if he was involved in the mess with Holden and the Dark Wolf? What if they were going to off me in the woods? Most of the pack would be at that party, but they'd be distracted. They could probably figure out a way for a non-shifted woman to get trampled to death by wolves.

We all learned early on not to mess with wolves in our human form. While we were supposed to have control over our wolf forms, instinct still drove us. We weren't as aware in that form. The animal parts got to drive some of our decisions. Which meant it was dangerous to be around as a fragile human. Especially someone like me who had yet to shift.

Kate hadn't come home last night, so I'd had all day to overthink every possible situation. I considered hiding when the knock on my door came. I could pretend I was asleep, or I could go into town and find something that was open. Okay, nothing would be open by sunset, but there were ways I could avoid being home.

As much as I tried to think of a way out of this, my mind reminded me that Dax was going to be alpha. There was very little I could do once he gained that title. Staying off his radar wasn't an option anymore, so the only other choice I had was to stay on his good side. He was bound to get bored of me eventually, right?

I ran a hand through my long blonde hair and glanced at the clock on the wall above the fireplace. *Shit.* It was going to be nightfall soon, and I was no closer to figuring out either what he wanted or a way out of it.

Resigned to go along with it, I headed to the shower and got ready for a night out. I figured I should look the part, play along, and maybe Dax would ease up. I doubted it, but what choice did I have? If he was planning to kill me, it wasn't like skipping tonight would prevent it. He was the alpha's son and if he wanted me dead, my boss did, too. It wasn't like Holden couldn't take me out just as easily. He'd done it with Darleen, and nobody even batted an eye.

It wasn't a comforting thought.

As I pulled on my jeans, a flicker of something else filled my chest. A nearly imperceptible sensation of restlessness mixed with desire. It reminded me of the time I'd thought I'd felt my wolf. I paused; my fingers frozen in the act of buttoning my jeans. There was only one thing I hadn't considered in all my ideas and thoughts today. What if Dax really did want me to shift?

I was the last one of my high school graduating class. It wasn't considered a lost cause until you reached twenty-two, but it was rare to shift so late. I expected it to happen sometime soon, but what if the full moon party could push up the timeline? While we'd been discouraged from being around shifted wolves in our human forms, we'd also heard stories of people shifting for the first time because someone they were with went through the change. As if one wolf called to the other.

At this party, I was going to be surrounded by wolves. My heart raced and for the first time all day, I felt excitement. I was curious to see what these parties were like, and I did want to shift. What if that's all it was?

Sure, Dax was after sex. That was glaringly obvious, but what if he really was trying to fulfill his role as a leader? I supposed it would make our pack stronger to have more shifters.

Someone pounded on my door, shaking me from my thoughts. I finished buttoning my jeans and pulled on my tee. After I grabbed my hoodie, I made my way to the front door.

Dax was waiting on my doorstep, the sun sinking low into the horizon behind him. He was cast in a warm glow, his hair shining, and his tanned biceps and forearms looking even more muscular in the light. Fuck. He was handsome. He had dark stubble across his cheeks and over his strong jaw. His full lips were quirked in a smirk, as if he knew I was checking him out. With a self-assured grin, he swept his arm away from my door. "Shall we?"

"Sure, let's get this over with," I said.

"Try not to sound too happy about it," he replied. "I don't want you too excited before we even arrive."

I bit back a smile at his easy sarcasm. I'd never seen this side of him, and I wondered how long it would last. Underneath this easy-going facade was the man who had his hand around my throat last night.

I locked my apartment, then turned to him. "I'm ready. Let's go."

It was odd climbing into the front seat next to Dax. Growing up, the only time he noticed me was if he was picking on me or hurting me. This was a mind fuck, for sure.

As we turned out of the parking lot, I looked over at him. His expression was neutral and unreadable but focused on the road ahead of him. I took a moment to assess him more. He was wearing dark jeans and a gray tee that was stretched over his thick arms and firm chest. I hated how handsome he was.

Dax glanced over at me. "You excited for tonight?"

I glared at him. "Are you serious?"

"I thought you might like the idea of finally getting to shift. This could be the night for you," he said.

"You are a literal contradiction. You know that?" I turned to look out the window.

"What are you talking about?"

"You honestly don't see it, do you? You tormented me for years, you beat the shit out of me in the ring, then you come into my work and threaten me so I'll go with you to some stupid party I'm not even welcome at?" I stared at him, not hiding my judgment in my expression.

"I thought you'd want to go," he said.

"Okay, forget about the fucking party. Why the hell do you have any interest in me all the sudden?" I demanded.

"I told you. I never noticed how gorgeous you were. And I have to admit, the way you held your own in the ring was hot."

"So, I'm just supposed to forget years of torment and melt into your arms?" I asked skeptically.

"Why not?"

"Because you choked me and demanded I come with you, you asshole," I snapped.

"Oh."

"Yeah, oh," I rolled my eyes and returned to the window. This night could not be over soon enough.

"I really was asked to bring you," he admitted. "My dad keeps tabs on the foundlings."

"That doesn't surprise me," I grumbled. Some of the kids I'd grown up with had entered into service with the alpha. It was supposed to be a great honor, but I knew he didn't pay. He simply counted their hours toward their debt. Nobody that had gone that route had earned their freedom. I supposed for some people, working for the alpha was enough. Not for me. I wanted to own my life.

"He keeps asking me about you," he said. "Wants to know if you have any special skills and shit."

"I hope you told him I don't," I said.

"I told him you could fight, but you weren't anything special."

To anyone else, those words might have seemed like an insult. I knew them for what they were. Being average would keep me out of the alpha's service. He had plenty of desperate people who wanted to work for him. If I wasn't important, he wouldn't bother with me. Because of my debt, if he called me to work for him, I'd have no choice.

I looked over at Dax. He had his eyes on the road, not looking at me. "Thanks."

He pulled the car into a dirt lot already packed with other cars, and parked. After he turned off the car, he looked over at me. "Look, Ivy. I thought I'd be with Stacey, but she found her true mate. My dad found his when he was nineteen. I have met every shifter in the pack and lots of shifters from other packs. My mate isn't out there. But I still need a partner. I can't be alpha without a wife. It's just how things work around here."

"You don't want me, Dax," I said.

"I do. You're by far the most beautiful single girl in town and you can hold your own. I want this to be your choice, but you will be mine. I'll give you as much time as I can, but it's going to happen either way."

"Are you insane? You can't just make someone be your partner. That's not how it works," I snapped.

Dax turned and grabbed my arm, pulling me closer. His dark eyes were wide and bright in the low light. He looked like a man possessed. I'd seen him angry before. I'd even seen him enjoy every second of hurting me or someone else. I'd never seen this look. It was like something came over him, driving his actions in a way unfamiliar to me.

"You are pack property. If I wanted to claim you right now, I could, and nobody would question me. You're lucky I want you to choose this on your own, but I won't wait forever." He released my arm, tossing it to the side as if I was something disgusting.

"You don't want me. We're nothing alike. If we were together, I'd make your life a living hell and you know it," I said.

"Maybe that's what I want. Nobody stands up to me.

You always have. All these years, even when it cost you, you never backed down. I need someone like that. Someone who can hold her own. There's nobody else. You're the only one who can handle what's coming," he said.

"You don't want someone defiant by your side. You need a pretty face you can drag along to all the things where you get to show off your power," I said.

"Someone like Stacey wouldn't last long in the days ahead," he said.

"What the fuck are you talking about? *The days ahead?* Is a comet heading for the planet? Zombies? I mean, what the hell could you possibly want me for? I won't hold your hand. I'm never going to satisfy you sexually. There's literally *nothing* between us."

His eyes swept down my body and I could almost feel his gaze as if he was brushing his hands over my skin. I shuddered, the violation of it oddly erotic.

"Don't even think about it," I snapped. My traitorous body might respond to his interest, but it didn't mean I ever wanted anything to happen between us.

"I don't have to make things happen on your terms. I can take what I want," he said.

"Try it and I'll bite your cock off, you piece of shit," I said.

He grinned. It was the look of someone who was completely unhinged. I expected him to hit me, to lash out. The smile on his lips was far worse. I scooted away, closer to the door. Something was very wrong with him. Something had changed.

Dax opened his door and stepped out, then he ducked his head in to look at me. "Have fun tonight. You can find your own way home or you can find me when it's over. Think about what I said. When you're ready to give in, I'll take you when you come to me on your knees."

CHAPTER TEN

I waited in Dax's car until he was out of sight. Shifters walked by, many paired off in couples or in large groups. Part of me longed to join them, to feel like I was part of something.

I'd always been an outsider, even more so since my classmates started shifting. Even Kate had shifted, making me feel isolated from her. I straightened, recalling that she would be here.

Finally, something was going my way. I could find her and ask for a ride home. Even if she was here with her new boyfriend, she'd drive me home. She might even do it now if she hadn't shifted yet. There was no reason for me to stick around and risk being stuck in human form around a bunch of wolves.

I exited the car and stepped onto the gravel parking lot. I took a deep breath, the scent of pine and cold winter air filling my nostrils. My breath out came in a cloud. I pulled my hood over my head and followed the other shifters toward the trees.

We were in the woods, the parking lot the only sign that anyone was around for miles. There were no structures, no paths, or roads. Simply a parking lot and a shit ton of trees.

The full moon cast a silvery glow, bright enough to see details without needing any additional light. I stepped into the forest, my feet sinking into the soft ground. Pine needles and patches of snow that hadn't melted yet lined the forest floor. It was colder in here under the trees and I regretted that I hadn't grabbed a warmer coat.

I didn't want to admit it, but I had specifically worn clothes I'd be okay with losing just in case I shifted. My wolf wasn't making any signs of reaction, so I wasn't hopeful.

The assembled shifters were fanned out around the trees, gathered in groups, moving deeper into the woods. So far, I wasn't impressed by the party. After everything I'd heard, I expected more.

I scanned the people ahead of me for Kate while maintaining distance. The last thing I needed was to run into Stacey or any of her entourage. While Dax might have made me come to this thing, he wasn't around now to explain why I was crashing an event intended only for full pack members who had shifted.

Ahead, I caught sight of flickering orange light. As I moved on, a bonfire come into view. Now, it was starting to look more like the parties I'd heard of.

Hidden deep in the thicket of the forest was a clearing. At the center, a bonfire burned. Benches and chairs surrounded the bonfire and off to the side were charcoal grills, tables with food, and several kegs. So this was the actual party.

I kept closer to the trees, afraid to be seen by the wrong people. I continued to look for Kate, but with all the movement and influx of people, it was difficult to find anyone I recognized.

Other than Dax, of course. I caught sight of him easily as he entered the clearing. He was greeted by friends who high fived or gave awkward man-hugs. From my inconspicuous space, I could see their smiles. Everyone gathered seemed to be in good spirits. It was almost contagious. I found myself wishing I could join in, but I knew that was risky.

At one point, Dax looked over my way, and our eyes met. I scowled at him, hoping he'd be able to feel how pissed I was. He winked, then went back to his friends. *Asshole.*

I tore my eyes away from him and continued to search for Kate. Finally, I found her. She was hanging on her new beau's arm, and she looked more relaxed and happier than I'd seen her in years. My heart sank. I couldn't ask her to leave this. She belonged here; she was part of this. She needed the time to run in her wolf form and she deserved the party with her boyfriend.

Feeling defeated, I blew out a long breath. We weren't that far from town. Okay, fine, we were probably ten miles out of town. But walking back was likely better than hiding here, waiting for a wolf to scent me. Besides, movement would make me warmer. I turned and took a few steps away from the clearing.

A roar of applause sounded from the crowd, and I looked back to them. Preston was near the fire, the rest of the shifters in a circle around him. He had his hands in the air and a smile on his lips. I realized I hadn't pressed too much when Dax had insisted that his dad was the reason I was here, and my curiosity took over. I stepped closer to the party, staying near a large tree to help conceal me so I could listen.

Preston calmed the shifters, then spoke in a clear, strong voice. "Full moon nights are the nights for all shifters. Our wolves thrive on our connection to the moon. It is our mother, our creator, our source of energy and life. As we do on all full moons, we let go of our fear, release our inhibitions, and allow our instincts to take control."

Something flickered in my chest. That strange sensation I'd felt before. I took a shaky breath, wondering if it really was my inner wolf.

"Tonight, you will be your wolf. Abandon your human side, allow your wolf the freedom of release. Shadow wolves, it's time to run." Preston pulled his shirt over his head and tossed it aside. Then he stepped out of his jeans, leaving him naked in front of the flickering fire. He was strong and muscular, an older version of his son. I had to look away. It felt far too personal to see him naked. Especially after what Dax had said to me earlier tonight.

Shifters were raised to think of nudity as normal, but I wasn't there yet. For a kid who was always in a scuffle, my skin was a glaring reminder of my last beating. I had never removed my clothes in front of anyone. I didn't even like changing for gym class. Sure, I was often late for class because I waited for a bathroom stall, but it meant I didn't have to show the bruises and scars on my skin.

Whoops and cheers echoed into the cold night air. When I glanced back at the bonfire, clothes were flying through the air. All the gathered shifters were stripping down. The crunching sound of breaking bones soon replaced the human voices as bodies folded and broke, reforming from human into wolf.

The flickering in my chest accelerated, my heart raced, my face felt hot. The feeling inside me turned from annoying to uncomfortable. Then it felt like I was being burned from the inside. My whole body felt like it was on fire. My head was spinning, and I buckled over, grabbing my stomach. I was sure I was about to vomit all over the forest floor.

Shooting pain radiated from my chest, racing through my limbs. I screamed. It felt like I was being ripped apart. This was it. I was dying. Something awful was happening to me.

I collapsed to my knees, my hands hitting the frozen ground. Panting, sweating, terrified, I had to work to get my vision to focus. When I glanced at my hands, I realized my fingers were gone. They'd been replaced by paws. Wolf paws.

I was shifting.

I think I was crying, but all I could hear was a rushing sound in my ears as my body contorted and bent into its new form. I knew this day would come, and unlike the more organized packs, the Shadow Wolves didn't have the aid of witches or magic to shift when it was convenient. Instead, we shifted sometime between eighteen and twenty-two. It came without warning, usually on a full moon, and always at night.

As the pain eased, I closed my eyes and took a moment to catch my breath. When I finally felt like I'd regained some sense of control, I opened my eyes. It was like looking at the world for the first time. Everything was sharper and brighter. I could see deep into the woods, far beyond the clearing with the fire. I could hear the footsteps of the other shifters around me. Soft feet padding through the underbrush, changing in pace and direction. My ears twitched, tuning into the cacophony around me. The breeze in the trees, the call of an owl, the howl of a far-off wolf.

I lifted my right paw and looked at it before setting it down and examining the other. My fur was dark gray. The color of a shadow. Wind rustled my fur, and I shook, feeling my new body move and react. It was both exhilarating and terrifying to be in this form.

I had to wonder if tonight was always meant to be my night to have my first shift, or if Dax had known that bringing me here would speed things up for me. Footsteps approached, and I tensed, leaning back on my rear legs.

Teeth bared, a growl at the ready, I waited for the intruder.

A huge black wolf emerged from the trees. He shook his head when he saw me, then let out a snort of air as he locked eyes on me. My tension eased a bit as my instincts took over. This was another member of my pack and my wolf wanted to be friends. The newcomer took a few cautious steps toward me and as he approached; I caught his scent. Woody and smokey and intoxicating. As soon as it hit me, it rolled through me, aligning the scent with the one male I was uninterested in seeing. I growled, letting Dax know I wasn't interested in playing.

He leaped forward, stopping just short of me, and nuzzled his nose against mine. I backed up, trying hard to maintain my anger, but it was melting away. Dax batted at me playfully and on instinct, I returned the gesture. He did it again and again, his wolf tapping me with his paws quickly, as if poking me. I batted him back and my wolf was elated. She was loving the playful interaction, and I didn't have any control over stopping her enjoyment.

Then Dax took off, racing through the trees. My wolf instantly jumped into action, giving chase. I tried to use logic, to tell myself that Dax was the last person I wanted to interact with in any form, but the ground under my paws, the wind in my fur, the sensation of weaving through trees was overwhelming. The more I tried to fight it, the harder it got. Running after Dax through the woods was too much fun.

I wasn't used to my new body yet, but it didn't seem to

matter. I adjusted to running on all fours, leaping over fallen logs and splashing through streams. I felt freer than I had in my entire life. Chasing Dax was exhilarating, and the longer we ran, the more I felt like I wanted to do this forever.

We raced onward, moving higher in elevation. The terrain grew rockier and the trees sparser. I didn't question anything. I just wanted to run. Finally, after what might have been hours, Dax stopped.

My wolf came to a halt reluctantly, and I panted heavily. All my muscles were burning, but I felt so alive. Dax looked up at the sky and I followed his lead, staring up at the moon. It was directly above us, a huge glowing white orb illuminating the hills around us.

I looked at our surroundings and noted we were at the top of a foothill. I could see our little town nestled below, bathed in the light of the moon. It was stunning. For once, our little shit hole on the Fringes looked peaceful, beautiful even.

Dax howled, loud and long. The tone caught something in me, pulling my gaze back toward the moon. I opened my mouth and joined in. The pure sweet sound of a howl escaped my throat, working in unison with Dax's.

When we finished, there was a heartbeat of silence before an eruption of howls filled the air. We were surrounded by the sound of our pack, hundreds of other wolves crying out to the moon. My heart was so full it felt like it might explode. How had I missed out on this my entire life?

CHAPTER
ELEVEN

FROM OUR PERCH on top of the foothill, I could see the city beyond the Fringes. In the center of the sprawl were high-rise buildings, giving way to shorter buildings as it radiated out. The city was densely packed compared to the tiny pocket of our town. Surprisingly, it didn't look as far away as I thought it was. I'd never left the Fringes.

By comparison, our single Main Street lined with businesses and side roads leading to residential areas almost looked like make believe compared to the scale of the city in the distance.

"It's beautiful up here, isn't it?" Dax asked.

I jumped, surprised to hear his human voice return. He was standing next to me, completely naked. I'd seen Dax shirtless countless times in gym class or at the swimming hole. But it had been a few years, and he had filled out a lot. I couldn't help but let my gaze drop from his chest, down his six-pack, toward the vee of his hips. Once I caught sight of his fully erect and proportionally large member, I looked up quickly. This was too intimate, and I was grateful I was still in wolf form.

As if my thoughts initiated it, my body shuddered, and I could feel the contractions as my wolf form gave way to my human form. *No, no, no*. Not now. I didn't want to be naked and alone with Dax.

I tried to take a few steps, hoping to get back to the cover of the denser woods, but my body wasn't responding. The change came fast, sharp pains shooting through me as my limbs broke and bent.

It didn't take long before I was hunched over on all fours, panting as if I'd been running for hours. The change back to human was rougher on my body and it took me a moment to collect myself.

"It gets easier," Dax assured me.

I looked up at him, then remembered that I was totally naked. The bright moonlight illuminated every inch of skin, showing all my bruises and scars. I covered my chest and turned away to hide as much as I could. "Why did you shift back before we were back?"

It had to be his fault, right? I didn't want to shift back, but seeing the other shifters transition to wolves had awakened the wolf inside me. It must have worked to bring me back to human as well.

"You shouldn't stay in wolf form too long your first shift," Dax said. "I was trying to help you."

"I don't want your help," I said.

"You don't have to cover yourself," he said. "It's not like I haven't seen a hundred naked women before."

"That's not helpful," I snapped.

He extended a hand. "Come on. I'll walk you back."

"Don't touch me." I stood on my own, keeping my arms crossed over my breasts. After everything he'd done to me, I didn't want anything from him. And I really didn't want to show him my body. It felt like giving in to his bizarre request for us to be a couple. Which was never, ever going to happen.

"Look, I had to piss you off in the car," he said. "It's the best way to get the wolf to show. Emotions, especially anger, drive our wolves. Why do you think so many shifters have their first transition to wolf after a big break up or during a fight?"

I'd heard that before. It wasn't exactly a secret that emotions were tied to our wolves showing. It was self-defense sometimes and often drove our first shift. I knew that, but I hadn't been in a hurry to shift. "What if I didn't want to shift yet? You ever consider that?"

"You can be mad at me all you want, but I'm not any different than anyone else in the pack. If my dad says I have to help you shift, I have to follow through," he said.

I narrowed my eyes.

"Why do you think I kissed you after the fight?" He grinned.

"Cause you're fucking crazy?" I suggested.

He laughed. "I was trying to get a rise out of you. After my dad saw us fight, he ordered me to get you to shift. He sees value in your abilities. I wish I could say I was holding back when we fought." He shook his head. "You've got serious natural talent."

"All of that was to get me to shift?" It seemed unlikely, but this was the Shadows and stranger things had happened. If the alpha really did demand it, he wouldn't have a choice.

"Is that why Stacey attacked me?" I asked. "Was she working on his orders, too?"

Dax's brow furrowed. "Stacey attacked you?"

"After the fight that night. Jumped me in the parking lot with a few other shifters. Something about keeping my hands off her man." I rolled my eyes. "I'm not sure if it's funny or sad that she found a mate that wasn't you a week later."

"We weren't even together that night. I broke up with her last semester," Dax said. "Don't worry, I'll take care of her."

"I don't need or want you to take care of anything. You've done enough." I walked away, watching for rocks as I traversed the uneven terrain in bare feet. "Did you really have to make us shift back up here?" I didn't even turn back to see his reaction, and I didn't expect a response.

"Yeah, probably not my best idea," he said.

I glanced over my shoulder. Had he just admitted he was wrong about something? That didn't seem like Dax at all. I was going to get whiplash from this asshole to nice guy routine.

"You know, I still think we'd be good together. If you ever feel like giving me a chance. We could go on a real date. Somewhere that isn't the Howler," he said.

"So running up a mountain and walking back down while naked isn't good enough for you?" I teased.

He laughed. An honest, actual, deep and, to my horror, sexy laugh. I wasn't sure I'd ever heard that before.

"Come on, they'll have blankets by the fire." He caught up to me and walked alongside me.

The two of us made our way through the woods in silence. My feet were numb when we returned to the clearing. I was shivering, but I wasn't as cold as I should have been. I realized the shifter powers were already taking hold. A little thrill rose in my chest. Did that mean I'd get the other perks soon, too? I should be stronger, and heal faster, in addition to running a lot warmer than I had pre-shift.

Dax led me to a stack of blankets and pulled two from the pile. I took one gratefully, wrapping it around my naked body. There weren't many people in human form around the fire, but more shifters emerged from the woods with each passing second. Knots formed in my stomach. I wasn't technically allowed to be here. "I think I should go."

"Stay. My dad wanted you here," he said.

"I'm not full pack," I reminded Dax.

"You're my guest," he replied.

I still wasn't happy about that, even if Dax had been trying to get a rise from me. Maybe I'd forgive him if he hadn't been a complete asshole to me as long as I'd known him. Or if he'd at least apologize, which he hadn't. I kept that to myself as I took in the increasing number of shifters returned to human form. Going off on Dax wouldn't improve my status in the pack. In fact, it could make it so my debt never got repaid, and I knew it.

I swallowed back the anger that surged in my chest. The whole system was broken. It wasn't my fault my parents dropped me at the foundling house. There was no punishment for parents who abandoned their child, but I was going to have to pay their debt simply because I existed.

"Speak of the devil," Dax said.

I turned in the direction of his gaze to see the alpha walking toward us. He was just as naked as most of the gathered shifters and I fought to keep my eyes at chest level and above. I had no interest in seeing if he and Dax's similarities extended beyond their general appearance.

"Since you're naked, it means either you just fucked Dax, which I suppose is possible after all that foreplay in the ring; or you finally shifted," Preston said.

Did everyone think that fight we had was considered foreplay? I blinked a few times, then fixed a smile on my face. "Shifted."

I didn't think he could get you in bed," Preston said.

My lips parted, and I wanted to say something snarky, but I felt a little bad for Dax. Weren't parents supposed to be supportive? Most of my experience about how families worked came from Kate's family. And her parents would never say something so demeaning to her.

"You impressed me in the ring. Was that really your first time?" Preston asked.

"Yeah. I mean, unless you count all the brawls as a kid," I said.

He slapped me on the back as if we were best friends. "That's what I thought. You're a fighter. I have use for someone like you. With some training, you could be spectacular."

"Um, thanks." I wasn't sure where this was going, but I wasn't getting a good feeling.

"I'm going to keep my eyes on you. I think you've got potential. I'll be watching you with interest," he said.

I forced a smile, unsure of how to respond. I wasn't even a full member, but I'd managed to gain the alpha's attention. That wasn't part of my plan. I was fine just blending in. At least until I paid my debt.

"I don't know, Dad," Dax said. "She just shifted tonight. She's going to need more practice."

"Of course she will," Preston countered. "She's got natural talent. An alpha knows these things."

It felt like I was living in another dimension. What was going on? Why was the alpha interested in me when he'd never noticed me before?

Preston and Dax were both watching me, and I felt like I had to say something. "Thank you for the kind words."

"When you're more comfortable with your wolf, come

find me. I might have a job for you. A way to pay back that debt faster," Preston said.

I tensed and tried to hide my disappointment. Working for the alpha never got anyone out of debt. That's all this was. He wanted another servant. "I'll keep it in mind."

"You do that," Preston said as he turned and left.

"You can't work for my dad. He's not what he seems," Dax warned.

I had no intention of working for the alpha, but Dax's words pissed me off. What right did he have to have any say in my life? I narrowed my eyes. "You brought me out here tonight and basically forced my shift. You dragged me into the ring to fight you and have pretended to have a bizarre interest in me. Yet, you're warning me against working for your dad? The beloved alpha of our pack?"

"There are things you don't know about him, okay?" Dax said.

I scoffed. "Coming from you, that means very little."

"Just don't rush into it, trust me," he said.

"I wasn't planning on it originally, but the fact that you're against it makes me question my decision," I snapped.

"Trust me on this. You don't want to work for him." Dax sounded genuine, like he was concerned about my well-being. It was really messing with my head.

Before I could say anything else, music filled the air and cheers erupted. I looked around and realized that the trickle of shifters had ballooned into a crowd, all in human form. People paired off, or gathered in groups and started dancing and swaying to the beat. Even I felt the pull to join in the fun.

"Want to dance?" Dax asked.

I turned to him. "Why are you being nice to me? We aren't friends. We've never been friends."

"I told you, I was trying to push you earlier," he said.

"But you have a history of being a dick," I said.

"And people grow up," he said. "Come on, would it kill you to do something fun?"

It had been a long time since I'd had a night off. And I'd never been to a party in the woods. Shit, I wasn't sure I'd ever been to any party aside from the sad holiday parties at the foundling house.

Dax extended a hand. "I'm a terrible dancer. You can ridicule me mercilessly if it helps."

I laughed. "You know how to sell it."

The two of us moved closer to the bonfire, and I tied the blanket around me like a toga. Some of the shifters had clothes on, but many were naked. The fire was warm enough with our shifter heat to keep the winter chill away.

Dax was right. He was an awful dancer, but despite that, I was having fun. A few songs later, I almost forgot about how terrible he had been to me in the past. Was it possible he'd matured?

We took a break to grab a drink. The night was going far better than I expected. I was actually having fun. But as I caught sight of Stacey and her mate heading our way, my shoulders slumped. I should have known it was going to come crashing down, eventually.

She approached the table and filled a red plastic cup with an overly generous pour of bourbon. Her eyes floated up to mine and her glare was intense. I stared back, unwilling to be the first to blink.

After a long drink from her cup, she finally took her gaze off me, turning her attention to Dax. "I see you ran out of reputable girls to fuck."

Dax closed the distance between him and Stacey in a blur of movement. He grabbed her chin and lifted her face so she was looking at him.

"What the fuck, Dax?" Stacey's mate stepped toward Dax.

Dax growled at him, then returned his gaze to Stacey. Her mate froze. Even I felt the authority behind that growl. He wasn't alpha yet, but he'd called on that part of him.

"If you ever touch Ivy again, I will kill you." His tone was deadly.

"Dax, that's not necessary," I said.

He shoved Stacey. "I'm serious. She's off limits to everyone."

Stacey let out a squeak that might have been agreement.

"Dax, stop it," I hissed.

He glared at Stacey for a moment longer. "Get out of my sight."

Stacey and her mate fled, leaving me alone with Dax.

He turned toward me. His jaw was tense and I could see the lingering anger flashing in his eyes.

"I can take care of myself," I snapped.

His expression softened. "I'm sorry. You're not mine. I had no right."

What the hell was going on here?

"Do you want to dance again?" he asked.

I needed some time to process all the weirdness of the night. Away from him. But I'd seen the flashes of anger and the power he could wield. I couldn't risk pissing him off.

"I'd like to find my friend Kate. I want to tell her I shifted. She'll kill me if someone else tells her first," I said.

"Alright. Find me later," he said.

I nodded, then made my escape. My head was spinning as I wandered around the crowd. This had to be the strangest night of my whole life. It took a few minutes, but I finally found Kate. She was wrapped around her new boyfriend. The two of them focused on each other, unaware of anything around them.

For a moment, I considered leaving them alone, but Kate really would be pissed if I didn't tell her first. I weaved through the crowd to reach her, then tapped her on the shoulder.

She jumped when she saw me. "What are you doing here?"

I grabbed her hand and pulled her away from her date. "Excuse me, but I need to borrow her."

He shrugged. "As long as I get to take her home at the end of the night, I don't care what happens in between."

"Cute," I deadpanned.

"My name is Ryan, by the way," he said. "I'm guessing you're the best friend and roommate she wasn't willing to introduce me to until I passed some kind of test."

"Nice to meet you. And it's not her test you should be worried about. It's the test I give you that really counts," I said.

He blinked.

"We'll be back," I said as I dragged Kate away.

"What is going on?" Kate demanded as soon as we were away from the crowd.

"I shifted," I said.

"What? Holy shit! Tell me everything," she shouted.

CHAPTER TWELVE

Kate listened with rapt attention until I finished explaining my night. I held none of the details back, including the invitation from the night before. When I finished, she was staring at me with wide eyes.

We were silent for several long moments. She blinked and shook her head. "What the actual fuck?"

"I know!" I was so glad I'd found her.

"When did Dax fall for you? Was this before or after the night you guys fought in the ring? Do you think he's secretly been into you since high school?"

"That's what you got out of this?" I asked.

"I mean, he's emotionally stunted and has no idea how to impress a woman, but it's obvious, isn't it?" She lifted her eyebrows.

"It doesn't matter if he likes me. He's fucking crazy," I said.

"Maybe he's matured a bit?" she offered.

I rolled my eyes. "Whose side are you on here?"

"Yours, always yours," she insisted. "And I'm not saying you have to marry the guy. He's not your mate. Why do you think I hadn't introduced you to Ryan? He's fun. The sex is fantastic. But we're shifters. If our mate shows up, none of our other relationships matter. They're all practice, or fun. Who gives a fuck if he was a dick as a teenager? We're all assholes when we're teenagers."

"I wasn't," I mumbled.

"You know what I mean. If you want to walk away from Dax, I support that. If you want to spend the night with him and not call in the morning, I won't judge."

I lifted a brow. "It sounds like that's what you're recommending."

"You deserve to have fun from time to time," she said.

Kate was gorgeous and confident. She'd honestly probably mentioned Ryan by name, but I never even bothered to learn it. He'd be replaced soon enough by some other guy. Kate wasn't shy about her sexuality. While she had a point about the mating bond, it wasn't likely to happen for either of us.

Shadow Wolves were rarely granted permission to leave our territory. Which meant we didn't mingle with other packs as often as some wolves. If we didn't meet our mate by the time we had our first shift, it was unlikely we ever would.

Sure, there were new shifters exiled to the Fringes every day. They spent years working to prove their loyalty before they were accepted as full pack, but they were around to add to the possible mate pool. Kate was a hopeless romantic who thought she'd find her true mate, eventually. I wasn't so sure. But what did I know? Stacey had found hers, so maybe there was hope for the rest of us.

"Listen, you have good instincts," Kate said. "Trust your gut."

"Thanks," I said. "Go back to your date before he worries I'm going to steal you away."

She laughed. "Thanks. You need me to come home tonight?"

"No, go have fun. I'll be fine," I said.

"Alright. Call me if you change your mind. Otherwise, I'll see you in the morning. And I'll bring coffee on my way cause we're out," she said.

I gave her a quick hug, then shoved her back toward the group.

I could hear Kate giggling as she reunited with her date, and a pang of longing went through me. I never let myself date anyone. Not that I had any offers, to be honest. Being a reject in a pack full of rejects was an odd situation. If I'd wanted to explore relationships, I was certain I could have found a hook-up. Possibly even something more long term if I wasn't too picky. I mean, Blake had been trying to get me in bed for the last two years. But guys always seemed like a distraction from my goal. Or they were flat out assholes like Blake. If I took Friday nights off to go out, I'd miss out on making money.

There was no bar to work a shift at tonight, just as there wasn't on any full moon. If I did act on the advances

Dax had made, I wouldn't be missing out on anything. Aside from my dignity, that was. Though sex wasn't a big deal around here. It wasn't like a future mate cared how many partners you'd had. I even heard some males talking about how they hoped for an experienced mate.

One of the perks of being a shifter was that we couldn't catch the diseases humans spread through sex. Add in that pregnancy was exceedingly rare, and it made for a culture of lots of random hook-ups. The only time anyone seemed to care was once they were mated. You did not cheat on your mate for any reason. In fact, it was shifter law that you had to be loyal to your mate.

All these thoughts continued to swirl in my mind while I watched the increasingly wild party unfolding in front of me. I could practically see inhibitions breaking down as shifters paired off and pulled away from the group. Some who had been clothed weren't any longer and a few couples were damn close to going to home base out in the open.

Desire coursed through me, catching me off guard. I had hormones just like everyone else, but aside from my fingers, I had very little experience. I knew how to get myself off, but some days it wasn't enough. For the first time, I started to wonder if I should just lose the v-card and see if actual sex was all that much better than what I could take care of myself.

I caught sight of Dax weaving his way through the crowd. He was wearing jeans now, but his chest was bare. In the flickering light of the fire, his chiseled chest and rippling abs looked even sexier than before. His hair was messy and wild and the smile on his handsome face was infectious. I had a sudden urge to use my tongue to trace that strong jawline. *Fuck me*. The curiosity and lust were working against logic, urging me to see how far I could take things with Dax.

"I was starting to worry that you found another ride home," he said.

"I was just watching the party," I said.

"You know, I just talked to my dad. He's going to change the rules starting next full moon," he said.

"What do you mean?" I asked.

"It wasn't right that foundlings couldn't attend. It's not like your loyalty is in question. He's going to change it so foundlings aren't cut out of pack events. Just cause your parents weren't able to care for you, doesn't mean you should be punished."

My heart melted, and I looked at Dax as if seeing him for the first time. Was it possible Kate was right? Had he grown up and changed?

"What's that look for?" Dax eyed me nervously. "If I didn't know better, I'd say you were going to bite me. And I'm not sure if that's good or bad."

"My expression is giving off biting vibes?" I asked.

"Just a little," he confessed.

"Maybe it's the good kind of biting," I said, attempting to be flirty. It wasn't a trait that came naturally to me. I was much better at sarcastic remarks and insults.

Dax smirked, and there was no denying the meaning in his expression. "I might be willing to take my chances."

I bit down on my lower lip to suppress a giggle. I was fucking terrible at this and I had no idea what I was doing.

"Come on, I want to show you something." Dax reached for my hand and guided me away from the party.

We walked for several minutes, heading deeper into the woods, neither of us speaking. My feet were unsteady on the forest floor and I stepped on more than one painful pinecone. The only perk was that my feet weren't freezing. That shifter heat had to be kicking in for me. "Not to be a party pooper, but the lack of shoes is making me want to turn back."

"We're almost there," he said.

With each step, the sound of the pack lessened. I started to worry that I'd made a mistake in trusting him. What if this whole thing had been a rouse to get me away from the crowd? He let people see that I was there, then he was taking me off to the middle of the woods. I'd fought Dax before and I was pretty certain I could at least defend myself enough to run back to the bonfire, assuming I didn't get lost on the way.

I was trying to decide if this was the beginning of a romantic interlude or the end of a serial killer story when I caught sight of a structure ahead.

"What is that?" I asked.

"That's what I wanted to show you," he said.

My shoulders eased as some of the tension faded. I

wasn't totally sure he wasn't going to kill me, but at least there was a possible reason to be out in the woods.

As we inched closer, I could make out the outline of a gazebo. The wood was slightly warped, and the paint was peeling. The roof was covered in a thick layer of pine needles, and one of the steps was missing entirely. I wondered how many people even knew this was out here.

We stopped in front of the decaying structure. The interior was just as worn down as the exterior. It had built-in benches that were nearly as covered in dirt and debris as the roof. Though it was ancient and had seen better days, I was instantly in love. It seemed like this magical thing in the middle of the woods, abandoned but hanging on. A memory from a time long ago.

"It's kind of amazing. How did you know this was out here?" I asked.

"My dad built it before I was born. A gift for my mom. She used to come out here to enjoy the woods. She was from one of the wild packs and grew up pretty isolated. Even our little town overwhelmed her sometimes. After she died, my dad stopped coming here. But I find it peaceful," he said.

There was so much emotion behind his words. All these years, I'd viewed him as this one-dimensional bully. Someone who enjoyed inflicting pain on others without ever stopping to consider that he might have pain of his own. Not that it excused him for his actions, but it made him into a deeper, more complex person than I'd realized.

We all knew the story of the alpha's lost mate. She'd

died when Dax was a baby and the alpha had been heartbroken. They say losing a mate is the worst kind of pain you can experience. Some shifters aren't strong enough to survive. Apparently, you can die from a broken heart.

I wondered if Preston had pushed past the agony for the sake of his child. That was not a question I was about to ask, though. "It's a special place. Thanks for showing me."

Dax took my hand in his gently, almost as if he was afraid I was going to pull away. He inched closer until we were nearly touching. Slowly, he lowered his face until his lips brushed against mine in a ghost of a kiss. He hesitated there, our lips ever so slightly touching. I breathed him in and could feel the warmth of his body. Nothing had ever been good between us, but this didn't feel bad, either. I wasn't getting alarm bells telling me to stop and while I wasn't getting an overwhelming rush to jump him, maybe not every connection would be fire and sparks.

I slid my hand to the back of his neck, then moved my fingers into his hair. With zero subtlety, I pulled his head to mine and our lips crashed together. His arms snaked around me, hands sliding under the blanket, making it fall in a puddle around my feet. I closed the space between us and my naked breasts pressed against his chest.

My body was on fire, ready for some release. It was odd being with Dax. I felt the hunger, but there wasn't any connection. I pushed the thought from my mind and deepened the kiss. It wasn't like we were settling down forever. This was just for fun, just for some release. I'd waited long enough, and I deserved to feel the pleasure I'd heard so much about.

Dax's hand rested on my hip, then moved to cup my ass. He pulled my hips closer and I could feel his hardness through his jeans. My hands began to explore his body, moving down his muscular arms, across his sexy back, finally landing on his waistband.

His fingers joined mine, working the button of his jeans open. The reality of our actions hit me and the part of my brain that reminded me of our lack of connection flared to life, beating out the rising lust. I pulled back and looked up at him. My chest rose and fell in great heaves, and I could feel the wetness between my legs. My body wanted this, but there was something that wasn't right.

"What's wrong?" He looked so concerned and for a moment, I almost went back to kissing him. But it felt hollow, shallow, wrong. It wasn't fun. I had never been saving my virginity, and I honestly never thought I'd care who my first time was with.

This wasn't about that. This was something else. That nagging sensation that Dax and I weren't compatible. As if I was being pulled somewhere else, which didn't make sense. There wasn't a single person in town I was attracted to. Sure, there were plenty of sexy, available males, but I'd never felt the need to jump into bed with any of them.

"I'm sorry. Honestly, I'm freezing." I pulled the blanket up around me, using the excuse of the weather. It was partially true. My libido had warmed me more than enough, but I wasn't about to tell Dax that I was turning him down because of some cheesy reason I didn't understand myself. I wasn't a romantic. I never had been. Why was I feeling this way all the sudden?

Dax smiled, then brushed his thumb across my cheek. "Another time, then."

"Yeah, sure," I said.

"Want me to take you home?" he asked. "You had a big night."

Dax, the perfect gentleman, was messing with my head, but the exhaustion of the first shift was starting to hit now that I'd told my sex drive to get her shit together. "Yeah, thanks."

We made our way back to the bonfire, passing several couples who had no concerns about their chosen partners tonight. My cheeks burned as I thought back to how strangely I'd reacted. Sex wasn't a big deal, so why was my brain making it into one?

To my surprise, Dax didn't even push for a kiss when he said goodbye at my door. As I closed and locked the door behind me, I shook my head and let out an exasperated sigh. What the actual fuck had happened tonight? Was I dating Dax now? Was that even something I wanted? Or was all this some random fluke?

I padded across the floor to the bathroom and dropped the blanket on the floor. I couldn't spend the rest of the night wondering about Dax. With any luck, he'd be back at school in a week and I could go back to normal. Hell, he wouldn't even be here for the next full moon. I could go with Kate and ask her to ditch her boyfriend d'jour. That could be fun. I had enjoyed being in wolf form. Running with someone I trusted, like Kate, would probably make it even better.

The hot water from the shower stung on my freezing skin, but I adjusted quickly. Soon I was cleaned up and ready for bed. I fell asleep thinking about how amazing the shift had been, while trying my best to not think about Dax.

CHAPTER
THIRTEEN

A SINGLE BARE bulb lit the empty basement. It was silent and eerie in the dim light. Everything about it was a little off, but I walked forward anyway, taking in how large the space looked without the crowd. Even the familiar scents of sweat and blood were missing.

I walked over to the bar, expecting to see Randy and Evan setting up. The counter was bare, no bottles or glasses. Was I that early for my shift? Why was nobody around?

Suddenly, the feel of the room shifted. An unusual scent caught my attention and I took a breath, trying to place it. It was smokey and comforting mixed with something familiar. Sage, maybe?

I turned and caught sight of a figure in the ring. The shadows hid the person, making it impossible to make out who it was. "Who's over there? Holden? Joe?"

The shadowy figure didn't speak. I should have felt

nervous, but there wasn't even a flicker of fear. Without concern, I moved forward, drawn to the newcomer like a moth to flame.

As I approached, the shadows seemed to shift, keeping the person shrouded from view. It should have seemed odd, but for some reason, it didn't bother me. I was too focused on reaching the ring to care.

Still unable to make out who was waiting for me, I climbed into the ring. The shadows receded, settling around the ring like a dark cloud, trapping me within the ropes.

My heart raced, but it had nothing to do with being enclosed. It was driven entirely by the male standing in front of me.

The Dark Wolf didn't say a word. His eyes swept down my body like a caress. My breath hitched, and I did the same to him, staring at his broad shoulders and muscular arms to his chest and waist, until I paused for a moment on the bulge in his jeans.

"Why do you still have your clothes on?" His voice was husky with lust.

My eyes snapped up to his, and I was suddenly held captive by his gaze. He moved closer to me, keeping his eyes locked on mine.

I tensed in anticipation of his touch. I wanted his hands on my skin, his mouth pressed against mine, my fingers in his wavy black hair. I wanted every inch of him.

When he reached me, our bodies collided as he swept me into his arms. Our lips met in a frenzy; the kiss intense and hungry. It was as if he was the only source of oxygen. My whole life depended on his lips on mine. He kissed aggressively, the pressure almost painful.

I wanted more.

His hands tangled in my hair, pulling me closer. I leaned into him, needing to feel his body against mine. It wasn't enough. Desperation crept in, and I felt an almost painful sensation of desire course through me.

I had to have him.

All of him.

It wasn't a choice. If I didn't have him, I was going to die.

It shouldn't have made sense, but I wasn't thinking clearly. My mind was fuzzy and overwhelmed. The only thoughts I could form were about how I needed to make this last forever.

When his hands moved to the edges of my tee, I broke away from the kiss and pulled my shirt off. No subtly, no hesitation. Taking off clothes would get me closer to feeling my skin against his. My lips longed to be kissing him again, but I needed the clothing to go away. I couldn't stand the thought of having anything between us.

The Dark Wolf yanked off his own shirt, then unbuttoned his pants. I worked quickly, stripping the rest of my clothes before I launched myself at him. His arms wrapped around me, pulling me in as our lips met in a collision.

My skin tingled, and little bursts of electricity sizzled where our bodies connected. I could feel my body responding, as if I had always been made for his touch.

Large hands grabbed my ass, and he lifted me up. I wrapped my legs around his waist, reveling in the closeness the new position brought. Every inch of my skin was on fire, the sensation driving me wild.

Without warning, he entered me. I gasped, pulling away from our kiss. With a growl, he pushed deeper until his full length stretched me to the max. I could feel him inside me, but there was no pain. Only building pleasure with each thrust. He pounded hard and fast, my body bouncing with each movement.

I gripped his shoulders, holding on while he continued to bury himself inside me. It was wild, and intense, and so right.

Panting and moaning, I gripped him tighter while the pressure built low in my belly. I could feel the orgasm coming. Little ripples of pleasure crashed through me, each one slightly larger than the one before.

"Come for me, Sugar," he said.

His words sent me over the edge. An explosion of pleasure made my back arch, and I closed my eyes while I tossed my head back to scream.

Breathless and completely satisfied, I opened my eyes and found that I was alone in my bed.

What the fuck? I stretched my hand over on my bed to make sure I was alone, then I sat up and looked around. The alarm clock on my bedside table informed me that it was the middle of the night. I ran a hand through my hair, moving it off my sweaty face.

That had been the most real dream I'd ever experienced. I caught my breath, then climbed out of my bed to peek out of my room. Kate's door was wide open and her lights were off. Thankfully, she wasn't home to hear what was probably a very loud performance.

I walked to my dresser and grabbed a fresh pair of panties because the pair I had on were soaked. Was this some kind of response to what I'd started with Dax in the woods? Was it the shifter part of me waking?

Forcing myself to take slow, calm breaths, I crawled back into my bed. Whatever it was, it was over now. The Dark Wolf was off limits, which meant he was a safe fantasy. That had to be what it was. It would have been far more disturbing to dream about Dax. At least it was someone I could never be with.

After convincing myself that it was a mixture of hormones and my first shift, I finally drifted back to sleep.

CHAPTER
FOURTEEN

THE ECHO of my dream was haunting my thoughts, keeping me from reality. My feet led me to the Howler from memory as I tried to convince myself that it wasn't a big deal. It had to be a reaction to getting close with Dax last night and cutting things short. Stupid hormones.

I shook the thoughts from my head and returned to reality as I approached the bar. Oddly, I wasn't the only one headed in that direction. Sure, it was the only bar in town and was usually packed. But we never had a line out the door. Especially not at three in the afternoon.

Shifters were gathered in a group in front of the Night Howler, and the door was propped open. Several people were standing in the doorway, as if they were the overflow waiting to get in. *What the fuck was going on?*

I picked up my pace and pushed my way forward. "Excuse me, trying to get to work."

To my surprise, the group did part enough for me to

reach the line at the door. I shoved past, getting more than one glare tossed my way. I didn't really care. Holden would have my head if I was late since we still hadn't replaced Darleen.

The interior was shoulder to shoulder, far more crowded than even a busy Saturday night. I managed to push and weave my way over to the bar where Kayla was leaning against the wall, watching the chaos.

I lifted the divider and stepped into the bar area. It was the only place that wasn't overflowing with members of the Shadow pack.

Kayla lifted her chin in greeting, and I made my way over to her. "What is going on?"

"Some big announcement, I guess. It's all over town."

"Where's Holden?" I asked. "How is he letting this happen? I don't see any drinks in hands. Not that we could get to customers under these conditions."

"We're not open for service right now, I guess," she said. "He told me to close the bar down about a half hour ago after the lunch rush and then people started showing up."

"He didn't give you any hints?" My stomach twisted into knots. I'd tried to ignore the fact that Holden was involved in something with someone outside our pack, but it crept in as a dark reminder that we can't trust anyone around here. It also reminded me that I'd just had a sexy dream about someone who was involved with killing a coworker. Somehow, I'd managed to ignore that information. The dream felt even more wrong now.

Maybe I was just as fucked up as everyone else around here.

I scanned the room and took in the gathered group, half expecting to see the Dark Wolf in the crowd. I recognized most of the shifters present. They were all high-level members of the pack. Many of them inner circle with the alpha. This wasn't some random gathering, and I got the sense that the invitation hadn't been open to everyone.

Unease crept in, making me feel restless and uncomfortable. Something very strange was happening. Why would Holden call a meeting with such an affluent group? He wasn't high ranking, and I thought he hated shifter politics. Then I realized he was probably just the venue and likely pissed that he was losing business to host something at the whim of the alpha.

"You think the alpha has some big announcement?" I asked.

"I haven't seen him here, but he could have come in the back. I thought he usually kept business to meetings with the elders or private events at his house or the Hall of Records. Did Holden gain some favor or something?" Kayla asked.

I smirked at that. "If anything, this would be a punishment for Holden."

"Good point," she agreed.

A hush settled over the crowd, and the hair on the back of my neck stood on edge. It was as if a strange sense of foreboding had settled around us. Focus moved to the stage, and I turned to see Dax step to the front of the platform.

"Where's Preston?" I asked.

"I don't know," Kayla whispered.

"Friends, I called you here today to share some news," Dax said, his tone somber.

An uncomfortable weight settled into the pit of my stomach. Whatever he was about to say, it was bad.

"Last night, after the full moon party, my father died." Dax's nostrils flared, and he sounded like he was holding back tears.

"What? That's impossible," Kayla breathed out.

I swallowed against a lump in my throat. How could this be? I'd seen him just last night. He was happy, full of life, strong.

Murmurs filled the room as the news sunk in. I think everyone was as stunned as I was. Preston wasn't considered old by human standards, let alone shifter standards. If he was dead, it hadn't been natural causes. Oh, shit. What if someone had killed him? First Darleen, now Preston? People died all the time in the Fringes. Things were rough out here, but a random waitress was not the same thing as the alpha.

"All of you gathered here were his closest friends and trusted allies. I wanted you to be the first to know. Especially since we have reason to believe that my father was murdered." Dax looked around the room, allowing the group to react before he continued. They gasped and cursed, and a rumble of disquiet rippled through the bar.

My mind was racing as I tried to consider the possibilities of what this meant. Was our pack under attack or was this a personal dispute? What did this mean for the Shadow wolves? Was it going to change anything?

"I know it is unexpected and I know I'm young for the position, but I hope I'll have your support as I assume my father's responsibilities. My first act as alpha will be to discover the truth behind this unforgivable attack on our pack and I will bring whoever is responsible to justice." Dax's jaw was tense, his lips in a tight line. His dark eyes scanned the room, his gaze deadly.

I had no doubt he was going to do what he said. In that moment, I saw the same ruthless boy I'd known growing up. He was going to find whoever killed his father, and he wasn't just going to punish that person, he was going to make their life a living hell.

"To the new alpha!" someone shouted.

Cheers erupted, accompanied by pockets of chanting Dax's name. It was an odd celebratory mood, blackened by the reason for the transition to power. I always thought it would be years before Dax held the title. And to be honest, I'd mostly dreaded it. I figured I'd be a full member of the pack long before it happened. Now, it was him I'd have to file my appeal with once I earned enough. After last night, I wasn't sure if that was better or worse than dealing with Preston.

The new Dax might be more mature, but the old Dax was predictable. I had no idea what to expect moving forward.

After the cheers subsided, Holden joined Dax on the stage. My brow furrowed, and I watched his expression carefully. Holden clapped Dax on the back, then whispered something to the new alpha. Then he stepped to the front. "Drinks on the house."

The response to this simple statement was deafening as the shifters roared their approval. My eyes widened, and I turned to Kayla. We were about to be very, very busy.

The next several hours were a blur. I was sweaty and exhausted and I couldn't keep track of the number of drinks I'd delivered. It was an odd sort of party. Half celebration, half wake. Several times, I caught sight of Dax, busy in conversations with well-wishers. Once, he locked his eyes on mine and winked. My cheeks burned. I couldn't handle him right now. It was too much. Dax was not my friend, yet I'd totally kissed him last night. Then, I dreamed about a stranger who was shady as fuck, so what did that say about me?

"Ivy!" Holden shouted as he maneuvered through the crowd.

"What's up, boss?" I asked.

He pulled his keys out of his pocket and held them out. "We need more whisky and two more bottles of vodka. Can you grab them from the back? The cheap stuff. Not the good stuff."

"You're trusting me with your keys?" I asked. "You're giving away liquor. You're suddenly chummy with Dax... who the fuck are you?"

He chuckled. "Just get the damn booze. Lock up when you're done."

I held out the tray I had tucked under my arm. "Trade you."

He grabbed the tray, and I took the keys. So maybe the whole world cracked. Maybe I was in some alternate dimension where Dax was kind and thoughtful and my boss was a decent guy. Probably not, but what other explanation was there?

Making my way through the crowd was easier without drinks in hand, and I was nearly to the kitchen when someone grabbed my ass. Not in a subtle, *oh sorry, I didn't see you there* kind of ploy. It was a full-on grab and squeeze. I rounded on the pervert, and without caring who it was, I wound back my arm and punched the asshole in the face.

"Fuck!" my knuckles screamed, and so did Blake.

His hands were on his nose, and blood streamed down his face. "You bitch!"

"I told you, it's never going to happen, Blake." I stared daggers at him, my jaw clenched.

He dropped his hands and bared his teeth. "I'm going to teach you some fucking manners."

I tried to take a step back, wanting to ground myself better, but Blake's friends had closed in around me. Not again. Why was I always getting myself into messes like this?

Blake grabbed my hair and pulled me toward him. I cried out in surprise and dropped Holden's keys on the ground. Blake's free arm pulled me in against him, locking my arms to my side. I squirmed, but every movement sent more pain to my scalp. Leave it to Blake to resort to hair pulling.

"I don't know what you've heard about me, but I'm not into having my hair pulled," I snapped.

"I've given you chances, Ivy. You've embarrassed me one too many times. It's time for you to pay for your sharp tongue," he said.

"Fuck you," I said.

He leaned down and whispered in my ear. "That's the idea, darling." Then he dragged his tongue from my jaw up to my forehead.

Nausea rolled through me, and I shuddered. "You had your fun, now let me go."

"No."

I twisted and turned, trying to free myself. I was supposed to have shifter strength now, but it wasn't going to help much against an even stronger shifter. I knew he couldn't follow through with his threats here in front of so many people, but I wasn't about to stay in his arms. I lifted my foot and slammed it back down on his toes.

Blake hissed and moved his foot away, but instead of me getting away, he tightened his grip. "You are such a bitch. When are you going to learn your place?"

"Do we have a problem here?"

Blake's friends moved aside, and the crowd fanned out, leaving a circle of empty floor around me and my captor. Dax strolled forward, a bored expression on his face.

"I said, do we have a problem here?" Dax repeated.

"This bitch disrespected me," Blake said. "I'm teaching her a lesson."

Dax's eyes flicked to me, his gaze dropping down my body, as if scanning every inch of me before he looked back up. "Are you hurt?"

"Only my knuckles," I said.

Dax smirked, then turned his attention to Blake. "Looks like your nose is broken."

Blake sniffed. "This bitch punched me."

"Then you deserved it," he said.

I had never seen Dax like this before. He was radiating power, calm, and authority. Everyone was focused on him, and it was as if he was feeding off the attention. He was every inch the alpha. A shiver ran down my spine, straight to my core. There was something incredibly sexy about this new Dax.

"You're on her side now? The foundling?" Blake sounded confused and offended. "Wait, oh shit. You're fucking her, aren't you?"

"He is not fucking me," I said. "But he's got a shot. You, on the other hand, will never be in my bed."

"You heard her," Dax said. "Let her go."

"But she's a foundling. She's not even full pack. You take her side over me?" Blake pulled my hair harder and my chin jutted up. I winced and bit back a yelp, trying to act strong.

"She's full pack," Dax said. "Her debt was paid."

Was he serious right now? As alpha, he had the

authority to do that, but was he just saying it to make himself look better? Letting Blake knock me around would be like old times. Nobody cared what happened to me, and I had very little protection. But if I was full pack, that changed things.

Blake suddenly released me and shoved me forward. I stumbled, and Dax caught me. Heat rushed to my face, and I quickly stepped back from his embrace.

"Show's over," Dax called.

Conversations started in earnest, but quickly returned to normal as everyone went back to their little groups and their drinks. Blake glared at me and I knew he wanted to say something, but with Dax standing right next to me, he didn't have the balls. He walked away, his friends following in his wake.

Dax leaned down and picked up the keys. "You dropped these."

"Thanks," I said as I took the keys from him. "And thanks for standing up for me."

I turned and took a few steps before I remembered about the debt. I doubled back. "Did you mean what you said?"

"Did you?" he teased.

"Don't make this about sex," I said. "I'm serious. Did you mean what you said about my debt?"

"It's a matter of adding your name to the registry," he said. "But yeah. Consider it done."

"Why?" I asked. "I can't get past the old Dax. You are seriously fucking with my head."

"My dad's gone. I can be who I want to be without having to fit some kind of expectation he wanted me to follow," he said. "Things are going to change around here, Ivy."

I didn't have a response for that, so I just turned toward the kitchen to go grab the booze. All I'd ever wanted was to be a full member of the pack. It didn't feel real. I felt numb, unable to accept it as fact. Afraid to get my hopes up, I pushed it from my mind. Right now, I needed to work and then I could start sorting everything else out. It was possible my life was about to change.

CHAPTER
FIFTEEN

My arms were full of bottles of alcohol as I walked back into absolute chaos. All the shifters were yelling and shoving forward toward the front doors. I looked behind me, half expecting to see a roaring fire driving everyone out.

I jogged to the bar and set the bottles down. Kayla was staring in the direction of the doors, watching the rush.

"What's going on?"

"Alpha challenge," she said, not taking her eyes off the doors.

"What?" I abandoned the bottles and raced toward the exit. How was this possible? Dax had only been alpha for a couple of hours. Who was already looking to replace him?

I burst through the doors, following the other shifters outside. Everyone was lined up on either side of the road as if waiting for a parade. Only, the main event was the two males in the middle of the street.

Stuart, our pack's beta, was staring down Dax. I found a space on the sidewalk where I could see better and waited, holding my breath. Stuart had been the beta my whole life. He was a good fighter and had a reputation for being tough as nails. Dax was so much younger and less experienced. I wasn't sure he could win against the older male.

"You don't deserve to run this pack," Stuart called. "You're too young, too weak. You can back down now and get out of this with your life."

"This is my birthright, and I'm not going to cave to you," Dax snapped. "You are a traitor. I am the rightful alpha, and you know it."

"No, you're an immature, dangerous boy who is going to lead this pack astray," Stuart said.

"Don't make me fight you," Dax said.

"Then concede. Let the grown-ups run the show," Stuart called.

My stomach twisted into knots and I found myself worried for Dax. I didn't want Stuart to hurt him. Why was the beta doing this? Dax was young, but he'd always been next in line. I thought the beta's family had been close with the alpha's family. Stuart and Preston had their differences, but they came across like brothers in public. How could he do this to Dax?

"Last chance, old man," Dax shouted.

Stuart pulled his shirt over his head. "Let's go."

Both men quickly removed their clothes and faster than I could have imagined was possible, wolves were standing where the human forms had been. I was impressed by the ease and speed of their shifting. Maybe Dax wasn't as inexperienced as I feared. He'd shifted with just as much finesse as his challenger.

The wolves charged, leaping into the air and clashing into each other in a flurry of snarls and teeth and claws. Dax's dark gray wolf landed hard on the asphalt, Stuart's brown wolf on top of him. Gasps and groans rippled through the onlookers as Stuart slashed his claws across Dax's face.

Dax snapped at the older wolf before throwing him aside. Stuart landed hard and Dax pounced on top of him, digging his teeth into the other wolf's shoulder. Stuart yelped, but rallied quickly. The two wolves grappled and fought, getting in attack after attack, matching each other blow for blow. Every time I thought one of them had an edge, the other rallied. They were so evenly matched I wasn't sure who would prevail. The thought made my throat tight and nervous flutters filled my chest.

I gasped every time Dax was on the outs, terrified that he was going to meet his end. My hands were squeezed into tight fists, my fingernails biting into my palms. Every time Dax got in a blow, I let out a breath. Every time he took a hit, I winced.

The brawl continued, the two wolves striking, clawing, and biting. They were a blur of fur and teeth; snarls and growls rising from the pair as gasps and murmurs rose from the crowd.

I wasn't sure how much longer either wolf was going

to last. Their movements were getting slower, and I wondered if either was considering yielding. Stuart leaped onto Dax's back, digging his sharp claws into the dark gray wolf's fur. Dax's wolf howled in agony and I sucked in a breath. Dax's wolf stumbled. He was struggling to move forward and wasn't able to shake off the brown wolf.

"Just concede," someone called. "There's no need to die for this."

I started to wonder if that was the right call. Dax didn't look like he was going to make it much longer.

The dark gray wolf bared his teeth and let out a dangerous growl. It was a warning, and I tensed, as if I could feel what was going to happen next. It was the same thing that happened in the ring with me. I thought I had him. I thought it was over, but Dax had been biding his time.

His next move was fast. Suddenly, the brown wolf was tossed from Dax's back and the younger shifter charged the other wolf. The exhaustion he'd been showing just moments before was gone. He was like lightning, moving with speed and precision. He seemed to float through the air as he leaped onto Stuart. Before the older shifter even hit the ground, Dax's wolf sunk his fangs into the other wolf's throat. When they landed, Dax leaped off, his muzzle covered in blood.

Stuart's brown wolf lay motionless on the asphalt, blood pouring from the gaping hole in his throat.

Dax's wolf stood proudly in front of his victim. His

chin high, his dark eyes scanned the crowd. It was as if he was challenging every other shifter there.

It was deadly silent for several heartbeats, then the crowd erupted into cheers, followed by chanting for Dax.

My heart hammered in my chest and my shoulders sagged as relief came with a long exhale. I hadn't realized just how worried I'd been for Dax until that moment.

He shifted back into his human self and strolled over to his abandoned jeans and tee. His back was covered in slashes and he was limping a little. I was sure he was trying to pass it off as no big deal, but he had to be in a ton of pain.

"Anyone else?" Dax asked as he wiped the blood from his mouth with the back of his hand.

"Long live the alpha!" someone shouted.

The crowd closed in around him, and that was my cue to leave. There might be something between us, but I wasn't part of this world fully yet. Always the outsider. Even if Dax was going to grant me the freedom I desired, I didn't feel like I belonged.

Holden was sitting on a stool, sipping brown liquor from a rocks glass. "How'd it go?"

"Dax is still alpha," I said.

He hummed, a noncommittal sound that was difficult to interpret.

I walked over to the bar and took the stool next to him. Holden reached behind the bar and grabbed another glass and a bottle of whisky. He topped off his glass, then poured some into the new glass before sliding it over to me.

We'd never had a drink together. And I'd never seen Holden drink while the bar was open. Not that we had any customers right now, but it was still an unsettling sight.

"What's going on with you?" I asked.

Holden glanced at me, then sipped his drink. His eyes dropped to my untouched glass. I took the hint and lifted it to my lips, taking a sip. It burned the back of my throat and I coughed a little.

Holden smirked. "You can fight, but you can't handle your whisky. Dax is going to chew you up and spit you out."

I set the glass down. "Holden, what the fuck is going on? Please, if you know something, just tell me."

He shook his head. "Not my place. Besides, I don't think you'd believe me if I did."

The door opened and shifters began to pour back into the Howler. Holden stood, then tossed back the rest of his drink. He blew out a breath before slamming the glass on the counter. "Back to work."

"Holden, don't do that to me. How long have I worked for you?" I said.

His lips twisted, and he looked like he was contemplating something very serious. "I need you in the basement tomorrow night."

I frowned. That wasn't what I was expecting. "Alright."

Before I lost my nerve, I tipped back the rest of the

whisky; the liquid burned all the way from my throat to my stomach. I didn't know why, but I had a feeling I was going to need that drink.

Somehow, things settled down, and business as usual returned to the Howler. Kennedy and Luke showed up for their shifts and both of them were pissed they missed all the excitement. I was tempted to tell Kennedy she could have all the excitement and bail on the rest of the night, but I wasn't ready to leave.

Dax was basically holding court in the corner booth, but he hadn't even so much as looked at me since he came back inside. Even when I dropped off drinks or food, he kept his gaze away from me, unable to look me in the eye.

So much for our newfound friendship, I guess.

After a few hours, things finally started to slow down. I took a minute to lean against the bar and closed my eyes. It had been a rather insane few days.

"Hey, I can finish up tonight if you want to head home," Kennedy said.

I opened my eyes. "You sure?"

"Yeah, you've been doing all those doubles. You have to be exhausted," she said.

I glanced over at Dax's table. He was surrounded by adoring fans. My heart felt heavy. Why was this getting to me so much? I didn't even want his attention before yesterday.

"Ivy?" Kennedy called.

I shook my head and looked at her. "Yeah. Sorry. I think I'm more tired than I realized."

"I'll close out those tables. Go home. Sleep," she said.

I nodded. "Thanks."

The walk to my car was blissfully uneventful. It was snowing and everything felt quieter than it had in days. I breathed in the thick scent of wet pavement and snow. It was peaceful and exactly what I needed. Tonight was for cozy socks and burrowing under all my blankets.

I drove home, wondering if Kate would be there or if she was spending the night with Ryan. A little flicker of jealousy reared its head when I pulled into my parking spot. Her car wasn't there, and all our windows were dark.

At least one of us was getting lucky. The thought startled me. Where had that come from? If I really wanted to get laid, it wasn't like it would be hard to find a volunteer. Besides, I was too tired to even break out my vibrator. Having a male over for company sounded like far too much work.

I had just managed to get my clothes off when I heard a knock on the door. It was probably my neighbor looking for a cigarette or something. I'd told him a million times that we didn't smoke, but every so often he came knocking and asked anyway.

Wrapping a towel around myself, I walked to the front door. "Go away, Jonas, I don't have any cigarettes or weed. Go ask someone else."

I opened the door and found myself looking up at Dax. "You're not my neighbor."

"I'm not, but I'm starting to wonder if I need to go kick his ass. Jonas, you say?"

"He's harmless," I assured him. "What are you doing here?"

"I wanted to see if you were okay," he said.

My eyebrows rose in surprise. "If I'm okay? You're the one who had to fight the beta. I'm fine."

"Can I come in?" he asked.

Can he come in? Dax, the alpha, the guy I couldn't figure out, wanted to come into my apartment while I was wearing only a towel. "Sure, come on in."

CHAPTER
SIXTEEN

WHAT THE FUCK was even happening in my life anymore? I didn't even recognize who I was. This wasn't me. I didn't have men over late at night, and I certainly didn't have any clout with the alpha. Shit was getting so strange.

"Have a seat," I said as I closed the door behind him. "I'm going to get some clothes on. I'll be right back."

"I don't mind what you're wearing," he teased.

"Nice try, but I'm not sure I'm ready to sit around in a towel with you." He'd seen me naked, and I'd spent most of the evening with him in just a blanket. But this was my apartment, and it felt far too personal.

Quickly, I ran to my room and threw on a pair of jeans, a bra, and a sweatshirt. I was behind on laundry, so commando was going to have to do. When I left my room, Dax was standing in the living room and he walked over to the couch. He winced as he sat.

He had to be in a lot of pain from that fight. Shifter

healing was good, but he'd been brutally attacked. I popped into the kitchen and grabbed the frozen peas and started the tea kettle.

When I returned to the living room I offered him the bag of peas. "I usually put the bag on my face, but everyone knows you were in fight so you could use it wherever it hurts the most."

"You have a lot of experience with that," he said.

It wasn't a question, so I didn't bother to reply. He knew what my life had been like. "Did you really come by to see how I was doing?"

"Maybe I wanted your company," he said.

I sat down on the coffee table so I was facing him, but not sharing the same couch. "You have a ton of adoring fans. People who would be happy to fawn over you and see to your every whim."

"That's why I came here," he said. "You hate me, which means you'll be honest with me."

"I don't hate you," I admitted. It was odd to hear those words come out of my mouth because I kind of always thought I did hate him. But maybe I didn't.

"I'm not sure I believe you," he said.

"You're the one who kissed me," I pointed out.

"If I'm not mistaken, you kissed me back," he said.

"After a few false starts on your part," I teased.

"See? That's why I'm here. You're the only one who doesn't treat me like I'm either made of glass or going to kill someone," he said.

"Are those the only options? Fragile or murderous?" I asked.

"I suppose for an alpha, it is," he said.

"I wouldn't want the job," I said. "That's a lot of pressure." I winced when I realized how insensitive those words were after today's events. "I'm sorry about Stuart. I never thought he'd do something like that."

"He was like a second father to me." He looked away, then pressed the bag of peas to the side of his face.

"That had to be very hard. I wish I had the right words to say." I wasn't sure how you consoled someone after winning an alpha challenge. The whole thing was supposed to be a sign of strength, but Dax was letting me see a peek at his vulnerability. I wasn't sure how much of that he wanted me to acknowledge.

"I expected someone to challenge me on day one. My dad always said it'd happen. Especially if I was still young. But I never thought it would be Stuart," he said.

"I think we were all surprised," I said. "Maybe it's better that you didn't keep a beta who was disloyal?"

"Yeah, maybe," he said.

The tea kettle whistled. "I'll be right back."

I prepared Dax a cup of tea using Kate's herbs. I still wasn't sure they worked, but it was all I had in my arsenal for taking care of someone who was injured. Usually, Kate was the one who did this for me.

When I returned, Dax had moved the bag of peas to his stomach. "Whatever you have, I can smell it from here."

"It's disgusting, I'm not going to lie, but Kate says it helps. I drink it every time I get injured," I said.

"You really drink that?" He wrinkled his nose in an adorable way.

I giggled. "Yeah, I do."

"Fine, hand it over," he said.

I passed him the cup, then took a seat on the couch, leaving a space between us. I watched him take a careful sip of the concoction.

"That's awful," he said.

"I know."

"It has to be good for you, right? Cause nothing this terrible tasting could possibly not be good for you."

"That's basically what gets me to go through with it," I said.

He set the tea down on the table. "I have to admit, I have an ulterior motive."

"Oh?" I quirked a brow. "You trying to get in my pants again?"

"Sadly, I don't think I'm up for that with the injuries. But maybe tomorrow?"

I was surprised that disappointment flared inside me. Was I hoping he'd come here and sweep me off my feet? *Seriously, Ivy, get your vagina under control.*

"I wanted to talk to you about your debt. About what I said at the bar," he said.

I perked up. "I should have said thank you for that right away."

"Don't thank me yet," he said. "I ran it by the elders

and they aren't going to let me just wipe it because I'm alpha."

My shoulders slumped, and a weight dropped into my gut. I should have known it was too good to be true. "That's okay. Thanks for trying. Honestly, I'm getting closer and I am fully capable of paying it off myself, eventually."

"I was serious about me and you, though. Every time I've said it, I've meant it. Even if I was trying to get a rise out of you, I think there's something special between us. I don't want to fight it. They'll expect me to marry and I know we don't have a mating bond, but Ivy... would it be the worst thing to be my wife?"

I blinked a few times as his words settled around me. "Are you proposing to me?"

"No, not yet. We don't have to move that fast. I want to take you out. Get to know you. But you have to know, that's where my head is. I'm looking for a wife and I don't have time to play the field. If you can't see yourself as some day being married to me, I won't waste your time," he said.

"Wow. That got very serious very fast." I wasn't even sure how I felt about him. This wasn't the same Dax I'd known, and I still wasn't sure I trusted him.

Sure, he'd defended my honor or some shit tonight when Blake had grabbed me, but I could have done that myself. I didn't need him for that, even if it was kind of great to see the look on Blake's face.

"Ivy, I know it's a lot. But there's nobody else. You're

real. You're honest. You're willing to throw a punch when needed, even if it's against me," he said.

I chuckled, feeling a little embarrassed. "This is big, Dax."

"If it's a fuck no, I'll leave. But if there's a possibility, why not explore it? You'd be the alpha's wife. Not just a full member of the pack, but the highest-ranking female in all the Shadow Wolves."

I swallowed hard. This was a lot. He'd brought this up before, but I dismissed it. Being with him would get me the belonging I always wanted, but I'd still be secondary to him. Wives had to submit. I wasn't sure I was the submissive type.

He was waiting patiently for my response, and he looked so sincere. What if there was something there between us? It wasn't like he was asking me to commit to marrying him right this second. He simply wanted to know if I was open to it, if things went well. "You're not asking me to commit now, right?"

"No, I'm not insane. We don't have a mating bond and realistically, the chances of either of us finding a mate are slim. We might as well see if we enjoy each other's company."

Moving beyond our past wouldn't be easy. "I'm not sure, Dax. We've got a lot of history."

"I'm going to be honest with you, Ivy. Part of why Stuart challenged me was because he thought I was too young and immature. Having a wife would make me less of a target. I'd look more serious. I don't want to rush into something, but you're the only one I can think of who would stand up to anyone who might challenge us."

"I'm a foundling," I reminded him.

"I don't care," he said. "And nobody else will once we're married."

"This feels too fast," I admitted.

"We can take some time to decide, but I can't afford to waste time if you can't ever see it happening," he said.

It seemed insane, but it wasn't like I had any better offers. And this one did come with paying off my debt. It would mean I'd have a huge savings I could use for something else. I wouldn't just be part of the pack, I'd be part of everything big. Besides, maybe people could change. "Alright. I'm willing to see where things take us."

Dax grinned. "You won't regret it, Ivy."

I really, really hoped I didn't.

He handed me the bag of peas. "I wish I could stay, but I think I need to go sit in a whole tub of ice and I'm not sure I'm ready to do that in front of you yet."

"Want to take the tea to go?" I offered with a grin.

"I think I already feel better from the sip I had, but thanks," he said.

I walked him to the door, and we stopped in front of it. It was nice to feel like things were starting to make more sense between Dax and me. Since he'd been home from school, I had seen a new side to him. If it stuck around for real, who knew where we'd end up.

Dax leaned over and gave me a gentle kiss on the cheek. "Sleep well, Ivy."

"You, too." I opened the door for him.

When he was out of sight, I closed the door behind him, then fell back against it as I let out a sigh. A squeal bubbled up inside me and I released it, feeling giddy with possibility. For once in my life, things were going my way.

CHAPTER SEVENTEEN

"You're kidding, right?" Kate stared at me, not masking the doubt in her expression. "I never would have thought he could take on Stuart. Especially after you held your own against him."

"I'm pretty sure he went easy on me that night," I reminded her. "You should have seen him in the fight. Stuart didn't even have a chance. Dax looked like an alpha."

She raised a skeptical brow. "You sound like a love-sick teenager. What the fuck is going on between you two?"

I'd given her the play-by-play of the alpha challenge but had yet to explain what happened later that night. After taking a steadying breath, the whole story spilled out. When I finished, I stared at her, waiting for her to break the silence.

"Wow. That's a lot. I mean, that's huge. Life changing huge." She leaned in; her brow furrowed with concern.

"Are you sure that's a good idea? You don't think he's playing you?"

"Maybe? But I think that would backfire if he was. It wouldn't look great for the alpha to string a girl along for no reason."

"I guess I honestly never thought you'd partner with anyone," she admitted.

I sucked in a breath. That hurt. "You thought I'd be alone forever?"

"Maybe not forever, but I figured you'd settle if you found a mate. It's not like we have a choice if that happens. But to choose to be with someone, especially the alpha…"

"I'm not marrying him right this second," I pointed out.

"No, but if you ever did, you're going to lose everything. You know how it works. The males get to call the shots. I just can't see you as the submissive type who has to ask permission to go out with friends," she said.

"I don't go out with friends now," I said. "All I do is work. That's my whole life. Until that debt is paid, I'm nothing in this pack. And even when it is paid, I'm still at the bottom."

"But you have freedom. If you were with Dax, you'd risk losing yourself," she said.

"You don't get it, do you?" Kate was my best friend, but she'd always been welcome in spaces I wasn't. She got warm greetings from other members of the pack while I got looks of mistrust and disgust. Even when I did pay my debt, I'd be treated differently. An outcast in the pack where I'd grown up. The Shadow Wolves were all I knew, same as Kate, yet she was treated as one of them. I would never know that feeling. Unless I elevated my status.

"I get it. I know life has been hard for you. I just don't want to see you get hurt," she said.

"How would this be any worse than the hurt I've experienced my whole life? How many times was I beaten up or left out simply because of who I am? I got a break from the violence after high school, but I'm working myself to death for a monster who murdered one of my coworkers," I said.

Kate blinked, and I covered my mouth with my hand. I hadn't wanted that to slip out.

"Wait, what?" She set down her cup of coffee and grabbed my shoulders. "Explain. Now."

"You have to swear never to tell anyone." I set my hands on top of hers. "Swear it?"

"Yes, of course."

"I was in the closet in the back of the Howler when I saw Holden with a man from another pack. They call him the Dark Wolf. I saw him at the fight that night." A shiver ran through me and my heart was racing. Simply thinking about the Dark Wolf was enough to do things to me. I really did need to get laid.

"What happened?" She leaned closer.

"They were talking about some secret and the Dark Wolf was worried that someone had found out what it was. Holden said he'd taken care of it. As in, he made sure

Darleen and her boyfriend were dead. I don't know why, but I know I can't afford to cross Holden and I sure as hell don't want him to know I heard that."

"Oh, shit, Ivy. Holden hosts those fights with the other packs and now he's talking with people during the day, too?" She shook her head. "I think you might need to tell Dax."

"You were just telling me how I shouldn't get involved with Dax," I said.

"Yes, but your other option besides Dax was working for Holden. If he's a murderer, that might not be worth it," she said.

I shouldn't have mentioned that to her. It made everything far more complicated. "I'm not sure I want to get in the middle of this. It's not like he'd be the first guy in the pack to eliminate another shifter. Nobody cares about people like Darleen. Or me. How easy would it be to make me disappear?"

"Darleen wasn't dating the alpha," she reminded me. "You've got the most powerful shifter in the pack on your side."

"What if things don't work out between us and I need that job with Holden? What if Dax believes Holden over me? What if Dax was in on it? He was fighting the Dark Wolf that night," I said.

"I don't know, Ivy," Kate admitted. "Maybe trust your gut?"

"My gut thought the Dark Wolf was the sexiest male I'd ever seen in my life and I wanted nothing more than to tear his pants off. Turns out, he's an accessory to murder. So, I'm not sure my gut is very trustworthy," I said.

She chuckled. "Your gut is just horny. Maybe you should go to Dax. Get laid. It'll probably help you clear your head. Once you have your first shift, your hormones go into overdrive."

"Well, I thought that way about him before my first shift, but to be fair the sex dream was after..." I glanced up at Kate and we both started to giggle. The tension of the conversation dissolved and things felt a little more normal.

We both took a sip of our coffee once the laughter had subsided and we settled into quiet. Finally, Kate turned to me. "Do you like Dax?"

I shrugged. "Maybe."

"Then you should give it a try. What's the worst that could happen?" she asked.

CHAPTER
EIGHTEEN

The excitement and anticipation in the basement were palpable. I knew I had sort of agreed to start dating Dax last night, but I couldn't help but hope I caught a glimpse of the Dark Wolf.

I shouldn't care. Especially since I knew he was involved in awful things with Holden, but my stomach was filled with flutters of anticipation. As I dropped drinks off, the crowd parted for me more easily. I wondered if it was because I'd dropped something last time or because the Dark Wolf had rushed to my rescue.

His dark eyes crashed into my memories, and I shook the thought away. Maybe Kate was right, and I needed to get laid. Dax was the alpha, and there wasn't any better match that a female could hope for. We were going to take things slow, figure out if we were a good fit. I should be daydreaming about him, not a strange wolf from another pack with questionable morals.

The crowd reacted with hisses and moans as the favorite in the current fight hit the mat. I glanced over and saw Chris, the owner of the hardware store, on his back. Josiah, a shifter who'd been a grade above me in high school, was standing over the older shifter. His shoulders rose and fell with rapid breathing as he stared down at his opponent.

"Vodka tonic," someone called, and I tore my gaze away from the fight and back to my job.

"You got it." I took a few more orders, then navigated through the crowd to the bar to get the drinks.

Randy and Evan were slammed tonight, making the drinks for walk up customers and for me. It seemed even busier than usual.

"Think we'll see Dax tonight for another round between you two?" Evan teased as he tossed a lime into a drink.

"I'd turn it down if he asked," I admitted. "Once was enough for me."

"If you won, you'd be alpha," he said.

"I wouldn't want the job, so I suppose I shouldn't risk it," I teased.

"That's alright," Evan said. "There will be enough eye candy tonight to satisfy you until you can go to him."

"What is that supposed to mean?" I asked.

"I hear the rumors. And who wouldn't be talking about the foundling who won the heart of the alpha?" Evan asked.

"What rumors?" I demanded. I thought we were

taking things slow. Dax and I hadn't even been on a date yet.

"They say he's off the market," Randy joined in the conversation. "Everyone knows it's you. The boy is smitten."

My cheeks heated, and to my surprise, I was flattered. Dax was sexy as hell, and I'd caught sight of his sweet side. Maybe we could live happily ever after. I'd never let myself consider that before and I was the last person I'd expect to ever call myself a romantic, yet here I was.

"Less talk, more work," Joe called. "I don't care who you're fucking. When you're here, you work."

I rolled my eyes and got back to the task of running drinks and returning empty glasses. It kept me busy, but my mind would wander from my job to Dax or the Dark Wolf. It was odd to feel so strangely divided between the two males in my head. It had to be the rush of the crowd and the anticipation of seeing the man who'd had a starring role in a very intimate dream. I fought against embarrassment, but that didn't make any sense. It wasn't like he'd know he'd done very naughty things to me in my imagination.

The night dragged on, and as anticipated, Dax never showed. He was probably mostly recovered from his injuries, but it wouldn't be a good idea to risk another alpha challenge so quickly.

"So, how did you and Dax end up together anyway? Was it that night in the locker room? I knew you hooked up with him post fight. That fight was so hot," Evan said.

"Seriously? I told you, we didn't have sex in the locker room. Can I get my drinks please?" I tapped on the tray.

Evan held his hands up in mock surrender. "Okay, girl, fine, keep your secrets."

I shook my head. This thing with Dax wasn't even official, and it was already causing issues. Could I actually handle dating the alpha?

Suddenly, a jolt raced down my spine. It was like a burst of heat, exploding in my chest and racing right down to my core.

The crowd roared, and it was as if the air around us was thick and heavy. I knew before I even turned around that he was here. Unease pooled in my stomach, and my heart raced. It was stupid, and it didn't make any sense, but I knew the Dark Wolf would be there when I looked.

Slowly, I turned to face the ring. He was there in his black hoodie, his back to me. Flutters and anxious ripples raced through me and I was nervous. As if he'd know I'd dreamed about the two of us.

"Ready," Evan called.

I grabbed the tray and forced myself not to look over at the ring. This was ridiculous. I was being courted by the alpha. I had a shot at everything I ever wanted. Freedom from my debt, belonging... I was closer than ever to being able to relax for the first time in my life. If Dax and I worked out, everything would change.

So why was I staring at the Dark Wolf as if he was a meal and I was starving? I couldn't help it. The pull to him was intense, drawing me in, even though I still couldn't see his face.

"Is that my drink?" A voice asked, breaking the spell.

I forced a smile on my face and tore my gaze away from the stranger. "Yeah. Here."

Quickly, I got all the drinks delivered so I wouldn't make the same mistake as last time and end up with spilled drinks during the surge of people.

Tray tucked under my arm, I glanced back, just as the Dark Wolf tossed his hoodie to the side. I didn't recognize his opponent tonight, but he was a burly bald man covered from his neck down in tattoos. He was strong, and he already looked pissed off.

Concern arose unbidden as I returned my attention to the Dark Wolf. He was all rippling muscles and *holy fuck,* I wanted to lick every exposed bit of his skin.

Shit. Shit. Shit. I felt my face heat, and I looked down, hoping nobody could tell I was flushing just from the sight of the man's back. What was wrong with me?

"It's time for the main event!" Joe's voice boomed from the speakers.

I needed to get away from here before I got pulled in with the spectators. I took a few steps but couldn't resist getting one last look at the sexy shifter.

His dark eyes caught mine and I swear I thought my heart was going to burst right through my chest. I stopped breathing, caught in his gaze like an insect in a spider's web. Internally, everything had turned to mush. If he'd asked me to do anything in that moment, I wouldn't have even questioned it. I could melt right into him and never look back.

Thankfully, he turned away from me and I stumbled backward, as if I'd just been released from a physical hold. Something was very wrong with me. It had to be the post-shifting hormones. I knew shifters had intense sex drives, but this was insane.

Before I made the mistake of looking at him again, I hurried to the bar to help Randy and Evan clean up.

It took far more willpower than I wanted to admit to avoid turning back with every reaction and sound from the crowd. I knew I'd get pulled in again, and even if I was interested in finding out more about the Dark Wolf, I knew he wasn't part of the Shadow Pack. Besides, a male that hot had to be claimed by someone else. My focus had to be on the same goal that had kept me alive all these years. I had to get out of my debt.

While there was a potential change to that plan right now with the possibility of being with Dax, I didn't know where that would take us. I had never been able to count on anyone but myself. What if we dated a while and he met his true mate? Or what if he lost interest in me? I was fascinating now because I stood up to him. There was a very real possibility he'd find that less endearing with time.

I had just finished wiping down the liquor bottles and setting them into the box to carry them back upstairs when a roar filled the basement. It was louder and more intense than the other reactions, and I couldn't help but look at the fight.

The Dark Wolf was standing in the center of the ring, his arms in the air, his opponent on the ground. I hadn't even noticed who he was fighting, and it was difficult to make out who it was while the guy was passed out on the ground.

"Victory to the Dark Wolf! Still undefeated!" Joe's voice boomed over the din of the crowd.

The Dark Wolf's muscles flexed and tensed as he pumped his fist in the air. He turned my direction and paused, our eyes meeting. My heart did the weird fluttering thing it seemed to do whenever I looked at him too long. I allowed myself a moment more to stare at him, then forced myself to look away.

Breathing out a shaky breath, I grabbed the trash bag. "I'll run this out."

"Take this one, too," Randy said, handing me another bag.

Gratefully, I lugged the bags to the stairs, careful not to look back at the ring. My life was confusing enough already without adding an infatuation for a stranger.

By the time I got back to the basement, the Dark Wolf was gone. I let out a long breath and felt some tension melt away. This was a good gig, and I was getting paid very well. I couldn't afford to lose this position. Holden might be awful, but I had to look out for myself.

Soon, we had everything cleaned up, and Holden

handed me my envelope of cash. "Any word on the next one?"

"Not sure yet," Holden said. "We're not quite sure how it's going to play with the change in leadership."

"Dax was down here last time, though. He didn't seem to care then," I said.

"He wasn't alpha then. He knows what really goes on down here. I'm not sure if he's going to tighten the reigns now that he has some power." Holden narrowed his eyes. "Maybe you can find out for me."

"I don't have that kind of pull," I said.

"I suppose that's for the best," he said. "I don't like that kid. He's trouble."

"He's the alpha," I said, surprised that I felt the need to defend him.

"That's what makes it even worse," Holden said. "Some people shouldn't have power."

The fact that Holden was so against Dax being alpha actually made me appreciate the young alpha even more. Holden wasn't what I'd consider a good guy. If he didn't like Dax, maybe it wasn't for the reasons I'd assumed in the past. Sure, Dax and his friends had been obnoxious and loud when they'd come into the bar, but the more I thought of it, it had rarely been Dax himself who caused the issues.

Stacey was the one who'd jumped me in the parking lot. Several of their friends had ended up in brawls over the years. But never Dax. Not once. He ran with the privileged, cocky assholes, but he was usually in the background. What did that mean?

"Well, let me know if you need me again." I covered a yawn. "I'm back tomorrow for lunch, so I'll see you all later."

"I need you to train the new girl tomorrow," Holden said.

"You finally hired someone?" I asked.

"Yeah. We'll see if she can handle it. You've got her at lunch and Kennedy can train her at dinner," Holden said.

"You got it, boss." I waved. "See you tomorrow."

Before anyone could say anything else, I took off. I'd made a lot of extra cash the last few weeks with all the extra shifts, but I was looking forward to having a night off every so often. A little part of me wondered if I was excited about it so I could go out with Dax. It was an odd sensation. I'd always been so focused on work, and it was fun to have something else to look forward to.

I was wondering about what kinds of things Dax and I could do for a date when I pulled into the parking spot in front of my apartment. Kate's car was there. I wondered if she'd broken up with Ryan.

When I walked into the apartment, I found Kate on the couch. Her posture was slumped and her eyes were red. I dropped my keys in the dish by the door.

This wasn't break up related. Kate never got this emotional over men. Unless things had been more serious than I expected. I sat down next to her on the couch. "What happened?"

"Stupid men," she said.

My brow furrowed. I wasn't expecting this from her. "What did he do?"

"I walked in on him with someone else," she said. "It wasn't like I expected him to be my forever, but we said we weren't seeing anyone else. Asshole."

I sat down next to her on the couch and pulled her into a hug. She hugged me back, then pushed away. "You smell like beer."

I laughed. "Yeah, I had to change the keg, and it got messy."

She sniffed, then wiped her face. "Well, you better get cleaned up cause we're going out."

"It's midnight," I pointed out. "And I worked all day."

She pointed at her face. "Do you see these tears?"

"Fine. But not too late," I said.

"Everything closes by four," she said.

I laughed. "I haven't been out that late, ever."

"Then it's time we change that," she said.

CHAPTER NINETEEN

I wasn't sure if it was a good idea to go out after my long shift, but Kate never asked for favors. She must have been far more into Ryan than I realized.

The Night Howler was the only bar, but we did have a club called the Dragon's Keep. I'd never been because it wasn't really a place I felt welcome. The full moon party was the first time I'd been to an event of any kind that I wasn't working.

Kate was a regular at the Keep, but this was the first time she'd insisted on dragging me along. I followed her to the front doors, tugging on the short skirt I was wearing. Kate was my best friend and if her getting to pick my outfit and drag me to a club would get her over the first breakup that ever threw her, I was willing to give it a try.

We paused at the front door as a bouncer looked us up and down. "Shifted wolves only."

"Don't be a dick, Ruben. I know the rules," Kate snapped.

My cheeks heated. I didn't realize that you had to shift to be allowed in. Now I guess I knew why Kate never invited me. I figured it was because she knew it wasn't my scene, but she didn't have the option to bring me.

"I know you shifted. How about your friend?" he asked. "Never seen her in here before."

I narrowed my eyes at the huge shifter. He had gray hair and a long gray beard. Add in his gut and he was giving off serious Santa Claus vibes, but without the whole cheerful demeanor. "I've shifted."

He lifted his brows and smiled. "Well, I hope I see you around more often, then."

Had he just gone from judging me to flirting with me? Um, hard pass. "Don't count on it. I'm just here to cheer up my friend."

"Ivy," Kate hissed.

"Everyone will know by tomorrow," I said. Gossip got around the Fringes with lighting speed.

"True." She sighed.

"Have fun, ladies," Ruben said as he stepped aside.

We walked into the club, the pounding bass vibrating in my bones. The entire space was lit with red and orange lights, casting all the writhing bodies in an eerie glow. The Dragon's Keep was mostly an open dance floor. Along the back, I saw a few tables and chairs and there was a balcony that overlooked the dance floor with more seating. Along the side was a mirrored wall with a bar in front of it.

The place was packed, the body heat making me instantly grateful for the tank top and skirt. It had been freezing on the walk from the parking lot, but now I was already at risk of overheating.

"We need drinks," Kate shouted as she grabbed my hand.

I kept hold of her as we made our way to the bar along the side of the club. The mirror behind it reflected the people dancing, making the place feel even more crowded than it was.

Kate flagged down the bartender while I looked around. There were several faces I recognized from high school or around town. Some of the people I'd brought drinks to earlier tonight at the fight were in attendance. I realized I wouldn't catch sight of the Dark Wolf in the crowd and my shoulders slumped a little. It didn't make sense to be pining over a pretty face, yet here I was. Okay, in my defense, he was a lot more than just a pretty face. He was the whole damn package. But he wasn't pack, and he was never, ever going to be an option.

Kate handed me a bottle of beer and then lifted hers in a toast. I couldn't hear a word she said, but I clinked my bottle against hers anyway. Then she dragged me to the dance floor. She looked so free as she danced, but I found myself looking around, nervous that someone was going to tell me to hit the road. Spending most of your life not fitting in will do that to you.

After several minutes of feeling self-conscious, I started to relax. Nobody was looking at us. Nobody cared I was here. Was it possible things had changed since school and I was the one who was still holding on? What if all those kids who gave me shit didn't mind that I was here now? It wasn't like any of it mattered. I had shifted, just as they had. And soon, I'd pay off my debt. We'd all be equal members of the pack. Well, in theory. We all knew there was status within the pack, but few of the kids I grew up with would rise to the highest levels.

Kate leaned into my ear. "I'm going to get a refill. You want one?"

"Sure." I handed her my empty bottle, and she took off toward the bar.

I probably should have followed her because I wasn't quite sure what to do alone on the dance floor. Just as I was considering trying to find her, someone tapped my shoulder. I spun around, expecting Kate, but was greeted by a pair of blue eyes and a smile.

"Want to dance?" A handsome shifter with sandy hair asked. I didn't recognize him, but maybe that was a good thing.

"Sure." We had come here to have fun, right?

Kate found me then and winked before melting back into the crowd. Guess I wasn't going to get that drink, after all.

"I'm Leo," he said.

"Ivy," I said.

He rested his hands on my waist. "Nice to meet you, Ivy."

"You, too. Are you new around here?" I asked.

"Moved here last year," he said. "Well, does anyone actually move here? I was sent here last year."

I wanted to ask him what he did to get sent here, but that seemed rather personal since we'd just met. Besides, I could ask Kate tomorrow and I was certain she could find out if she didn't already know. It was probably best to just enjoy the dance. It wasn't like I was going back to his place.

We danced for a few songs, and I was surprised how much fun I was having. There wasn't any pressure with Leo. He was fun and a great dancer.

"Thirsty?" he asked.

I nodded.

"I'll be right back," he said.

I looked around for Kate while Leo was gone and found her grinding against Ryan. Looked like they'd made up. I wondered if that's why she wanted to come out tonight or if it had been a coincidence.

Before I could think too hard on it, Leo was back. He passed me a beer. "Bartender said you were drinking this earlier."

"Thanks." I took a sip.

We started dancing again. Leo moving a little closer to me, but still careful to move slow. I was impressed by what a gentleman he was.

Suddenly, someone grabbed him and, in a flash of

movement, a fist landed in Leo's face.

Cries of surprise rose above the music, and I scrambled toward the scuffle. Leo was holding his nose, blood gushing down his face. Dax was standing in front of him, his shoulders rising and falling in heavy pants. "Hands off, asshole."

"What the fuck, Dax?" I shouted.

Dax charged forward and grabbed the beer bottle out of my hand, then threw it to the ground. The bottle shattered into pieces.

I took a step back, nearly stumbling backward. The room was spinning all of the sudden and I wasn't feeling quite right.

Dax was at my side, his arm around me seconds before I slumped over on him. It was too difficult to stand up. "What's going on?" I slurred my words, but I hadn't had that much to drink.

"Get him out of here," Dax growled.

"What's happening?" I managed, my vision was blurry and I couldn't focus on anything correctly.

"I watched that asshole drop something in the drink. I'm so sorry I didn't get to you sooner. I lost him in the crowd for a bit," Dax said.

"What?" I wasn't sure if I was even speaking out loud anymore. Everything was like it was in a dream. Was I even awake?

I fought like hell to keep my eyes open, but I lost the battle. My body went limp and the last thing I remembered was Dax holding on to me.

CHAPTER TWENTY

My head was pounding, and I wondered exactly how much I had to drink last night. I opened my eyes and squinted into the watery sunlight. Panic surged through me and I bolted up, looking around the unfamiliar room.

The events of last night crashed in around me and I recalled dancing with someone and the drink and a fight. I tensed as I looked around the room until my eyes found a familiar form sitting in a chair.

"Morning, sunshine," Dax said.

He was in boxers and a white shirt, and the chair he was sitting on was covered in blankets. I was in his bed. *Oh shit.* I slept over at Dax's house. "What happened last night?"

"A piece of shit tried to drug you. Well, I guess he succeed in drugging you," Dax said.

I groaned and fell back into the bed. This was so typical. The one time I go out and do something fun, I end up like this. I sat back up as another thought hit me. "Where's Kate? I went to the club with her."

"Don't worry, I let her know you were with me," he said.

"And she was okay with that?" I was skeptical.

"My place is much closer, and we were able to get the doc here to check you out. We both agreed it was better not to move you," Dax said.

"Wait, Kate was here?" I was even more confused.

"She insisted. She wanted to make sure you were cared for," he said.

"That sounds like Kate," I said.

"She promised to do some really terrible things to me if I hurt you, so if you'd let her know you're safe, I'd appreciate it," he said.

I chuckled at that, then winced. I'd had a lot of headaches over the years and this one was trying for the worst of all time award. "What exactly did he give me?" Human drugs didn't work on shifters, but there were other things out there.

"We're looking into it," he said. "He's locked up, and we'll be investigating everything about him. He's going to wish he'd never set foot in the Fringes."

Warmth spread through my chest. Despite what had happened, I felt safe here with Dax.

"Kate dropped by a packet of that tea. Made me promise I'd give it to you," he said. "I'll go make it."

"Wait, she was here this morning, too?" I tossed the blankets aside and climbed off the bed, instantly regretting it. Everything was spinning, and I had to sit back down.

"Easy, it's going to take some time for the drug to wear off," Dax said.

"What time is it? I have to be at work," I said.

"You can't work like this."

"You don't understand, Holden will fire me. I need that job," I said.

"Let me talk to him," Dax said.

"No." I wasn't about to start letting someone else fight my battles. Besides, I knew Holden didn't like Dax. The new alpha demanding I get a day off would backfire spectacularly. "Do you have a phone? I should do it myself."

Dax walked over to a desk and I noticed my purse was hanging over the side of the chair. "If yours isn't charged, I can get give you mine."

He handed me my purse. "I better go make that tea. I know how scary Kate can get."

I smiled as I imagined Kate chewing out Dax, the kid who used to be the biggest bully in school, who was now the alpha. She'd always been like that, though. When we were younger, she used to stand up for me then, too. I hated when she did because I worried they'd turn on her. With her dad's connections, though, she was never a target. She'd probably saved my life more times than I realized by stopping fights.

It felt strange to be sitting here in Dax's room after all the history between us, but I needed to call Holden before

I let myself process anything else. My phone still had some charge, so I quickly called the Night Howler.

Holden answered. "Howler."

"Hey, Holden, it's Ivy," I said.

"Where the fuck are you? You're late," he snapped.

"I was drugged last night. I'm not going to make it to the lunch shift," I said.

"I was counting on you," Holden said.

"I didn't choose to have someone spike my beer," I replied.

"Fine. Be here for the dinner shift or find a new job." He hung up.

I tossed my phone back into my purse. That tea better work on getting whatever this was out of my system. Knowing that I needed to be back on my feet quickly, I tried standing up again. This time, I was prepared for the unease. Nausea rolled through my stomach and dizziness hit once again. I breathed through it, forcing myself to take a few steps forward.

As I walked, I could feel myself improving. It was helping to move around. While I knew it would be some time before I was back to myself, at least I could walk without falling over.

I stopped in front of the desk, leaning on the chair for a break. I'd never been inside Dax's house, and I certainly never thought I'd be inside his bedroom. It was a large room taking up the top level of the house. The ceiling was slanted from the roof, making the edges of the room hardly usable for someone as tall as Dax.

He had a small couch shoved into one corner and bookshelves along the other. Aside from the bed and the desk, there was an oversized chair, which might have been where Dax slept last night. A shiver ran through me. Had he actually spent the night in the chair at my bedside? I was certain there had to be other rooms with beds in this house. Why would he stay in here with me?

I glanced over at the desk and a file folder caught my eye. The words *Ivy Shadow* were written across the tab. Like all foundlings, I'd been given the last name of the pack since I didn't have one of my own. My brow furrowed, and I leaned a little closer to the folder to make sure I'd seen it correctly.

There was no mistaking it. Dax had a folder labeled with my name. I reached out to touch it just as I heard footsteps. I turned and watched Dax walk into the room with a steaming cup of tea.

"You weren't kidding," I said. "I can smell it from here."

"I have my doubts about this, but since we don't know what he gave you, I figure it can't hurt." He handed me the cup.

I accepted it, then looked back to the desk. "Why do you have a folder with my name on it?"

"I told you, I was trying to get your debt wiped. Pack has a folder on everyone. I was looking for a loophole." He scrunched up his face. "Don't tell. I'm not really supposed to take those things out of the records office."

"Not even the alpha has that authority?" I asked.

"The elders take their jobs very seriously. While my title holds the most power, they are there with the final say. Apparently, they're big on keeping tabs on records," he said.

"Is it weird? Being alpha, I mean?" I asked.

"I miss my dad," he said.

My eyes widened, and I felt like such an asshole. I hadn't dwelled on the fact that in order for him to be in this role, he'd lost his father. And after the alpha challenge, he'd lost the other man who had been like a father to him. "Fuck. I'm really insensitive."

He chuckled. "You're not. I just think it didn't cross your mind. I was lucky I had a dad. You never had that."

That was true and helped explain why I never thought about it, but it didn't make me feel better. If I was a better friend, I'd have been worried about how he was feeling during all this change. Not just for the adjustment of the title, but also for what it cost him. Though, I suppose I was also new at this whole being friends with Dax thing. If that was even what we were.

"Are you doing okay?" I asked. "With everything. Your dad, Stuart... it's a lot."

"I'm figuring it out one day at a time," he said. "I'll feel better when we find out who is responsible for my dad's death."

"Do you have any leads?" I asked.

"I think it might be an outsider. One of the Umbras maybe," he said. "But we're not sure yet."

For a moment, I wondered if I should say what I knew

about Holden. What if he had something to do with this? What if that was what he was discussing with the Dark Wolf?

If I turned Holden in, he'd be punished, even if he wasn't involved. In the odd chance he got off, he'd know I snitched. I'd be at risk of following in Darleen's footsteps. I couldn't chance it without more information.

"Why don't you sit down before you fall over?" Dax suggested. "You're leaning against that chair pretty hard." He took the tea from me and led me to the couch.

I had to duck to sit on it, and once I was settled, I realized it wasn't much larger than the oversized chair in front of the bed. Dax passed back the tea.

"Did you sleep in the chair all night?" I asked.

"Do you think that's creepy?" he asked.

I shrugged and took a sip of the tea.

"Cause if you think it's creepy, I definitely slept in the other room," he said.

"I don't think it's creepy," I said.

"Good, cause I slept in the chair."

"Thank you, by the way," I said. "Not for the chair thing, but for the other thing. For getting me out of there. I don't know how I let myself get fooled by that man."

"I'm glad I was there to help," he said.

"Where is he now? Leo, I think his name was," I said.

"He won't bother you again," Dax said.

I swallowed hard. His words sounded so final. I wished I felt a little sympathy for the missing man, but I couldn't find any. Someone who tried to drug a girl wasn't going to be missed. The world was probably better off without him.

We sat in silence for a while and I focused on the steaming drink in my cup. I was about halfway through the awful tea and I was actually starting to feel a little better.

"When you're feeling better maybe you and I could go to the Keep. I can promise you I won't put anything in your drinks," he said.

"I'd like that," I said, surprised that I meant it. I finished the tea, then stood. "I should get going. I have to be at work tonight."

"You know, I probably could get you out of it if you wanted me to," he said.

"No, thanks though," I said.

"You don't have to keep working there," he said. "If you and me work out, you won't have to use that money you've saved. You could move in here with me, do whatever you want."

"That sounds too good to be true," I said.

"I know it's hard to trust people after all you've been through, but I'm not the same kid I was so long ago," he said.

"I know that," I said. "But I'm still not ready to give up one of the few legit jobs in the Fringes."

"I understand. When you're ready, I'll be here," he said.

For some reason, as the two of us walked down the steps to the front door, I got the strangest sensation that I should run. It came on quickly. An almost overwhelming urge to flee. I pushed the feeling down, trying to ignore it. I was on my way out the door as it was, but also I was with Dax, who had saved me last night.

As soon as I stepped outside, the sensation eased. It wasn't gone, but it was better. Maybe it was a delayed reaction from last night's trauma.

My car was parked in front of Dax's house. "Wait. How did my car get here?"

"Kate drove it over for you." He fished my keys out of his pocket.

My heart thundered. He'd had my keys this whole time? It was impossible to turn off the strange alarm bells in my head. Dax hadn't done anything wrong. I wasn't restrained, I had access to my phone, and he'd had my car brought to me. Why was I freaking out?

I grabbed the keys, hoping that would help tamp down some of the rising anxiety. "Thank you."

"See you around, little flower." He winked.

I got into my car and drove back home. It wasn't until I was in my apartment with the door locked that some of the fear started to subside. What was that? Why had I freaked out like that?

For once, I was glad Kate wasn't home. I didn't want to have to explain this newfound anxiety. Figuring it was a lingering effect of the previous night, I headed to the shower. I still had to be at work tonight and I needed to be more clear-headed than I was now for a shift at the Howler.

CHAPTER
TWENTY-ONE

THE NEW SERVER, Grace, was fantastic during her training shift with me. She got the hang of it quickly and wasn't easily thrown off by our rowdier customers. By the next day, I started letting her take tables by herself and I wasn't quite as stressed as I had been the last several weeks. I might even get an actual day off on occasion.

The end of the week was going to be the big test for her, though. Holden had another fight scheduled and Grace and Kennedy would be running the floor. It meant that things would be easier for Kennedy, who had taken all the tables herself when I'd been working the fights, but it was a big deal for Grace. Instead of working one or two tables at a time, she'd do the job the same as the rest of us.

Dax had stopped by a few times, and while he'd mostly been mobbed by other patrons, he had managed to remind me that I owed him a night out. I was actually looking forward to spending time with him, but the transition to alpha was keeping him just as busy as I was. With any luck, I'd get that night off and a night out very soon.

When I showed up for work on Friday night, there was a sign on the front door. There weren't any patrons smoking outside, and it felt far too quiet.

I walked up to the door so I could read the sign. *Closed due to illegal activities.* My brow furrowed. What the fuck? What did that even mean? Every business around here was shady as hell. Every *shifter* around here was shady as hell. Aside from the fights in the basement, what could Holden have done that would get his bar closed?

I leaned in a little closer to the sign and noticed the symbol on the bottom corner. I'd only seen a handful of times, but I still quickly recognized the alpha's symbol. Dax did this. He was the one who got my workplace closed.

Pissed and confused, I spun around and stormed back to my car. My pulse raced, my mind whirred. Could he possibly be doing this because of me? Dax knew about the fights, but I doubted he would know about what Holden did to Darleen. My stomach clenched as guilt squeezed my chest. I should care more about the fact that I was working for a murderer, but all I could think of was the fact that I'd lost my path to freedom. I needed this job.

Dax's house was a few blocks off of Main Street. It was part of a row of large, Victorian style homes that had been some of the original structures in town. The Fringes had once been a mining town, but shifters had started taking over slowly. By the time the mines were dry, the humans headed to the city, and the shifters stayed.

Sometime before I was born, a deal was struck with a coven of witches to ward our lands. Humans thought it was nothing more than a patch of woods. They couldn't enter, but the spell made it so they didn't even come near. It was a complex bit of magic, but somehow they'd pulled it off and it was still going strong all these years later.

When I arrived at Dax's house, I had to park across the street. Eight cars were parked along the street on his side and none of those cars had been there when I'd left last weekend.

I could sense the unease in the air. Something big was going down, and I had a feeling I was walking right into the middle of it. If I was less pissed, I might have turned around and gone home. What right did I have to demand answers from the alpha? Dax and I were in a strange place. We were possibly dating, but hadn't actually gone on a date yet. What did that make us? We weren't friends exactly, but we weren't yet lovers. The only thing I knew was that for the first time, we weren't enemies.

Flutters replaced the tension I was feeling. Dax was the last man I thought I'd get involved with, but he had been doing everything right lately. Surely, he wouldn't care if I showed up to express my anxiety at not having a job anymore?

I hesitated in front of his door, my fist poised to knock. Last chance to flee. Suddenly, the door opened and a shifter nearly walked right into me.

"So sorry, didn't see you there," a large male said. His brow furrowed. "Ivy?"

"Mika?" I was staring at another former classmate. Mika was tall and broad, with dark skin and green eyes. Aside from Dax, he'd been the other heartthrob at my high school. A year older than me, he'd dominated the school, only backing down to the future alpha when needing to keep the peace. I never got the sense that he was friends with Dax, but I suppose as alpha, there wasn't much choice.

"I heard about you two, but I didn't believe it," Mika said.

"What's that supposed to mean?" I snapped defensively. I was so tired of being looked at as less than everyone around me.

"I always thought you were way too hot for everyone in the Fringes," he said with a shrug. "I figured you'd be out of here."

"I can't leave. I'm a foundling," I reminded him. Yet another wonderful perk of my position. If I left, I would have a bounty on my head. Foundlings were technically pack property.

"Oh yeah, that," he said. After an awkward pause, he inclined his head toward the house. "You heading in?"

"I guess so," I said.

"I'm sure I'll see you around," he said as he stepped aside to let me pass.

I walked into the house and Mika closed the door behind him. No turning back now.

Voices floated toward me, their tones sounding angry and tense. When I turned the corner, I caught sight of a dozen shifters sitting around a huge dining room table. They were talking over each other, slamming hands on the table, and some even jumped up from their seats as they spoke.

I knew I was walking into something I probably shouldn't see, but until I saw the frustrated expression on Dax's face, I didn't realize how big it was. I got the distinct impression I didn't belong here, and I took a careful step backward, hoping to slip out without notice. They were so engaged in their conversation, it might be possible. Then I stepped on a board that squeaked. I froze, my whole body tensing.

A dozen male shifters looked up at me, the conversation ceasing. Dax's expression softened immediately. "What are you doing here?" He stood and walked toward me.

"I didn't mean to interrupt. Mika let me in, but I can go." Suddenly, this felt like a very bad idea. It was as if my insides were clawing at me, telling me to get out. I made a mistake coming here.

"What's wrong?" Dax looked every piece the concerned friend, but something was off. Maybe he was stressed and didn't expect me to walk in on him. I wasn't sure I'd be thrilled with him showing up while I was in the middle of something.

"I just wanted to ask about the Howler," I said. "I went for my shift and saw the sign."

He brought his hand to his forehead. "Of course, I should have told you. It all just happened so fast."

"She works for Holden?" An older shifter I didn't recognize asked.

"She's a waitress. She has nothing to do with this," Dax said, a note of a growl in his tone. It was a command and I could feel the pull of the words, even though they hadn't been directed at me.

I swallowed. It was one thing to know that Dax was alpha; it was another to see the power he now wielded being applied.

"What's going on?" The curiosity was now outweighing the strangeness of this situation.

"Holden isn't who you think he is," Dax said.

"Holden's an asshole," I said. "What do you think I think he is?"

Dax chuckled. "I told you all she has nothing to do with this. She just worked there."

"Dax, tell me," I said.

"Holden was caught working with the Umbra Wolves. They were planning to overthrow our pack," he said.

I covered my mouth with my hand as the shock of the whole thing settled around me. How had I not seen this? It explained the conversation I'd overheard and why Darleen was dead. I had wondered if he'd been mad about the fight or if he'd been involved with Preston's death, but I could never quite find resolution with what I'd heard.

I lowered my hand, then kept my voice to a whisper, "Those wolves at the fight."

"I should have seen it then," he said. "But I was naive and thought it was about money and entertainment. Now, I know why my father had the rule in place to keep the other packs out."

I considered sharing what I'd heard, but the gathered shifters already seemed suspicious of me since I'd worked for Holden. I couldn't admit I'd heard something weeks ago that I'd kept secret.

"What's going to happen?" I wanted to ask about my job and the bar, but it sounded too selfish to ask that specifically.

"Holden will go on trial before the elders and we'll investigate this. It'll be alright." He pulled me into an unexpected hug.

My breath hitched, and I sunk into him, reveling in his warmth. When I was wrapped up with him, the alarm bells faded. I liked the feeling of his body close to mine. Maybe it was time to stop fighting it.

He released me, then cupped my cheek with his hand. "I know you were counting on that job. I'll ask around and see what I can find for you."

"Did you say she needs a job?" The older male asked.

Dax took a step back, dropping his hand from my face. I felt cold and empty, already missing his touch.

"Don't even think about it," Dax said.

"She's small. We need someone who can get in and get out," he said.

My brow furrowed. I was smaller than average for a shifter, but I didn't really like to be reminded about it.

"It's far too dangerous," Dax said.

"It would pay her debt. Isn't that what you want for her?" the older shifter asked.

"Not like that. She wants to pay her debt herself," Dax said.

"And this would allow her to do it. In a single night."

"What are you talking about?" I asked.

"No, Ivy. It's too dangerous," Dax said.

"She'd have the whole team with her," another shifter added. I recognized him as Xander Lee, one of my former classmates. "Having someone her size would make it easier."

"I really don't want to involve her in this," Dax said, but it sounded like some of the fight had gone from him.

"Maybe you all can explain what you're talking about?" I suggested.

"We need proof of the conspiracy," Dax said. "We're sending in a team to find the information."

"Breaking and entering, you mean?" I asked. "Why can't you just search Holden's house?"

"It's not at Holden's house. He's been communicating with one of the Umbra heirs. We need the information to prove it to their alpha. It's the only way to do this without causing war," Dax said.

"We're no match for the Umbra forces if they attack us," Xander said. "We have to solve this diplomatically."

"You think breaking and entering is diplomatic?" I stared at the group of shifters. Sure, we live in the Fringes, and things were different here, but even they had to see the hypocrisy in the situation.

"If we accuse the alpha's son without proof, it'll be dismissed, and then he'll destroy the evidence. We have no way of knowing if Holden is the only informant. We could be days away from an attack," the older man said.

"Why would the Umbras attack us?" We were the outcasts. Even they sent their criminals to live with us. They needed us in an odd way. I knew that long ago, they'd controlled our lands, but we'd coexisted since then.

"We're the first step," Dax said. "They intend to take over all the packs. We're their first stop. They'll claim any of our warriors they can to join their cause and they'll suck us under their rule."

I didn't like the sound of that. Who wanted to live in a place where every aspect of your life was dictated by the alpha? I'd had a taste of that with my limitations, and I couldn't imagine it being worse.

"She'd be safe. The team is solid," Xander said.

"The question is, can she fight?" The older shifter asked.

Dax glanced at me, then looked back at the group. "She can fight."

"What do you say, Ivy? Want to help your pack?" Xander asked.

My pack. That was all I'd ever wanted. I wanted to be officially part of the pack and have a place I belonged. If I did this, I was helping save my pack from destruction. It would earn me some respect and I would be able to pay off my debt.

"If she does this, I want her debt wiped," Dax said.

"The council will agree to that," the older man said.

I sucked in a breath and tried to contain my glee. Did that just happen? In exchange for breaking in and stealing some documents, I'd get my debt wiped?

"I won't be alone?" I asked.

"You'll be with our experts," Xander said. "Our smallest member is out, as she's pregnant. You'll have everything you need. It should be quick. In and out."

I glanced at Dax, curious to see if he had anything else to add. He nodded once, as if giving me his blessing. I wasn't sure why I cared what he thought, but it helped encourage me. "Okay, I'm in."

CHAPTER
TWENTY-TWO

My life was in a strange place. Dax's house was a buzz of activity, and I was right in the center of it. I wasn't sure if it was the fact that I'd agreed to steal documents for the pack or if it was because Dax set a protective hand on my lower back every time we were close. Whatever the cause, I was welcomed as part of the group. For the first time in my life, I didn't feel constantly aware of my status as a foundling.

I met all the pack elders and each of them interacted with me the same way they treated everyone else. I listened to conversations and plans while trying to make sense of what was going on. This was private pack stuff; things I never thought I'd be a part of, even after paying my debt. It was exciting to be included.

The other members of the team I was now a part of joined the elders and we began to pour over maps and strategies. I focused on learning the plan, paying careful attention to the escape routes that were drawn on the map.

My stomach did a flip every time they mentioned pieces that were my role. I was the one who had to climb through the window and do the actual work of stealing what we needed. The rest of them would cause distractions and keep the getaway car ready.

It was terrifying, but I knew there was a whole team to support me and keep watch. With several distraction plans and intel that the Umbra estate would be largely empty, I was feeling pretty confident by the time all the details were explained.

The doorbell rang, and I stood, grateful for the break to stretch. Pizzas were brought into the kitchen and the group filed out of the dining room. I lingered behind, taking a moment to process how quickly everything in my life had changed. It was overwhelming in the best possible way. This was what it was like to be one of the regular shifters.

"Hey, Ivy, we're going to go out to run tonight," Frankie, one of the wolves on the heist team, said through a mouth full of pizza. "You should come. It can't hurt to practice a little."

"I don't think that's a good idea," Dax said. "She's only shifted once."

"Even more reason to practice. If we have to get out fast, wolf form is much better," Frankie said.

"You're leaving tomorrow night. She'll wear herself out if she goes tonight," Dax said.

"She'll be fine," Frankie said.

Dax growled low in his throat. "I said *no*."

"Alright, man, you're the alpha." Frankie turned and walked back to the kitchen, leaving me and Dax alone.

"Dax," I hissed. "What the fuck?"

"I'm sorry." He moved closer and reached for me.

I stepped back. "I know you're the alpha but you're not in charge of me."

"I just get so crazy about the thought of sharing you with anyone," he admitted.

"It's a run in the woods, not sex," I said.

"If you end up having to hide out after, it could be days before I see you again. Selfishly, I don't want to share you tonight."

My breath caught, and my stomach flipped for an entirely different reason. Dax and I had been moving toward couple status, but things kept getting in the way of even going on a date. "Are you asking me out?"

"I'm asking you *in*," he said, his voice husky.

My body reacted to his words, knowing exactly what he had in mind. "That could be fun."

"I've been dreaming of getting you alone for so long." This time, when he moved closer to me, I didn't pull away.

He wrapped his arms around my waist, his strong hands pulling me into him. I lifted my chin so I could look into his dark eyes.

His hand moved to my chin, and ever so slowly, he lowered his lips to mine. It felt like an eternity as I waited for his kiss. When our mouths connected, it felt like a burst of tension released. Our lips moved in unison, the kiss gentle and sweet. I never expected such tenderness from Dax. His tongue brushed against mine and a shiver went all the way to my core.

When he pulled away, I had to resist the urge to grab his shirt and yank him back to me. We'd have time for that later.

Dax smirked. "As soon as I get these freeloaders out, it's me and you. Alone. All night."

"I can't wait." My words came out breathy.

Dax licked his lower lip as if savoring the taste of our kiss. I bit down on my lip, working to rein in the need coursing through me. I'd never been with a man before, but this felt right. Tomorrow night I was going to do the most dangerous thing I'd ever tried, so why not let myself enjoy one of the best parts of life tonight?

Anticipation simmered low in my belly as I forced myself to eat and smile and pretend that everything was normal. The group of shifters started to break off, getting smaller as people left to go home. It felt like hours dragged by, but it wasn't as long as it seemed until Dax and I were alone.

I helped him clean up the paper plates and beer bottles, the two of us working together in silence. We were just picking up trash and wiping the counters, but I could feel the sexual tension sizzling around us. I wanted this. I wanted to be with Dax. Our relationship had unfolded unusually, but in a pack where anonymous sex in the bathroom wasn't out of the ordinary, I shouldn't be too surprised. At least Dax was making an effort to prove himself to me.

He was the alpha, and I had a feeling if he wanted to push me, he could have. Nobody would have stopped him, and any objections I made would have been ignored. If he'd done that, he would have ruined everything between us, but based on what I'd known of the teenage version of him, that was more of what I expected. This new side was surprising and really, really hot.

Dax stood in the middle of the kitchen, his hands on his hips. "I think it's good enough. What do you think?"

My stomach twisted into knots. Who knew cleaning could act as foreplay? "Yeah. Looks good to me."

I hardly registered his warning growl before Dax had me in his arms. His mouth crushed against mine as he pushed me up against the island. I tangled my fingers into his dark hair, pulling his head closer to me as we deepened the kiss. Our tongues battled as we devoured each other. It was angry and heavy, and the kiss felt almost the same as our fight. This was how things should be between Dax and me. We were irrational and feisty and nothing about our strange romance was, by any means, a traditional love story. It didn't feel like it was about love. It was about releasing tension and for now, that was enough.

His hands slid down to my hips, and I felt his thumb

slip under the waistband of my jeans. I lowered my hands to my jeans and, after unbuttoning mine, I reached for his.

He pulled away from the kiss and I whined, already missing the feel of his lips on mine. With a wicked grin, his gaze raked down my body, taking me in. When his eyes flicked back up to meet mine, he reached for my shirt. "You have far too many clothes on, my flower."

"I could say the same about you." I stood on my tip toes, and pulled his head down to mine. Instead of kissing him, I sucked his lower lip into my mouth, then lightly bit him.

He groaned, then began kissing me again, even more hungrily this time. His hand worked its way under my shirt, sliding up my stomach until he reached my breasts. His touch was warm even through the fabric of my bra, but he didn't stay above the bra for long. Soon, the bra was pushed above my breasts and he was cupping me and teasing my nipples with his fingers.

I moaned into his kiss, my back arching as his expert touch sent ripples of pleasure through me. I reached for his jeans, wanting to feel him the way he was feeling me.

He pulled away. "Not yet. I go first."

My brow furrowed, but I didn't get a chance to say anything before he lifted me and set me on top of the counter. I kicked off my shoes and waited with bated breath to see what he was going to do next.

"I'm going to make you beg for more." Dax tugged my jeans and underwear off in one movement, then tossed them aside.

He lowered his head and my breath hitched as I realized what he was doing. Dax, the Shadow Pack alpha, wanted to go down on me. I kept my thighs together, feeling a little self-conscious. I hadn't expected this. I figured we'd have sex and that would be it. I didn't think it would get quite this intimate.

"Relax," Dax said as he gently pushed my thighs apart.

"I've never done this before," I admitted.

"I know," he said. "We'll take it slow."

I nodded, still feeling a little nervous. I wasn't sure why it was bothering me; I wanted to have sex with him, but I hadn't thought it through. I always kind of figured my first time would be terrible and quick. I never imagined a situation where I'd be cared for and my needs would be taken into consideration. All those stories from classmates about their first time made it seem like the first time was just this thing you did to get it over with. I realized I had tried to tell myself that was what it would be like with Dax, but I never really believed it. There was something more between us than a one-night stand.

Dax stood between my thighs. "Lean back. Try to enjoy yourself."

I laughed nervously. "I'm trying."

Dax's brow furrowed. "We don't have to do this if you're not ready. It can wait. I'll still be here when you get back. I'll be here in a week or a month or a year."

I melted right there. "You'd really wait a year?"

"I don't want to wait, but I know you're worth it," he said.

Oh shit. I was in so much trouble. This wasn't just sex. I was pretty sure I was falling for Dax. How the fuck did that happen?

I bit down on my lower lip and nodded, then I leaned back on my elbows as he instructed. I felt so exposed and vulnerable, but I trusted Dax. His head settled between my legs and I held my breath, unsure of what to expect. All I knew was what I could do with my own fingers, so all the sensations were different. Feeling his body heat and his warm breath against my sex was already more stimulation that I was used to.

His lips pressed against my clit, gentle and warm and I relaxed a little. So far, it wasn't too strange. Then his tongue flicked over the nub, and I gasped. He did it again and again and I felt the remaining tension leave as the sensation of his tongue on my body sent me to places of pleasure I'd never reached on my own. How had he done that so quickly?

He changed pace and direction, licking, sucking, and using his fingers. My eyes rolled into the back of my head and I moaned wantonly as all sense of self-consciousness was replaced by pleasure.

Slowly, he dipped a finger inside me and I sucked in a breath, startled by the new sensation.

"Is that okay?" he asked.

"Yes," I breathed.

His finger returned, sliding in and out. He was gentle and slow. Combining the new sensation with the movement of his tongue on my clit. My breathing grew rapid, and I could feel the pressure of an orgasm building.

All of the sudden he did something with his finger, hooking it inside me so it reached a place that made my back arch. I gasped as a jolt of pure sensation rushed through me.

"You liked that," he said, his voice husky and deep.

I gasped and looked at him, our eyes meeting. "What was that?"

"I forgot how fun virgins can be," he said.

It was an odd comment, but he moved his finger inside me again, and all thoughts vanished. He continued to work his fingers and his tongue until my hips were bucking wildly and I was gasping for air. It didn't take much longer before I was gripping the countertop as an orgasm came crashing through me.

Ripples of pleasure were still rolling through me as I pushed myself up to sitting. Panting, I stared at Dax. "That wasn't anything like I expected."

"It gets better," he promised.

I grinned. "Don't I get a chance to make you feel good?"

"Don't worry, you will." He grabbed my hips and pulled me to the edge of the counter.

At this height, my bare pussy was lined up at his waist. I could see the erection through his jeans and desire roared deep inside me. I wanted more. I wanted every part of him.

Dax lowered his jeans, revealing his very large cock. I

swallowed hard, unsure of how that was going to fit inside me.

As if aware of where my thoughts were, Dax gently moved a stray lock of hair from my face. "We'll go slow."

Before I could respond, he claimed me with his mouth. I wrapped my legs around him, pulling myself as close to him as I could. I could feel his cock against my inner thigh. My whole body felt like it was on fire with desire. I wanted him inside me. The anticipation was driving me wild.

I pulled back from the kiss. "Dax, I want all of you."

"You sure you're ready?" he asked.

"Please," I begged. "I need you."

"Oh, god, you have no idea how sexy it is to hear you say that."

He grabbed my ass and angled himself so he was positioned better. I felt him push up against my entrance. Nervous flutters filled my chest, and I dug my fingernails into his back. This was what I wanted, but I was still a little unsure of how he was going to fit.

"Relax," Dax said.

I looked up from his massive cock, and his calm expression and smile reassured me. Everyone was probably nervous their first time. Dax kept one hand on my ass, but he grabbed the back of my head with the other, pulling me in for a much softer, gentler kiss.

As our lips moved together, he pressed into me. I gasped. Dax deepened the kiss, distracting me from the stretching my body was doing. He went in a little deeper and I winced. It was a little uncomfortable. So far, the fingers were much better. Why was this such a big deal?

Dax bit down on my lower lip hard just as he pushed into me fully. The pain on my lip mixed with the pain I felt from his cock, but both eased quickly. It was still uncomfortable, but Dax thrusted out and in slowly a few times, allowing my body to adjust. After a moment, it didn't feel uncomfortable anymore. It felt full in a good way.

I relaxed, letting my body take over, my hips moving with Dax's, our bodies finding a rhythm. He eased into it at first, then increased his pace, burying his cock deep within me. My body adjusted, and I gasped for air as pleasure replaced the initial discomfort.

Dax leaned down, his mouth claiming mine as he continued to piston into me. His hands explored my body and all the sensations built until I could feel a rising crescendo. A wave of pleasure was building deep in my core, threatening to explode. I dug my fingernails into Dax's back and he moaned into the kiss. The sound sent me over the edge, and I pulled away from the kiss as I cried out.

The climax rolled through me in ripples before exploding again and again. Just when I thought I couldn't take anymore, Dax thickened inside me. He thrust one more time, then groaned as he found his own orgasm.

For a moment, he was still, eyes down, panting. Then he looked up and smiled. He lowered his face to mine and kissed me sweetly before pulling out.

My whole body felt hot and far more relaxed that I had

in a long, long time. I understood why people enjoyed this so much. If not for the fact that I was a little sore, I might have grabbed Dax and insisted on another round.

He helped me off the countertop. "My shower is large enough for two."

I took his hand and the two of us headed upstairs.

CHAPTER
TWENTY-THREE

I woke to watery winter sunshine streaming in through the curtains in Dax's room. Stretching out my arms, I reached for him, longing to bury myself into his warmth. I only felt cool sheets and pillows.

I turned to where Dax had been when I fell asleep, finding his side of the bed empty. I glanced over at the clock on the bedside table. It was already eleven in the morning. No wonder Dax was out of bed. I guess all those double shifts I'd been working caught up to me.

A pang of sadness made my muscles tense at the realization that I wasn't ever going to be working at the Howler again. I hated the job, and I was counting down to when I'd get to leave, but I thought it would be on my terms. There was something so unfinished about the way it went down.

I should be celebrating. Tonight was the night I was going to finally gain the thing I wanted more than anything; my status as a full member of the pack. Why did I feel so uneasy, then?

I hugged my knees to my chest and looked around the room, trying to give myself a moment to let everything about the last twenty-four hours sink in. I was in Dax's bed, again. Only this time, it wasn't because he was rescuing me. A little rush of excitement welled up inside me at the memories of last night. I'd had sex for the first time and it was amazing. It wasn't the horror stories I'd heard from other girls. And it was with Dax, of all people. In a million years, I never would have thought the two of us would be anything other than civil at best. Instead, I felt giddy just thinking about him. What was wrong with me? It wasn't even the way Kate talked about hooking up with guys. This was something different.

My eyes widened. *Shit*. Kate. I hadn't been home all night, and I hadn't left a note. While she was often out, I never was. She was probably worried something had happened to me. I scrambled off the bed and looked around for my purse. Then I remembered that it, along with all my clothes, were downstairs.

I crept to the doorway and peeked out, listening for any signs of visitors. We were meeting here tonight before we went out for the heist, and I wasn't sure if anyone else was arriving sooner.

There were some faint sounds, like muffled conversation, but I couldn't tell where they were coming from. I tip-toed out the door to the top of the steps and peered down. There wasn't any sign of anyone, but I could hear better now. Dax was talking with somebody, and I couldn't yet tell if it was a phone call or in person.

A wicked thought filled my mind. If I crept down naked, I had a feeling the phone call would end quickly and we might be able to get in another round. I was a little sore from last night, but I was eager to experience sex with Dax again.

I stood still and listened, trying to determine if it was safe to go down without clothes. A second voice joined in, and my shoulders slumped in disappointment. So much for round two. It was probably going to have to wait until I returned from tonight's events.

I turned and took a step toward the room, but a bit of conversation caught my attention.

"She really doesn't know?" the other voice asked.

Who were they talking about? I crept back to the stairs and listened carefully, trying to tune into the heightened senses I was supposed to have as a shifter. Not that I'd taken any time to practice yet, but they were supposed to be there once you shifted.

"I told you, she has no idea," Dax said.

"I can't believe she never caught on," the mystery shifter said. "You'd think something would have happened to tip her off."

"There's a lot she doesn't know," Dax said. "I'm lucky I even found out. The elders hide everything in those files of theirs."

It felt like someone had just dumped ice water over me. I tensed and a rushing sound filled my ears. Was he talking about me? I recalled the folder I'd seen in his room the other day. Without waiting to listen to the rest of the conversation, I raced back to his room and stopped in front of Dax's desk.

There was nothing on it. *Fuck.* What had they been talking about? It had to have been about me. What did Dax know about my past that I didn't know, and why was he sharing it with someone else?

I almost didn't hear the footsteps in time. With a leap, I crossed the room to the opposite side and tried to look like I wasn't freaking the fuck out.

Dax peeked in around the door. "Hey, you're awake."

"Yeah, trying to remember where I put my clothes," I said.

"That would be the kitchen," he said. "But I have company down there. Work never seems to ease for the alpha."

I smiled. "Do you need me to go?"

"Of course not." He walked over and planted a kiss on my cheek. It didn't feel the same way it had last night. After what I'd just heard, it felt like I was playing house.

"You okay?" Dax asked. "You seem tense."

"I'm just a little sore," I said.

He cupped my cheek and looked down at me. "It'll pass. I'll give you a few days to recover before we do it again if that helps." He winked.

I reached up for his cheek and then rose to my toes so I could kiss him. It was a quick kiss, but I hoped it was enough to ease his mind. I didn't need him to know I'd heard him. I had to do some digging on my own first. What if he wasn't even talking about me at all?

Okay, fine, I knew he was talking about me. What other file would he be talking about? He'd had mine on his desk last time I was here.

"Help yourself to whatever's in the closet." He released my face and walked toward the door.

I blew out a relieved breath. Last night, being around Dax had felt so right. Today, I was regretting everything. What if I made a huge mistake?

As I dug through his closet, I started to feel a little better. So what if Dax found something weird in my file? I was going to do this job tonight and by tomorrow, I would be a free wolf. Once I was a full member of the pack, I'd ask him what he found. If I wasn't happy with his answers, I could walk away. If all he wanted from me was sex, he'd already gotten it. What was the worst that could happen?

I suppose he could make me vanish the same way Holden made Darleen vanish. Or worse. He was the alpha. What if it was nothing? What if the file said who my real parents were, and they were Umbra wolves? That would be slightly scandalous if we got serious, but it wouldn't be the most interesting thing that had happened around here. Even if something was strange in my file, something else would happen and they'd forget about me.

After this thing was finished tonight, I could worry about this more. But right now, I had to stay focused. I was so close to my goal I could taste it. I was finally going to be a full member of the Shadow Pack.

I headed downstairs and found my purse in the dining room, slung over a chair. My phone was nearly dead, but I had enough battery to send a quick text to Kate, letting her know I'd stayed over at Dax's. I didn't elaborate, and I knew it was going to drive her crazy, but I wasn't sure how to explain over a text. Slipping my phone back into the bag, I left the dining room to go find Dax.

When I wandered into the kitchen, I found Dax with his friend Xander. I got the sense that the two of them were close yesterday. I wondered if he was Dax's choice for Beta. I knew there was a whole process with nominations and approval by the elders, but I wasn't sure of how it all went down. I wouldn't be surprised if Xander ended up with the title, though.

"You're here early," I said by way of greeting.

"Or maybe you're up late," Xander said.

"We had a busy night." I kept my tone light and definitely insinuated that Dax and I were intimate.

Dax's chest expanded a bit like a peacock, and I breathed a little easier. Whatever he was up to, I wanted to find out without alerting him to my concerns. Keeping his ego stoked was my best play. That was one thing I was certain had never changed about Dax. He enjoyed the spotlight for all things. When we were younger, he'd take it for the negative as well as the good.

The thought sent my stomach into knots. What did I really know about Dax now? I had a sinking feeling I'd been played, at least a little. I thought I was smarter than that, but maybe I wasn't. All I knew was that I was going to have to be far more careful moving forward. I wasn't used to being part of the in-crowd and I wasn't sure if they played by the same rules as the rest of us.

"Coffee?" Dax passed me a steaming mug. "I feel like an ass for not knowing how you take it, but I didn't have any of Kate's herbs sitting around."

I accepted the cup. "Black, and I'm grateful you don't have the herbs."

"I'm grateful you don't need them," Dax said.

"I'm missing something," Xander said.

"No, you're not, trust me," I said.

Dax smiled, and it sent a little rush of heat into my chest. Okay, so maybe I was still taken by him. He could be quite charming and it was kind of fun to have an inside joke between us.

I took a sip of the coffee. It was good, dark coffee, and it made me feel a little less unbalanced. I sat at the table and looked over at the two males, waiting for one of them to speak. They'd been happy to talk before I arrived. Another point for the theory they'd been talking about me.

"So, what time is everyone else arriving?" I asked.

"Sunset," Dax said. "We've got a little time."

"You might, but I've got some things to prepare." Xander stood. "I'll see you in a bit."

Dax waved to his friend, then walked over to where I was sitting. "I know you have a big night tonight, but how about we squeeze in that first date? It's a little backward from tradition, but I have a feeling you don't mind if we skirt convention. The Diner serves breakfast all day."

My stomach growled at the thought of food. "Alright, but I'm going to need to change into clothes that belong to me if we're going out."

"You look amazing in my tee," he said.

"I know that, and you know that, but you have a reputation to uphold. You're the alpha. I'm a foundling. Shouldn't I at least look like I made an effort to be seen with you?" I asked.

"Will it make you feel better if you change?" he asked.

I nodded. "It won't take me long. I can meet you there in an hour."

"Okay. I've got some stuff to go over, anyway." He leaned down and kissed me. "Can you see yourself out?"

"Yeah," I said.

Dax left the kitchen, and my heart thundered against my ribs. I was so confused by the whole situation. I tried not to read too much into Dax needing to work; he was the alpha and we were planning something big tonight. It made sense. But that folder and the comments kept forcing their way into my mind.

The only thing I needed to do right now was talk to Kate. She could be my voice of reason. If she thought I was blowing things out of proportion, I'd believe her. If she thought I needed to run for the hills, I'd pack a bag. My own head was far too mixed up to think clearly. I wasn't even sure which direction I wanted Kate to point me.

There was a part of me that wanted things with Dax to

be real and uncomplicated and hot. Sex in the kitchen and brunch on a cold winter's morning sounded like perfection. But I couldn't let myself get there completely while I wondered what he might have been saying behind my back.

I took one more sip of the coffee, then I dumped the rest in the sink. It was a waste, but I was in a hurry.

CHAPTER
TWENTY-FOUR

My phone was officially dead when I reached my car. I hoped the text I'd sent to Kate went through. I also hoped she was at home. It was Saturday, and she usually spent the day working on projects in her room. There was a chance she'd stay over at someone else's place, but last I heard the brief interlude with Ryan at the club hadn't lasted.

I blew out a relieved breath when I saw Kate's car in her parking spot. As soon as I opened the front door, I was tackled by my friend.

"Where have you been?" she demanded.

"I'm guessing my text didn't go through," I said as I pried her arms off me.

Her brow furrowed, and she walked to the couch where her phone was sitting. She glanced at it too quickly to even read it, then looked back at me. "Okay, so I missed your text. But I'd already called everyone I could think of before you sent that. Including your work only to find out it's fucking closed."

"Wait, you called people? I don't know anyone. You mean you called my work?" I said.

"No, I called all the girls you work with and I even called Dax. Asshole didn't pick up the phone," she grumbled.

My cheeks heated.

Her eyes widened. "You were with Dax? All night?"

"Okay, don't freak out. I have so much to tell you," I said. "The least of which is that I slept with Dax."

She squealed. "Finally. How was he? Is he as big as they say? Did you do it again this morning?"

"Stop." I knew she'd continue to pepper me with questions if I let her. "Yes, we slept together. Once, last night. Yes, he's a big as they say. But that's not what I need to talk to you about."

She sat on the couch and patted the spot next to her. "Tell me."

I joined her and considered which topic I should open with. Did I tell her I'm going to be part of a break-in tonight or that I suspected Dax knew something about my past? Even as the thought crossed my mind, I felt stupid. Compared to crossing into enemy territory and stealing documents to prevent a war, Dax knowing something about my past didn't sound like it was a big deal.

My whole life I'd been angry at my parents for what they did to me. I wasn't sure finding out anything about them would change my feelings. I wasn't even sure I wanted to know. What if I was overthinking the whole thing?

"Ivy, what's going on?" Kate asked.

I snapped out of my thoughts and turned to Kate. "I have a chance to wipe my whole debt out tonight."

"Why do I get the sense that I'm not going to like this?" she asked.

"It's pack sanctioned and I won't be alone." I wasn't sure how much I should tell her. A few minutes ago, I wanted to spill everything and now I was overly aware of how she'd worry.

"Hey, did you know that the pack has records on all the foundlings?" I asked.

"No, but it makes sense. Don't they have a record on all full pack members? I mean, we aren't as hard-core as the Umbras, but they do keep tabs on us."

"True," I said. "So, I saw a folder at Dax's with my name on it."

"Did you get to open it?"

I shook my head.

"Well, as fascinating as it might be to find out about little foundling Ivy, I'm far more interested in this job you have. Explain."

"I guess we're at risk of a war with the Umbras. It's why they closed the Howler. Holden was working with them," I said.

"Shit, Ivy," Kate said. "Everyone knows Holden is a grumpy old asshole, but I never thought he'd go against the pack."

"Me neither," I said.

"I know you worked there, but what does this have to do with you?" she asked.

"We need proof of what he was working on with one of the Umbra heirs. If we can prove it to their alpha, it could prevent a fight," I said.

"And your role is..." Kate let the words hang in the air.

I squirmed a little, feeling like a fraud before I'd even done anything. I was a waitress, not a thief. "I'm helping them steal the documentation."

"Like from Holden's house?" She looked hopeful.

"No, not from Holden's."

"Fuck, Ivy, you're going into Umbra territory?" Her expression was a mixture of judgement and fear. It matched exactly how I felt internally. I shouldn't be doing this. I had no experience, and it felt wrong. I'd been so proud of how I was working to pay my debt without going into a life of crime. Yet, here I was.

"It will pay your debt?" Kate seemed to have collected herself quicker than I expected. "As in just finishing off what you owe, or will this be enough?"

"It's a clean slate once I do this. The heist in exchange for pack membership." I needed that money I'd saved to help me survive until I found something else I could do for work. If we proved Holden was a traitor, his bar wasn't going to open again. At least not with him as the proprietor. There was only one punishment for betraying pack: death.

"You won't be alone?" Kate confirmed.

"There's a whole team. This is what they do. They were just short a smaller member to fit in tight spaces."

"I don't know how I feel about this, Ivy."

"I know." The odd comments and the folder were nearly forgotten. Realistically, they were a much smaller priority than me risking my life for this mission. Once it was over, I'd ask Dax. There had to be a reasonable explanation.

"You sure about this?" Kate asked.

I nodded. "It's all I've ever wanted. You don't know what it's like to be on the outside all the time."

"I know how hard it's been for you. You deserve this. You should have been made full pack years ago," she said.

"Well, with any luck we can celebrate tomorrow," I said.

"This is happening tonight?" she said.

"Yep."

She took a deep breath and let it out slowly. "Okay. But when it's over, I want all the details about you and Dax."

"Promise," I said.

I TRIED to ignore the stares of the other customers as I slid into the booth across from Dax. It had to be odd seeing us together. Hooking up at a full moon party was one thing, having brunch in public was entirely different.

I'd spent years telling myself I didn't care, but it was hard to always be reminded that I didn't really belong.

"How's Kate handling everything?" Dax asked.

I hadn't even slipped off my jacket yet. "How'd you know I talked to her?"

"She's your best friend, right? I remember how close you two were in high school. She even threatened me a few times," he said.

I shrugged. "You probably deserved it."

"I one-hundred percent deserved it," he admitted.

A server stopped in front of our table, two mugs of coffee in her hands. "Coffee for both of you?"

"Yes please," I said.

Dax tapped on the table. "Right here. Thanks."

"Do you know what you're having?" she asked.

I hadn't even looked at the menu, and I quickly grabbed it.

"Blueberry pancakes and bacon," Dax said.

My stomach growled. "That sounds amazing. I'll have the same." I handed the menu to the server.

"We like the same breakfast food," Dax pointed out. "That's a good sign."

"Who doesn't like blueberry pancakes?" I asked.

"You'd be surprised. There's some real weirdos out there." He smiled, and it looked so genuine and warm.

This morning, I'd been uncomfortable around him after what I'd overheard, but now I wasn't feeling as uncertain. He wasn't the same guy he was when we were younger. I'd tried to tell myself I'd wait to ask, but I had to know. "Dax, I'm going to ask you something and I want you to be totally honest with me."

"I'm pretty sure that's a trap, but I'll play," he said.

"It's not a trap," I said. "I just can't stop thinking about something."

"If it's about Stacey, I promise you it's over. Even if she hadn't found her true mate," he assured me.

"It's not that." I looked into his eyes, hoping I'd be able to catch his reaction to my question. "I over-heard you talking this morning. I don't want to be paranoid, but I got the sense you were talking about me."

"Which parts did you hear?" he asked.

His expression hadn't changed, and he didn't appear phased by my question. Between that and his response, I felt a little unsettled. "Was there more than one time you could have been talking about me?"

"Probably," he said. "I didn't spill all the details, I swear."

My eyes widened. "No, not sex. Something else."

"Oh, that," he said. This time, he looked down, breaking eye contact with me.

Anxiety spiked. He looked like I'd caught him in a lie. "Was it something to do with what was in that folder?"

"Of course not," he said. "I wouldn't share that with anyone."

"What exactly is in there?" I asked.

"Notes about your health as a child, check-ups, when you potty trained, first words, grades, things like that. I was hoping it would give me more, to be honest." He shrugged.

I winced. While that wasn't interesting, it sounded like

there was lots of room for embarrassing pieces of my past. "So, what were you talking about then?" It was possible the *she* in his conversation hadn't been me, but my instincts told me not to pull back. When I'd been at my apartment, I thought I could let it go. I was wrong.

"You sure you want to hear this?" He grabbed my hand.

His touch was warm and comforting, but there was a part of me that was desperate to pull away. I resisted, forcing myself to lean into the comforting part of the touch until he told me more information. "Just tell me so I'm not worried all night."

"I didn't want to freak you out, but they found Darleen's body," he said. "I know you worked together, and I really don't want you to know the details. Especially since Holden was your boss." His thumb caressed the back of my hand. "I'm just so grateful we caught him before he could do anything to you."

"That's what you were talking about?" I asked, feeling a little numb. I already knew Holden was the one who killed Darleen, and I probably should have acted surprised about that part. "I mean, that's awful. So it wasn't the Umbra Pack who killed her?"

"We found her body in Holden's back yard." He shuddered as if recalling something gruesome. "I can tell you more if you'd like, but I'd rather not. It's pretty disturbing. I didn't want you to find out."

"I don't think I want to know more details," I admitted. I should be concerned about Darleen and Holden and the whole mess, but I was mostly relieved that Dax wasn't hiding things from me to hurt me. "Thank you for telling me."

"Of course," he said. "But maybe we can change the subject? It's not exactly the conversation I imagined we'd have on our first date."

"Yeah, you're right." I tried to scramble for anything that wasn't related to the chaos of the Shadow Pack. My mind whirred with thoughts of the alpha challenge, and Preston's death, and Holden. There wasn't much else in my life to talk about.

"So, blueberry pancakes are a good start," Dax said. "But the serious question is thick crust or thin crust?"

I laughed. "Thin crust."

"Oh, we are so compatible," he said with a grin.

The waitress returned with our pancakes and set them in front of us. She topped off our coffee. "Anything else I can get for you?"

"I'm good," I said.

Dax already had a bite of food in his mouth. He gave the server a thumbs up.

"Alright, if you need anything, let me know." She turned, then spun back around. "I heard about the Howler. I know you worked there. It probably doesn't pay as well, but we've got openings here if you need it."

"Thanks," I said. The thought of having to start waiting tables again made my stomach clench. I'd hated working at the Howler, but the excellent pay helped me to get through it. I wasn't sure I could handle the crowd here.

Most of my customers were so much nicer after they had a few drinks in them.

"I'll put in a good word for you," she said before turning and walking away.

"You know, you could just take me up on my offer," Dax reminded me.

"Well, thin crust is a promising start," I said. "But I need more time."

"Sounds like date number two will have to be pizza. What would you say to a night in? Pizza, movies, maybe some other nocturnal activities..."

While I was eager for another round with Dax, his comment sent my mind in another direction. "What about shifting? I've only done it once. I honestly don't even know if I can do it on my own. I'd love some lessons."

"Sure. We could do that one of these days, but I'd rather get to know you better first. We can shift any time," he said.

I was a little hurt, but it wasn't like I was in need of learning how to control my wolf. What need did I have for shifting? I'd have lots of full moon parties ahead of me to get out and run. Most wolves around here only shifted once a month, and that was good enough for them.

"Favorite movie?" he asked.

"Anything scary," I said.

We chatted about movies and music, and Dax told me about college and what he'd been doing before his dad died. The time flew by and soon we were both done with our food and we'd lingered a while.

I took a final sip of my coffee. "We should probably leave so she can have the table."

"Good point. And don't you dare offer to pay." Dax threw some cash on the table and a moment later, the server stopped by to pick it up.

I probably would have argued with him, but I was technically unemployed.

"I'll be right back with your change," she said as she reached for the money.

I quickly added the amount in my head, curious if Dax would leave a good tip. When I'd waited on him, tips were okay, but never spectacular. Most of the time, though, it was a group of them all chipping in together, so it was hard to know who was putting in what amount.

The server returned and dropped the change on the table. "Have a great day."

"Thanks," Dax and I said in unison.

He stood, not making a move for the cash on the table, leaving it all behind. I was impressed; he was a good tipper. It might not be a very scientific theory, but I would stand by my belief that the good ones left better tips than the assholes. Who would have guessed that Dax was a generous tipper?

I tugged my jacket on and stood. Dax offered his hand, and we walked out together. I could feel the stares on us as we left, but this time, it didn't bother me.

CHAPTER
TWENTY-FIVE

I DIDN'T EXPECT to arrive at a house full of people. The elders I'd met last night and the whole crew I was joining for the heist were already gathered.

"I thought you said sunset," I whispered to Dax.

"I guess they were eager to get going," he said.

I didn't even want to ask why they were all inside his home while he was away. I knew the pack owned the alpha's house, but I didn't realize it was fair game for them to show up any time they wanted. Maybe this was an unusual circumstance? Probably not. I was pretty new to seeing deeper into pack politics, but I already figured out that the elders had more to do with decisions than I realized.

"We wanted to run through everything one last time," Patrick said, not even waiting for us to take our jackets off.

I nodded and hoped it wasn't a sign of how the rest of the night was going to go. Sure, it was important that the guy running the operation was good at his job, but this was a little much. We'd been over the details a hundred times last night and we had an hour drive ahead of us. There was time to discuss it on the road. Why take up the last few hours everyone had to rest?

"I'm going to talk to the elders while you go over this again." Dax took my jacket and walked away.

I turned back to Patrick. "Did anything change since last night?"

He scowled. "Maybe this doesn't seem like a big deal to you, but if any of us don't pull our weight, we're all fucked."

"I understand that," I said. "Especially since I'm the only one going inside the house. I think I'm a little more at risk than you."

"I'm the one in charge. If they catch us, you can bat your eyelashes," he said.

"Seriously? What is your problem?" I asked.

"My problem is that the alpha replaced a trained thief with his flavor of the week. This is serious shit. It's not something to just get an adrenaline rush," he said.

I scoffed. "You think I want to do this? Oh, no. You are mistaken. I'm doing this as a favor to the pack. Not that I owe you a damn explanation."

"Just know that if you don't pull your weight, we won't either," he said.

"I'll do my job," I said. "And you better do yours."

"I'm good at my job. This isn't my first time and it won't be my last. But I am not a babysitter."

"I never asked you to be," I said. "I just want to do this thing, get it over with, and get back."

"So you can fuck the alpha?" He sneered.

I lifted my brows. "What am I missing here? Are you mad because you want to fuck the alpha?"

He growled. "The shifter you replaced is my mate, and she's home because she's carrying my child. I will go home to them."

"That's all any of us want. I'm not here for some kink. I'm here to do the job properly," I assured him.

He seemed to relax a little, and I did as well. His freak out had nothing to do with me. He was afraid he wasn't going to make it back home, and I was the easiest to take it out on. "Listen, I know you don't know me, but I'm a foundling. I never met my parents. I'd never want that for anyone else."

His brow furrowed.

"And before you judge me for not being full pack, this job will get me there. It's worth more to me than you'll ever know."

"Alright," he said.

"Now, is there really something we need to go over or are we good?" I asked.

"We're good," he said. "We leave in thirty."

I glanced at the clock on the wall. How was it nearly sunset already? My stomach twisted into knots. I wasn't ready for this, but as I said to Patrick, I was going to do my best. This was my ticket to freedom. To owning my life. I'd have choices and options that had been unavailable to me in the past. Everything was going to change.

Trying not to overthink what was coming, I made my way over to Dax. Right now, his presence was the comfort I needed.

I stood with him while he talked about pack politics. None of it was as exciting as I hoped. Finally, I was able to drag him away for a quick goodbye. Dax started running through a list of horror movies, trying to decide what we should watch for our next date. It was a good distraction, and I found myself looking forward to the company more than the film.

"Hey, lovebirds, say your goodbyes. It's time to go," Patrick called.

Dax grabbed hold of me and pulled me close, lowering his head to mine. He kissed me hungrily. I was drawn into it, meeting his passion.

Someone cleared their throat, and Dax eased up and released me from his grasp. My pulse raced, and I was warm all the way to my core. The kiss had left me longing for more.

"Hurry back," Dax said, then he turned to Patrick. "Bring her home in one piece, you hear me?"

"You got it, boss," Patrick said.

Still feeling a little breathless from Dax's lips on mine, I followed the group out of the house. We climbed into a large black SUV and now my heart was racing for an entirely different reason.

We were about to drive right into Umbra territory and break into the home of the alpha.

Fuck me. What was I thinking when I agreed to this?

I took a seat next to Frankie, grateful to not have to sit by Patrick. I think we'd cleared things between us, but there was definitely still tension there. Marsha was driving, and Keith was next to her in the passenger seat. Patrick and Farrah took the back row behind me.

The crew was quiet for a while as Marsha drove away from Dax's house. We sped through the Fringes, leaving my hometown behind in a matter of minutes. Last time I'd left the Fringes, it had been for the full moon party and it was in the opposite direction. This time, we were heading toward the city. My stomach tightened and nervous flutters filled my chest. It was too late to turn back now.

"You'll feel us pass through the ward in a few minutes," Marsha said.

"Is this your first time out of the Fringes?" Farrah asked.

"It is," I said. "Unless you count the full moon party."

"That's still our territory," Patrick said.

"Is it true you've only shifted once?" Farrah asked.

"Yeah," I said.

"Tell me why she was chosen for this job," Farrah mumbled.

"She's the alpha's pet," Keith said with a growl.

So nobody here liked me. "I can do this, and I will do it well."

"You better," Keith said.

Heavy silence hung around us, and I was having more than a few regrets.

"Just stick to the plan and you'll be fine," Frankie said.

I wasn't sure if I should respond or keep quiet. Before I could decide, a burst of ice passed over me. It was so cold it was painful. The sensation only lasted a heartbeat, then it was gone.

"That was the ward," Marsha said. "You're officially out of Shadow territory."

"Are we already in Umbra territory or is there a neutral space between?" I asked.

I heard some laughter from behind me.

I rolled my eyes. "It was just a question."

"Everything outside the Shadows might as well be Umbra territory," Marsha explained. "They technically control the city, but they don't follow the rules the other packs abide by. They make their own and nobody is willing to stand up to challenge them."

"Why don't the other packs care?" I knew the Shadows didn't have the numbers or the resources. We were barely able to support ourselves and the new members that joined. But we were unusual for a pack. We were born of necessity, taking in the outcasts. Other packs had histories going back hundreds of years. They had power, money, resources, warriors... surely one of them would be interested in keeping the Umbras in check.

"The other packs are so far away, they don't care," Frankie said. "There are only three packs in North America. Four if you count us. We're basically in the Wild West out here. No other packs want our territory. Especially since the Umbras claimed human cities."

"Cities. Plural?" I had learned about the major packs in school, but it was a basic overview. I knew approximate territory and the names of alphas. Well, I had at one point at least. I wasn't sure I could recall them now. It wasn't like I had a lot of use for naming alphas for far away packs while waiting tables.

"They've got operations in every major city from Denver to the west coast. As long as they don't cross into Senka or Tari territory, nobody seems to care," Frankie explained. "Most of the packs avoid human cities. The Umbras took the opposite approach."

"Why would they want to be around humans?" I asked.

"Why is anyone willing to take risks?" Patrick asked. "For money and power."

I swallowed hard. His words felt like a personal attack. Was that what we were all doing here? I was here to gain my freedom, but why were the others here? Nobody in the Shadows did things for the good of the pack. There were always strings attached. My debt was massive, and this was risky enough that the elders agreed I'd be even with what I owed. The others had to be getting paid very well.

Ahead, I saw the lights in the city sparkling like beacons. When I'd viewed the city from afar, I'd thought it looked beautiful. Now, it looked like a warning.

CHAPTER
TWENTY-SIX

We were surrounded by cars on all sides as we sped down the road. I'd never seen so many cars in one place, and it was a little freaky. I had a car, but I used it to drive distances I probably could walk. Seeing the city grow larger as we approached gave me a new appreciation for our little town.

Sure, there were downsides to the Fringes, but I was already feeling overwhelmed by the sheer amount of buildings and vehicles. I knew that many of those buildings housed hundreds of humans. My skin crawled just thinking about how close I was to them.

Shifters were forbidden from revealing themselves to humans. It was dangerous to be too close to them. Of course, the Umbras chose to live with them. It made sense with their reputation for violating every rule without concern. I'd always heard they played human politics from the background, but I wondered if they weren't as secretive about it as we'd been led to believe. What if they were up front with humans? How would they react to meeting a shifter? Did they keep their secrets from everyone or just the masses?

There were so many questions spinning in my mind as we drove by the towering buildings. I watched humans walking along the crowded streets. They were bundled in heavy coats against the chill. Shifters could tolerate the colder weather better than humans, so seeing their fluffy parkas was a little amusing. We never needed anything more than a basic jacket. Those giant parkas couldn't be comfortable.

I watched a group of teenagers run by in tees and jeans, and I wondered if they were shifters or just really dumb humans. Without being up close, it would be impossible for me to sense who was human and who was a shifter.

A strange realization dawned on me. In theory, I'd know the difference, but I'd never tested it out. This was the closest I'd been to a human and the only time I'd seen them in real life.

I continued to gawk at the city around me, noting the steam coming up from the manholes and the overflowing trash cans. My nose wrinkled. Who would want to live in such a place?

We passed by a bar with a crowd of people standing around outside. They blew smoke from cigarettes and stood around tall metal objects with glowing red tops. Many of them were in far too few clothes for how cold it was. Even I wouldn't want to wear those little skirts in this weather. Humans were odd creatures.

"Their car was picking them up for the charity gala at five, so they should be gone by now," Marsha said. "We'll drive past first, to check for any signs of them, then we'll park a block away as planned. We walk in groups of two. Do not break protocol."

We'd turned off a road lined with skyscrapers and were suddenly on a street lined with mansions. One after another, sprawling structures of stone and marble. Gorgeous remnants of a time long passed. I knew these buildings were all over a hundred years old.

They'd once housed the most elite humans in the city. Now, many of them were occupied by shifter families and a couple had been turned into businesses or museums. I would have liked to look around one of them, but I wasn't going to have time. My job was clear. Get in, get the documents, get out. No lingering.

"There it is," Patrick said.

Everyone's heads turned to the right, and I followed their lead, looking for the Umbra's mansion. I'd seen photos of it, but it was odd to see it in its natural state surrounded by a huge stretch of green lawn. Compared to its neighbors, it was a smaller, almost unassuming building. Pictures of it on its own made it look much more impressive. Don't get me wrong, it was still a mansion, but I expected them to have the largest on the street.

The property was surrounded by a wrought iron fence,

but the gaps between the bars were large enough to see everything clearly.

Marsha drove a little slower as we passed the front gate. I stared at the dramatic driveway, noting that there was no sign of cars or life at all. If we timed everything correctly, the house would be empty.

The Umbra alpha and his family were attending some kind of charity gala in the city tonight. I had been too embarrassed to ask what a gala was, but I got the sense that it was a party for rich people. It didn't really matter. Whatever it was, it got them out of the house.

"Ivy, you remember what you're looking for, right?" Patrick asked.

"Yes. I'm looking for correspondence between the alpha's son and Holden. I should be able to find something indicating his communication on the desk in his office. I'll grab anything I can find. Journals, letters, whatever." It felt silly repeating the information we'd gone over a dozen times.

"Good. It's vital we find something, so don't leave empty handed," he said.

"We're sure we're going to find anything?" Farrah asked.

"They found no evidence on his computer so they think the communication was being done the old fashioned way," Patrick reminded her.

"You do know we only get paid if we find something," Farrah said.

I tensed and turned to look at her. "What if there's nothing there?"

"There has to be. They wouldn't send us otherwise," Patrick said.

"What if they're smarter about covering their tracks?" I asked. The thought had crossed my mind earlier, but they'd never said I had to have evidence to get paid. If that applied to my debt, it was even more vital I find something that would prove the Umbra's intentions.

"Find something. Anything. If you can't find something that connects Holden or proves the malicious intent against our pack, find something we can use against them," Patrick said.

"Like what?" I asked.

"Fuck, we are so screwed," Farrah said. I could almost hear her eyes rolling.

"First time, okay, just a little guidance," I snapped.

"Anything that makes them look bad. Photos with the alphas's dick in a place it shouldn't be. Anything incriminating."

"Blackmail material. Got it," I said.

"Maybe there's hope for her," Farrah said.

"Don't count on it," Kevin said.

I ignored him and tried to reframe what I was looking for. I would only have ten minutes before the guards would be back to check on the room, so I was going to just grab whatever I could. Fuck looking for specifics. We could sort out whatever I took when we were back home.

Marsha parked the car. My pulse skyrocketed. *Fuck. Fuck. Fuck.* It was really happening. This was it.

I tried to hide my panic. The last thing I needed was to make the others doubt that I could do this. I opened the car door and stepped out, just as I was supposed to do. Chin held high, I paused for a moment until Patrick was next to me.

The two of us walked down the street. He held up his elbow, and I slid my arm though his so the two of us could appear to be a couple.

He moved closer to me and leaned down so he could speak quietly. "You'll have ten minutes once you breach the room. We'll be on the permitter in case anything goes wrong. If something is off, you bail. But try to get anything you can before you leave. The alpha won't be happy if we come back empty handed. It doesn't matter if you're fucking him. I've seen Dax's bad side, and he makes Preston look like a goddam saint."

I swallowed hard. That wasn't the pep talk I was expecting. We circled the block, passing the Umbra's house and turning onto the street behind them. When we reached the Holly House, a mansion that had been converted into a museum, we stopped.

Holly House was a gorgeous old mansion that had been well cared for. With three stories and balconies that wrapped around every level, it was like something out of a dream. The best part about it was that it had once had acres of apple trees. While most of the orchard was long gone, one half of the yard was lined with row after row of trees that went right up to the edge of the Umbra property line. The trees were going to provide some cover for me as I attempted to cross into the mansion beyond Holly House.

The two of us walked up to the plaque in front of the house and acted like we were reading about the home's past. My heart was pounding so hard in my chest I was certain Patrick could hear it.

In the distance I heard a siren, but it faded quickly. My breath came out in clouds as I stared with unfocused eyes at the sign. There were photos and words, but I wasn't taking in anything other than the general shapes. The signal would come any second and the waiting was killing me.

An alarm blared, and I nearly jumped out of my skin despite the fact that I knew it was coming. Farrah and Kevin had broken into one of the larger mansions to set off the security system. All the cops would be on their way there and all the curious neighbors would be looking to that house to see what was going on.

"Go," Patrick said.

I bolted toward the museum, running through the grass toward the trees. Once I was in the orchard, I felt a little more protected. Though, the lack of leaves made the skeletal trees less protective and a lot creepier. There wasn't time to wonder if they were providing the cover I hoped for. If I was going to pull this off, I was going to have to turn off the doubts in my mind and go on autopilot.

It wasn't easy, but I pushed through, ignoring all the warnings inside telling me I was insane for going along with this.

Finally, I reached the end of the orchard and I stopped next to a large tree to catch my breath. I glanced down at my watch and noted that I was right on time. The team might be giving me a lot of shit, but they were precise. So far, everything they'd planned was working.

Putting my faith in their planning, I walked up to the iron bars and slipped between them. They didn't even brush against my sides. Seriously? This was the part I had doubted. I knew I was small, especially for a shifter, but why have a fence if people like me can slip through?

Still in shock that I got past the first hurdle, I raced across the dead grass to the house. My stomach was in knots and I fought against nausea as I found the window I was instructed to use.

Part two was completely dependent on the Umbra's hubris. We'd been told they had no security system in place. Which meant as long as we dodged the guards on patrol, there would be no indicator we'd entered the home. I was doubtful that they would have a house without an alarm, but I guess I had to trust our information.

I peered into the window. "Fuck." I was looking into a hallway but it was supposed to be an office. Either our information was wrong, or I miscounted.

I glanced around and quickly counted the windows again. Each passing second weighed on me like a bomb ready to explode. We were supposed to have a ten-minute opening without guards, but this was supposed to be the correct window.

I hesitated for a moment, wondering if I should turn back. If we had the wrong intel on the window, what other information was incorrect?

Patrick's words rang through my mind, reminding me that I needed to come back with something. Anything. I couldn't come all this way and not try for something to buy myself my freedom.

Steeling myself, I moved to the next window. The blinds were closed, so I had no idea what it was. I quickly peeked inside three more windows. Only one had the shades up and it was clearly a bathroom and not an office. Go figure the one room you'd think you'd want privacy in had a clear view inside.

I was about to leave when I noticed that I could see into another room across the hall. The light was on and I could make out the built-in bookcase and a chair. It was either a library or an office.

Time was running out, and I hadn't even breeched the building yet. *Fuck it.* Carefully, I popped out the screen and tried lifting the window. There was a little resistance, but I pushed past it and the lock gave. Just as we'd been told, the Umbras had recently re-done their windows and all the locks were faulty. I didn't pry as to why that was or how we knew, but at this moment, I was grateful.

Holding my breath, I slid the window up and listened for any signs of alarms or guards. All I could hear was sirens wailing in the distance, probably parked at the house we'd used as a decoy.

I hoisted myself up and climbed through the small opening. While other members of the group may have fit through the second story windows, they wouldn't have fit through any on the first floor. They were all far too narrow for most shifters. But the windows weren't the reason I was asked to do this. Someone could have risked climbing the fence I'd slipped through, but it made things much harder for a fast escape. Since I could run right through the gate, I could get out at any point if I needed to flee from a different direction.

The bathroom smelled like lavender and lemons. It was almost overwhelming, and I gagged a little. They were scents I usually enjoyed, but I had a feeling my shifter senses were finally kicking in. Good timing. I would take any help I could get.

I took a few cautious steps toward the hallway and found that the ancient wood floor was blissfully free of squeaks. They might have shit windows, but they had good flooring people. The hallway appeared empty and the room across the hall did look to be an office.

A flicker of hope mingled with excitement. Now that I was inside, I was running on pure adrenaline. *Get in, get out.* I crept forward and entered the office. A lamp on the desk illuminated the space, but otherwise it was empty. Things were finally going my way.

Quickly, I shuffled through the papers on the desk. They had the Umbra family crest on the top of them, which sent my blood pressure through the roof. I was actually inside the Umbra's mansion. Holy Fuck. If anyone had told me I'd ever step foot in here, I would have said they were insane.

The papers didn't look like what we were looking for, but I remembered that I was running out of time. I swept them into a neat pile and then turned to the drawers. The top drawer was full of pens and office supplies, the middle drawer had blank envelopes and paper. The third drawer was full of files. Dozens of them. I froze for a moment, overwhelmed by the volume of papers to choose from. How was I supposed to know what to grab quickly?

The tabs were labeled in some sort of code with random words like apple, fox, and key. Frustration made my chest feel tight. I was here; I had access to what was probably really important stuff, but I couldn't carry it all out.

Overly aware of the clock ticking down, I skimmed through the files. After a moment, I caught sight of a paper with the words *Shadow Pack* on it out of pure luck. It was in the section labeled *fox*. I grabbed the whole chunk of papers and the file. Then I quickly added everything that was on top of the desk. This was going to have to be enough. I was out of time.

I retraced my steps back to the bathroom, then I climbed out of the window. My heart was beating so fast it was practically humming and I could hear the blood rushing in my ears. I was so close to getting out of here unscathed. So close to paying my debt and getting everything I wanted.

There was no sign of guards, no indication that anyone had noticed we were here. I closed the window behind me in the hopes that nobody would notice the missing file until morning.

My mind was doing a little victory dance as I cut back through the orchard to the rendezvous point. We had contingency plans, but it didn't look like we needed them. It was taking more willpower than I expected not to cheer in celebration. I was off of Umbra land, and I was nearing the sign.

I could see Patrick waiting, his head down, gaze fixed on the historical information as if it was the most interesting thing in the world. I burst out from the orchard and raced across the grass, only slowing once I reached the sidewalk. Carefully, I tucked the file under my arm as if I was simply out for a stroll with a pile of documents.

Tossing my hair aside, I felt a wide grin spread across my face. I'd done it. After all their doubts and concerns, the team wouldn't be able to give me any shit on the way back. I did exactly as I was supposed to.

Patrick looked up from the sign, his face obscured by a hood. My body went rigid and cold spread down my spine.

Everything had gone according to plan, but there was one problem. The man smiling at me was not Patrick.

CHAPTER
TWENTY-SEVEN

I moved the papers to my hands, then I took off at a run, clutching them as tightly as possible. I had to make it to the alternate rendezvous location, but I had to lose my tail first.

Pumping my free arm wildly, I pushed ahead. My lungs burned and my legs resisted. I'd been running for several minutes and I'd passed nobody on the street.

Unsure if I was even being pursued, I risked a backward glance. I was alone. What the hell was going on? Slowing to a jog, I glanced around some more. Had I imagined the whole thing? Or maybe it was some random person messing with me. Maybe I wasn't even being followed at all.

I looked back once more, again seeing no signs of anyone. I was walking now, hoping not to draw attention to myself. Once again, I tucked the file under my arm and tried to look like I wasn't up to something.

That's when a figure on all fours emerged in front of me. The creature was large, and almost perfectly blended with the shadows. With a growl, the wolf moved closer to me.

I spun on my heels, but before I could run, another wolf came at me from behind. Growls encircled me and, for the first time, I realized what they meant when they said we could feel other wolves. I didn't need to look around to know I was surrounded.

My throat and tongue suddenly felt far too dry. I licked my lips, and tried to come up with a plan. I was a solid fighter, but going against wolves while I was in human form was suicide.

I could try shifting, but I didn't know how to fight as a wolf. And to be honest, I wasn't even sure my wolf would respond. I wasn't feeling any signs of my wolf. That whole shifting in life-or-death situations would be really helpful right about now. *Nothing?* My shoulders slumped. So much for getting any help from my inner wolf. Not that it would help much with these odds.

"Hey, look, I'm sorry." I set the file down on the ground. "I'll just leave this here and I'll go. Everything's here."

I stood, my hands up where they could see them. "I'm going to go now. Sorry for the inconvenience."

When I took a step to the side, a wolf quickly moved next to me. It snapped its jaws at me and I jumped back. "Look, you got it back, just let me go."

The wolf growled, closing in on me.

I backed up a little more. I never thought I was going to go down like this. "I'm sorry, okay."

A deep, rumbling growl made the hair on the back of my neck stand on edge. My heart thundered in my chest and I sucked in a breath. There was something about that sound that went deep into my soul. I turned and faced a massive black wolf.

He bared his teeth, growling again. The sound made my legs feel like jelly. I stared at him, our eyes meeting. I got the sense that I knew him, but that was impossible.

The wolf lifted his head, and I instinctively knew he wanted me to follow him. I hesitated. Nothing good was going to come from this. Why couldn't they just be in human form so I could attempt to get away? We were in a human city, after all. Terror gripped me when I realized that they had no concerns about shifting in a human city. I knew the Umbras ran everything from under the humans, but this confirmed just how deeply rooted they were here.

"What if I don't go with you?" I asked.

The wolf took his gaze off me for a moment and grunted something. The other wolves closed ranks, surrounding me.

"Alright, I guess I don't have a choice," I said.

The massive wolf growled again, then turned. A nose pressed into my thigh, urging me forward.

"Hey, I'm following. No more touching," I snapped.

The wolf behind me growled.

"Don't growl at me. I'm following. You keep your snout to yourself." I had to bottle up the urge to fight back.

I was probably screwed either way, but if I started fighting the wolves, there was a good chance their instincts would take over and one of them would rip my throat out. At least by following them, I had a chance that they'd shift back into human and I could reason with them. Or at the very least, try to fight them in that form.

As I walked along with the group of wolves, it struck me as odd that I was still alive. I'd heard so many conflicting reports of how the Umbra pack behaved, but I thought for sure getting busted breaking and entering would be one of those no warning kind of punishments.

Unless they wanted me to talk.

I balled my hands into fists and considered my next steps. We hadn't discussed any protocol for what to do if we were captured. Was it like in the movies where I just gave my name and kept my mouth shut? Or should I spill? Would it be better or worse for me to explain that we had a traitor in our pack we were trying to build evidence against? If our target hadn't been one of the alpha's kids, maybe that would get me some understanding. If I explain, I'm throwing a high-ranking Umbra under the bus.

There was no way I would win in this situation. Keeping quiet makes me look even guiltier, but explaining the truth was going to get me silenced permanently. Why had I thought being officially part of the pack was worth this?

The elders and the team all made it sound like such an easy job. The Umbras were supposed to be away all night, and I was in and out in less than ten minutes. I knew I did my part. Where had Patrick gone? Why had he left his post? How had he been replaced by an Umbra wolf?

Dread fell into my stomach like a weight. What if they'd all been captured? What if the betrayal by Holden ran deeper? Someone had to have tipped off the Umbras.

Or our intel was bad.

Either way, this was far deeper than Holden and I had no way of warning my pack.

The group of wolves led me to the front of the Umbra mansion. It was more impressive up close. Huge columns lined the two-story entryway, supporting an expansive balcony. A giant glass door sparkled at the center of a wide set of steps. On either side of the door were tall evergreen trees decorated with glowing white lights. How festive.

I marched up the stairs, still surrounded by wolves. They stopped at the front door and I looked around at my captors. "Am I supposed to go inside?"

One of the wolves shuddered and started to bend and break, the body twisting as the change took hold. A moment later, I was staring at a very tall, very naked male. He had long, dark hair that was hanging in front of his face. His hand raked his hair out of the way and he stared down at me with intense green eyes. Damn, he was sexy. And I had a feeling he knew it. I hated him already.

I forced myself to keep my gaze on his face, resisting the temptation to look lower. From the build of his shoulders and chest, he didn't miss workouts.

Sexy wolf grabbed my upper arm and dragged me toward the door.

"Hey, I can walk, you know," I said.

"I can't risk you running," he said.

"Do I look stupid enough to run?" I asked.

He growled, then pounded on the door. "Keep your mouth shut, Shadow Scum."

I raised my brows. "Shadow Scum? That sounds very unpleasant, but I think you could do better."

The door opened and my captor dragged me inside. My jaw dropped as I walked across the marble floor. The exterior of the mansion was beautiful, but this was opulence and wealth on a scale that only existed in historical fiction about Renaissance France.

From the marble floors to the hand-painted wallpaper to the pedestals holding priceless sculptures and pottery, everything about the entryway screamed excess. I made a mental note not to touch anything. It was so over the top; it made me uncomfortable. Far more museum than home. "You live here?"

"You might want to keep your mouth shut," he said.

It was the second warning he'd given, and I probably should listen, but I got mouthy when I was nervous. "You wouldn't have to hear me at all if you just let me go. I gave back the papers."

His hand was on my cheek before I saw it coming. I gasped, surprised by the sting of the slap. "Did you just slap me?" It was a little insulting. Who slaps someone?

"Be grateful I didn't do worse," he said.

I risked a glance behind me and realized the door was closed and there was no sign of the other wolves or even whoever had opened the door. By the looks of the place, it was probably a servant and if I was lucky; they weren't paid enough to get involved in anything physical.

I lifted my foot and slammed it down on the bare foot of my captor. He grunted, but gripped me tighter. Quickly, I turned and kicked up, landing my foot right in his goods.

With a yelp of pain, he released me and grabbed himself. I bolted for the front door, throwing it open and running hard without looking back.

I was halfway across the lawn when sharp teeth closed in around my leg, pulling me to the ground.

I cried out as the teeth dug deeper into my flesh. Searing pain radiated from where the fangs pierced my skin, moving up my leg. I tried to pull myself free, but the pain intensified. My vision darkened, and I tried to pull free again. Instead, I fell face first.

The wolf released me, and I clawed at the ground, pulling myself forward. When I tried to put weight on my injured leg, it gave out, causing me to end up on my ass.

The wolf was circling me, his maw matted with my blood.

I was panting, trying to ignore the throbbing in my leg. When I looked for an escape, I noted that we were no longer alone. The other wolves had returned.

My attacker shifted back into human form. The beautiful shifter's mouth, chin and chest were covered in blood. He looked like the killer he was.

"I tried to warn you," he said.

"I'm a terrible listener," I said.

He scooped me up, tossing me over his shoulder as if I was nothing more than a rag doll. I had a clear view of his ass which, to my utter disappointment, was spectacular. Dammit. Another case of an asshole getting blessed by the sexy genes.

"Please, just let me go. I swear I'll never come into your territory again," I said.

"You're still pretending you were just after some documents?" he said.

"Of course I was. I gave them back. What other reason would I have?" I asked.

"You're either a very good liar, or your pack kept you in dark. I'm not sure which is worse." He carried me across the grass, back to the house I'd just run from.

"What are you talking about?" I asked.

"I'm going to say it again, if you have any sense of self-perseveration, stop talking."

This time, I listened.

CHAPTER
TWENTY-EIGHT

THE WOLVES FOLLOWED US. The pain in my leg was making it difficult to concentrate, but I worked to keep myself calm. I was going to have to take any chance I had at escaping. The only thing keeping me going was the fact that they hadn't killed me yet. They needed something from me, but I wasn't sure what it was.

For some reason, these wolves seemed to think I was involved in something bigger. That didn't make any sense. Dax wouldn't agree to anything that would have put me in harm's way, right?

We were walking downstairs now, my leg bumping against the shifter's chest. I winced and closed my eyes, breathing through the pain. At least I was getting more blood on the asshole.

The temperature was cooler than it had been seconds ago, and I opened my eyes. The opulence was gone, replaced by cement walls and unfinished steps. My captor reached the bottom, and we walked across more cement. The space was lit with bare bulbs, casting creepy shadows on the floor. For a moment, there was nothing but cement. Then, I noticed iron bars. Unfortunately, they weren't close enough together for me to slip between them. "You have got to be fucking kidding me."

"Where did you think I was taking you?" the shifter asked.

"We don't have dungeons in the basement where I come from," I snapped.

"Are you sure about that?" He sounded amused.

"Pretty sure." Though, as I said it, I wasn't. What if there was a dungeon in the basement of the Alpha house where Dax lived? It wasn't like I asked him or explored it. I didn't know what that house held.

My captor stopped in front of a cell. Another naked shifter, a woman, stepped around him and I heard the creak of a door. We moved forward, and I was dumped on a cot.

"If you behave, I'll have someone bring you supplies to clean up that bite," he said.

"You wouldn't have to do that if you hadn't tried to chew off my leg," I said.

"You aren't in any position to be telling me what I should and shouldn't do," he said as he left the cell. He slammed the door and the female shifter handed him the keys.

"Keep up that smart mouth of yours. I'm sure it'll go over well when my brother arrives," he said.

"Let me guess, you're the bad cop?" I said.

He chuckled. "Darling, I'm the only good cop in the Umbra clan."

I glared at him, unwilling to let his words get to me. It didn't matter, anyway. Even if I talked, it wasn't like they were going to get what they wanted from me. Clearly, they thought I was part of some larger conspiracy and they were going to be disappointed when they got nothing of use from me.

My captor and the female shifter walked away, leaving me alone in the cell. As soon as they were out of sight, I pushed myself to standing. Wincing, I shifted my weight to my good leg. I should probably be trying to stop the bleeding from the puncture wounds, but if there was any way of getting out of here, I had to find it now.

I reached for the bars, feeling foolish, but you never knew. They had shit windows and huge gaps in their fence. It was possible they'd cut corners down here, too. I grabbed the metal pole and shook, but released quickly as a burst of pain bloomed across my palms. *What the fuck?* I looked down and noted that my palms were red, as if they'd been burned. They probably rubbed the iron down with Wolfsbane. Assholes. Good thing I hadn't touched the fence on my way in. I made a mental note not to try that again. The bars weren't my ticket out of here.

Next, I looked around at the cinderblock walls. There were no windows, and the only light was from the bulb hanging in the hallway. The cot was pushed into one corner and in the other corner was a bucket. I wrinkled my nose when I realized that was probably supposed to be the toilet. I really hoped I was out of here before I needed to use that.

Footsteps alerted me to company, and I limped to the cot as quickly as possible. The female shifter had returned. This time, she was dressed in jeans and a white tee that did not hide the fact that she wasn't wearing a bra. Her long blonde hair was in two braids that nearly reached her waist.

She locked bright blue eyes on me. "You probably won't be alive long enough for it to matter, but they sent me with this for you." She tossed a roll of bandages into the cell. Then she reached down and set a bottle of something on the ground right near the bars.

"Am I supposed to say thank you?" I asked.

"You could, but I don't give a shit either way. Madoc's on his way down. I've never seen anyone survive an interrogation from him. Any last words you want me to send along to your pack if your alpha even cares enough to ask about you?"

My stomach flipped. My alpha. Dax. Was he worried about me? Had the rest of the group returned, or were they here in another one of these cells? "Where are my friends?"

"The shifters that turned you over to us and then fled? You sure they were your friends?" It sounded like a genuine question. Her tone didn't sound mocking. If anything, it sounded a little sad.

"What do you mean, they turned me over?" If she was

willing to give me information, I might as well take it. I wasn't sure if it was true, but I hated the fact that I knew it could be. It was the only thing that made sense. Someone had to have tipped the Umbras off.

"You're dead soon, anyway," she said. "Don't make the mistake of defending the pack that didn't have your back."

She turned and walked away, leaving me with a million unanswered questions. Her words could have been crafted to confuse me and make me feel abandoned. There was no denying she'd done a good job of setting that up. The problem was, I didn't know enough about the shifters I'd been with to trust them. It couldn't have been all of them. There had to be some loyalty to our mission; to our pack. What if there was one traitor in the group? Or what if she was messing with me and they'd killed or captured the others? Or what if they got away but couldn't figure out how to get me out?

I wasn't going to know until I got back to my pack. That had to happen. There were too many unanswered questions, and I refused to believe that Dax would have sent me as a sacrificial lamb into the lion's den.

The footsteps receded, and everything was silent. I looked over at the bandage and the bottle. My leg was killing me and I knew I'd lost a lot of blood. Carefully, I put the weight on my good leg first, then took a step forward. My injured leg gave out from under me and I bit down on my lower lip to keep from screaming. This bite was going to take time to heal, even with shifter healing.

Grateful that nobody was around to watch me, I

crawled forward, dragging my injured leg behind me. I grabbed the bandage and the bottle of clear liquid. It was labeled as alcohol and a sniff confirmed that it was what it said. There was a chance they could have laced it with something, but I wasn't sure what that would accomplish if their goal was to question me.

I set the bottle back down, then got to work gingerly rolling my jeans up so I could uncover the bite. The fabric stuck to the blood and every time I bumped the wound; it sent a rush of pain. With a hiss, I finally got the last of the fabric free.

My leg was swollen and angry and the blood covered all signs of the puncture wounds that I knew were under there. I was amazed I was still moving at all with how bad it looked.

Jaw clenched, I popped open the alcohol and poured it on my leg. I screamed, unable to hold it in this time, but I bit it back quickly. Panting and wincing, I finally washed the blood off enough to see the bite. It was a perfect series of holes on the top and bottom, the exact shape of the wolf's teeth.

Anger replaced the pain. Who goes around biting people like that? A little voice inside reminded me that I was the one who broke into their house.

Now that I had the bandage wrapped tightly around my leg, some of the adrenaline and fear had worn off. I was starting to feel foolish for even getting involved in this in the first place. What was I thinking?

I barely got started on my self-loathing when footsteps sounded. I crawled back from the bars and hoisted myself up onto the cot, trying to look like I was bored.

As soon as the newcomer was in view, my heart felt like it skipped a beat, then it began to race wildly, uncontrollably.

I'd know those dark eyes and that handsome face anywhere. It had haunted my dreams and made me feel things I couldn't explain. Despite the fact that I knew I was his prisoner, and he was an Umbra, my body still reacted. Heat flooded my cheeks, spilling into my chest. My lips parted and my eyes widened. I suddenly felt more alert and alive than I had since my capture.

Even in a cage, seeing the Dark Wolf was enough to break down all my defenses. "You must be Madoc," I managed.

"And you have to be the stupidest shifter I've ever met," he said.

CHAPTER
TWENTY-NINE

"What? No snappy comeback?" Madoc smirked and took a step closer to the bars. I had the overwhelming sensation to walk over to him and claim him with my tongue. Something was very, very wrong with me.

"All those visits to the Fringes weren't just for the fight, were they?" I said. "I saw you with Holden. I know it's your fault my friend is dead."

Calling Darleen a friend was a stretch, but she'd been pack. It didn't matter what my libido thought of this shifter; he was my enemy. It was insane that I needed to remind myself of that, but here we were.

"What I do with my time is none of your concern," he said.

"It is if you want me to talk." I hadn't planned on saying anything, but my curiosity was piqued. Besides, I had come with the intention of getting proof about Holden's betrayal. While a conversation wasn't proof, it was possible I could get some information. I'd need that if I ever made it back to my pack.

"What makes you think I won't just condemn you to death?" he asked.

"If you were going to, you'd have done it already," I said.

"What's your name?" he asked.

"When are you going to let me out of here?" I asked.

"What's your name?" he repeated.

"Why are you working with Holden against my pack?" I asked.

Madoc opened the door to the cell and was in front of me before I could rise from the bed. Not that my leg would support me, but I would have tried.

His legs touched my knees, and he peered down at me as if I was something disgusting. My stomach rolled uncomfortably and disappointment pooled in my gut. I hated how he was looking at me, and I hated that I cared.

He leaned down and set his hands against the wall on either side of my head, boxing me in. "You will answer my questions, or I will make you answer them."

"If you get answers, I get some, too," I said.

"That's not how this works."

I glared at him. "Then I guess we both lose."

He growled, the tone low and threatening. My body responded with a rush of heat to my core. Seriously, something was very, very wrong with me. Sure, the guy was hot. Okay, he was probably the most attractive male I'd ever seen, but he wanted me dead. I should be fighting him, not getting wet from his threats. Maybe I hit my head, and this was some kind of brain injury response.

"Your name," he demanded.

"Your connection to Holden," I replied.

Suddenly, his hand was around my throat and he thrust me against the wall. I had a flashback of Dax doing the same thing. Then Dax was gone from my mind, replaced by an explosion of white light. My whole body felt tingly and warm. Madoc released me and the strange feeling vanished.

He took a step back and stared at me, his eyes wide. "This isn't possible."

My brow furrowed. "What are you talking about?"

"Your name, woman," he spat.

"Fuck. You."

He roared in frustration and raked his hand through his hair. Then he stormed off, slamming the door behind him.

What the fuck just happened? I sat in stunned silence for a moment, waiting for him to run back in. He'd slammed the door, but he hadn't bothered to lock it.

The seconds ticked by, and there was no sign of him returning. No sounds at all. Was this some kind of trick?

If it was a mistake, I was wasting time sitting here. I pushed myself to standing and tested my injured leg. It was holding weight a little better but it still hurt like hell. I couldn't rely on it to support me if I had to do anything too athletic. I had to hope the coast was clear and I could limp right out of here.

The whole idea sounded ridiculous, but what choice did I have? Quietly, I limped toward the door, then used my foot to push it open. I wasn't going to make the mistake of touching it again. The hall was unguarded, and I was able to get a better look at my surroundings. There appeared to be three more cells, but all of them had their doors wide open. None of my pack members were here.

So far, this was proving to be a relatively easy jail break. But then again, this was the family who didn't have alarms or proper locks on their windows.

I crept down the hall and found the stairs also unguarded. Anxiety spiked as I climbed the stairs. I knew I was bound to run into someone soon. Would I be strong enough to run? Or would it be better to try to fight? With my leg, neither was a good choice. I'd have to rely on instincts. Just do whatever felt right.

The one thing that might help would be to shift. In theory, I'd heal faster, and I'd have three good legs to run on. It would probably be easier to sneak out, too. But I couldn't rely on that ability yet. I needed more practice. So much for not worrying about learning how to use my wolf.

When I reached the top of the stairs, I turned the doorknob as quietly as I could. The knob didn't make a sound, but the door squeaked as I pushed it open. I winced and held my breath, waiting for someone to charge me.

No attack came.

I wasn't sure if I should feel cocky or worried. This wasn't how escapes were supposed to go, were they?

Nobody in sight, I tiptoed toward the large front door. Out of the corner of my eye, I caught movement and froze.

To my right was a formal living room complete with floral print couches and polished wood furniture that looked ancient and far too ornate to actually use. A fire flickered and crackled in a wood fireplace. Madoc stood in front of it, a decanter of brown liquor in his one hand, two rocks glasses in the other. As in, he could hold both of them in one palm.

I started to wonder how those huge hands would feel against my bare skin. I could think of a lot of excellent uses for those fingers.

Shit. I had to stop fantasizing about him. This was an Umbra wolf. He wasn't my friend and he could never be my lover.

Madoc stood frozen in the room and it took me a second to realize that he wasn't making any moves toward me. Was he going to let me escape?

Testing my theory, I took a few steps toward the door, then glanced back at him. He remained where he was.

I got all the way to the door, my hand on the brass doorknob, when he cleared his throat.

What a drama queen. I rolled my eyes, then looked over at him. "What?"

"You can leave, or you can stay and we can figure out what to do about the little problem between us," he said.

"What problem?" I demanded.

"Our mating bond," he said.

"Our what?" My eyebrows pulled together. "Are you insane?"

"I don't like it either."

"We don't have a mating bond," I said.

"You can't tell me you didn't feel it when we touched," he said.

"I have no idea what you are talking about," I lied. I turned the doorknob and opened the door.

"If you leave, the bond is just going to drive you mad until we find our way back to one another," he said. "Why do you think I'm willing to let you go? With our bond, I can track you anywhere."

I had wondered why it was so easy.

"I'll be able to find you any time I want if you don't come running back to me first," he said.

I took a step outside into the cool night air, but I didn't leave. I stood right outside the door, weighing his words. Was he telling the truth or was he trying to get into my head?

When I looked back, Madoc was standing in front of the door. "Tell me you don't want to rip my clothes off right now."

The idea of sex with Madoc caused a throbbing need so strong I clenched my thighs together. "Fuck."

"Come back inside," he said.

"I don't want to." I was confused and freaked out and still far too turned on.

"You don't really have a choice." He inclined his head toward the ground.

I looked down and noticed that I was back inside the house and I didn't even recall returning. "What did you do to me?"

He turned and walked back to the fancy living room, then set the glasses and decanter down on a table. He filled each glass. "Have a drink."

My body seemed to move without my consent, taking me into the room where Madoc was waiting.

I sat on the couch across from the one he was sitting on, doing my best not to wince from the pain of moving my leg. Madoc pushed a glass across the table, then lifted the other glass to his lips.

My eyes watched him take a drink and reflexively, I licked my lips as I imagined what it might be like to kiss him.

Madoc grinned. "I bet I could get you to do anything I wanted."

I tore my gaze away from his luscious mouth. "You're an asshole."

"I am, but it looks like I'm your asshole."

CHAPTER
THIRTY

"This is a mistake," I said. "Or a trick."

"If you really thought it was a trick, would you have turned around and come back inside? Please tell me I didn't get stuck with a mate who is that stupid." He took a sip of his drink.

I narrowed my eyes. "Who are you? Everyone else is gone, and they left you behind. Why are you even here?"

"Someone had to stay and deal with you," he said. "And I hate all parties where we have to pretend to be human. It's unnatural."

"So they really are out at a gala?" I asked. "Does that mean you're what, head of security or something?"

He smirked. "Or something."

"What's your name?" he asked.

"Who are you, really?" I already knew he was an Umbra Wolf, and I got the sense that he was high ranking. He was the brother of the shifter who bit me, but were they inner circle or were they part of the family itself? I could almost feel his power, but I knew he wasn't the alpha. What if he was the Beta? That would complicate things even more.

"No more questions from you until you answer mine. A name is the least you can give me," he said.

"Fine, it's Ivy," I said. "Now tell me who you are."

"You haven't told me who you are, Ivy."

Hearing my name on his lips made my breath shaky. I wanted him to say it again. Over and over. Shit. If this was what a mating bond felt like, I wasn't a fan. I didn't like the lack of control. Who would want this?

"Ivy..." he let the word linger and I had to fight against the desire to walk over to him and sit on his lap.

"Ivy Shadow. I'm a foundling. A nobody. I have no rank, no power, no family. You happy now?" I spat.

His brow furrowed. "Not what I expected."

"Your turn," I demanded.

"I'm sure you've heard of me," he said.

"I saw you fight under the name *Dark Wolf*." I scoffed. "What kind of a name is that, anyway?"

He grinned. "The kind that women scream during orgasm."

"You are infuriating," I said. "The fates are punishing me."

"You won't have to worry about the fates much longer," he said.

I tensed. "I thought mates couldn't harm each other."

"I can't harm you, but my brothers can. So if you want my protection, you better start talking."

"I don't have anything to say," I said.

He tossed back the rest of his booze, then stood. "That's a shame. You have such a pretty face. I'd hate to see anything happen to it."

I glanced toward the door.

"Go ahead. Shift, run. I could use the workout hunting you down. I'll even give you a head start."

I swallowed. This was another trick, I was certain of it. But it was also a chance. What if I could outrun him? He was so cocky he might really give me a head start. What if my team was still waiting at the back up meeting site?

I took a deep breath and called to my wolf. I had no idea what I was doing and wasn't sure it would work, but it was worth a try.

For a moment, I felt a familiar sensation deep inside myself. Instinctively, I knew it was my wolf. Just as soon as it swelled to life inside me, it faded, leaving me feeling more alone and hollow than before.

"What's the matter?" Madoc said.

I couldn't admit that my wolf wasn't there. "I'm not going to play your games."

"That's a shame. I would have liked the workout." He stepped closer to me and made to grab me and I stepped back, avoiding his reach.

I wanted to fight him and knock him down so I could run, but my body wouldn't let me strike him. Everything tensed up, resisting the commands to hit or kick. As much as I wanted to deny it, the only thing that would cause this kind of reaction was the mating bond. It didn't allow us to hurt our mate. At least I knew he couldn't harm me, either. That was the only good thing to come of all this.

"Are you taking me back to the dungeon?" I asked.

"Your friends ambushed our alpha and tried to kill him. So, yeah, you're going back to the dungeon," he said.

"We didn't try to kill the alpha," I said.

"I hate that I find it adorable when you lie."

"I'm not lying." I walked away from the couch and moved to the marble entryway. My leg was feeling a little better and while I still couldn't put my full weight on it, it didn't feel like it was going to give out on me.

"We know all about the plan," he said. "And I'm sorry to be the one to tell you that the rest of your team is probably dead. At least last I heard, my brothers had them surrounded."

He was trying to get in my head. I couldn't let that happen. I kept my eyes locked on him. The front door was so close and I might not be able to shift, but I had to make one more attempt. Once I was locked back in that dungeon, I couldn't count on him leaving the door open again. I still wasn't sure why he even did it in the first place.

"There was no plan to kill anyone." I took a step back, my eyes still locked on Madoc.

"If you're being honest, that means they didn't tell you the truth. Now, was that because they didn't trust you or were you always meant to get caught?" He asked. "Hard to believe they'd sacrifice you, but stranger things have happened."

His tone made it sound like he knew a lot more than he was letting on, but I was certain it was an act. Madoc looked so calm. His shoulders were relaxed and his arms hung by his side. He didn't appear to be ready to run after me, but I knew better than to overestimate him.

If only I could shift. *If you're in there, now would be a great time.* I tried to encourage my wolf, one last attempt at getting her to appear.

There wasn't even so much as a flicker. *Thanks for nothing.*

"Were you serious about giving me a head start?" I asked.

His lips turned up in a wicked grin. "You have sixty seconds."

I didn't hesitate to turn and run through the front door. Arms pumping, lungs burning, I ran for the orchard. The trees were bare, but they might provide at least a little cover.

I didn't bother to count as I ran; it was probably futile, but I had to try. Weaving around the trees, I hoped I was throwing my scent enough to give me a chance.

My legs ached, and my injured leg was starting to give with each step. I wasn't going to be able to run much longer. I pushed forward, hoping to make it to the street. I didn't know much about humans, but if I shouted for help, maybe I could create a scene. At the very least, it would prevent Madoc from shifting.

Unless he'd already shifted.

Suddenly, my leg gave out, and I went down hard. Panting and desperate to get free, I pushed myself to standing. Searing pain came from the bite, radiating up my leg. How long did shifter healing take? Come on, leg. Work with me.

Limping along, I continued toward the street. I needed people, an audience, anything to cause a distraction.

Out of nowhere, Madoc appeared in front of me. He was in human form and fully clothed, which meant he hadn't shifted.

"No way you gave me sixty seconds," I said.

"I wish I hadn't. I'm honestly disappointed," he said. "So what does that make now? Two unsuccessful escape attempts?"

"You don't need me," I said. "If someone really tried to kill your alpha, you have bigger problems than a girl who broke in for some papers."

"Ah, yes, the papers," he said. "Holden told me you were smart, but I think he made a mistake. I'm so glad I didn't let him invite you to join us. That would have been a terrible mistake."

"You were talking about me with Holden?"

"That's what you got out of that?" He laughed.

"Stop toying with her," another voice called.

I turned and saw three males walking toward me. "What is all this? You told me they were away."

"I'm a very good liar," he said. "Take her to the dungeons."

I braced for a fight, keeping the weight on my good leg. Arms in front of me in fists, I glared at the males walking toward me.

They looked amused, but continued moving closer. I punched the first male who reached me. He let out a surprised, shocked kind of sound. As I pulled my fist back to punch him again, I was grabbed by someone else.

Kicking and twisting, I worked to free myself. "Let me go."

"Keep her quiet," someone shouted.

"Better yet, knock her out," another said.

The last thing I saw was a fist coming toward my face.

CHAPTER
THIRTY-ONE

My head throbbed, and I groaned as my eyelids fluttered open. It took a moment for my eyes to adjust to the dim light. I pushed myself to sitting, and the room spun, making me close my eyes for a moment as I adjusted.

I was back on the cot in the cell. Twice I'd tried to flee, and twice I'd been stopped. The memory of my conversation with Madoc came back to me all at once, making my head spin for an entirely different reason.

Was he really my mate? Or was he messing with me to get me to talk? I could feel something between us, but who wouldn't react when around a shifter as sexy as him?

I rolled up my jeans to check the bandage on my leg. It looked clean and fresh, no signs of blood. Someone must have changed it for me. Carefully, I unrolled it, revealing the skin beneath. The bite marks were healed up, leaving fresh scars in their place. Wonderful. More marks to show just how battered and abused my body had been all these years.

"You awake yet, sleeping beauty?" A male voice called.

I rose from the cot and walked closer to the bars just as the shifter who'd bit me arrived.

"You are awake. How was the nap?" he asked.

"Are you here to let me out so I can go home?" I asked.

"You don't get it, do you? You're not going home ever again. You broke into our house. If I was calling the shots, you'd already be dead," he said.

Well, that was interesting. "You do know you're not going to get any of the information you want from me?"

It was probably a stupid thing to say, considering that it was likely the only thing keeping me alive.

"I'm not sure how you managed to get by Madoc or why he sent me instead, but I'm not going to argue. He always gets to have all the fun. Now, it's my turn. And I can promise you, you won't get away from me."

This male was Madoc's brother. I remembered that bit of information. Yet, he didn't seem to know that Madoc claimed we shared a mating bond. Either Madoc was messing with me, or he was keeping it a secret.

I heard the click of the lock, then the squeak of the hinges as the door was pushed open. He stepped inside and closed it behind him. The keys jingled as he shoved them into his jeans pocket.

Panic made my chest tighten. Madoc had said he couldn't hurt me, but his brothers could. Was that what was going on? How much of this was I going to have to take?

I glanced longingly at the door. It wasn't locked, but my captor was standing right in front of it.

"We're going to try this again, darling," he said. "I want names. I want details. And most of all, I want to know when they plan to strike again."

"Do you want me to make things up? Because that's the only way you're going to get answers from me," I said.

"It's Ivy, right?"

"Well, you know my name, don't you think I should know yours?" I asked.

His brow furrowed, as if my question confused him. "You don't know who I am?"

"Should I?" I didn't hide my skepticism.

"You don't even know who lives in the home you were breaking into?" He sounded dubious.

"I didn't ask a whole lot of questions," I replied.

"Do you even know this is the Umbra Estate?"

"Yeah, I knew that. I might be from the Fringes, but I got that part," I said.

"Willow," he called.

The woman I'd seen earlier appeared in the hall outside the door. "What do you need, Cavan?"

"Can you bring me the documents our guest tried to steal?" he asked.

"Cavan?"

"Yes, Cavan Umbra. Second born son of Erwin Umbra," he said.

Oh, shit. Madoc was one of the alpha's sons. That mating bond thing better be a hoax. I had enough confusion with Dax right now to add in that mess.

"So you're the alpha's son. Am I supposed to be impressed?" I asked. "I would have thought they'd have security or trained professionals to handle the riffraff like me."

"I've had plenty of training," he said.

"If it matches your ego, I might be in trouble," I said.

He took a step forward and slapped me across the face. I winced and my eyes watered, but I bit back the pain.

"So this is what the Umbra pack does? Beats up helpless women? So far, you're no different than the Shadow Pack," I snapped.

"I have the papers," Willow called.

Cavan reached through the bars to grab them. "Thank you. You can return to your post."

Willow gave me what almost looked like a sympathetic expression, but it passed quickly.

"This is what you risked your life for?" Cavan threw the papers down at my feet.

I kept my eyes on him, my jaw clenched. I had no idea what was in the papers I'd grabbed, but I didn't know if it was better or worse for him to realize I was out of my element here.

"Take a look," he said. "Go ahead."

"No, thanks, I'm good," I said.

He moved so fast that his hands were on me before I

could react. With a sweep of his foot, I was down, catching myself only just before my head hit the cement.

"Look at them," he demanded.

Blood boiling, I glared at him. "I told you I didn't want to."

"I'm not giving you a choice," he said.

Reluctantly, I sat up, then picked up the paper nearest me. It was an order form for lumber. I grabbed a few more papers and found more invoices and receipts.

"It's nothing. So let me go," I said.

"It's proof that you were the decoy." His tone was calm and resigned. It was scarier than the anger he'd spoken with earlier.

"If I was a decoy, I was just as in the dark as you are," I said.

He grabbed my hair and pulled me back, then leaned down so his face was near mine. "Your pretty face might work on my brother, but it won't work on me. When I return, you better have something of value for me or I'm going to make you wish we'd killed you when we caught you."

Cavan released his grip from my hair and I eyed the door, wondering again if I could make it through before he caught me. Another slap hit my cheek, the force catching me off guard. I fell to the side and reached for my stinging face.

"Don't even think about running again. Next time I have to take you down, my teeth will hit an artery." He walked toward the door and this time, I didn't even look up to watch him.

Feeling defeated, I moved back to the cot and curled up in a little ball. The papers were still scattered around the floor, a mocking reminder of how badly I'd screwed up.

I'd done this for a chance at freedom. Instead, I was more a prisoner than I ever had been. Had my life really been that bad? Sure, my childhood was hell, but I'd had a brief respite the last two years. I had a decent apartment with an awesome roommate. I splurged on brand name cereal and generally enjoyed my existence. I even missed my shifts at the Howler.

Despite all I had, I wanted more. I wanted the respect that came from being a full pack member. And if I was being honest with myself, I wanted the parties and the invites to run in the woods in wolf form. I wanted to belong.

Now that I was trapped, I wasn't sure it was worth it. Why had I cared so much?

I stayed on the cot until I had no choice but to get up to use the bucket. I hated myself so much in that moment. In a million years, I never thought this was where my life would take me.

Without windows, I had no clue if it was day or night. The only way I could count how much time had passed was from simply guessing. My stomach growled, and I was feeling a little nauseous from lack of food. The more time passed, the more aware I was of how dry my mouth was.

I guess the only good news was that I hadn't had to use the bucket again.

After what had to be hours, I heard footsteps. I considered standing, but didn't see much of a point. I sat up on the cot, watching to see who had come to torment me.

Willow stood in front of the bars, a plate of food and a bottle of water in her hands. "Hungry?"

I could smell the food from here, and my stomach roared in response.

She set the food down right outside the bars. "It's here if you want it. They didn't mess with it, I made sure of that."

"Cause I should trust you?" I said.

"You shouldn't trust anyone, didn't your pack teach you that?" she asked.

"I guess I missed that day in school," I said.

I waited until I didn't hear footsteps before going to grab the food. I had to fold the paper plate a little to fit it between the bars, but I got it through. Food consisted of a peanut butter and jelly sandwich and apple slices. I was so hungry; I didn't care if Willow had been honest. I ate the sandwich and the apples, then drank half the water. I'd save the rest for later since I didn't know what was coming next.

Time moved impossibly slow in the empty cell. I busied myself by checking for any way out several times.

When I came to the same conclusion as the first time, I finally took a seat in the middle of the cell on the floor.

Watching the bars, I waited.

And waited.

My eyelids grew heavy, but I resisted the temptation to sleep. Someone was going to come back here, and I needed to be prepared. I fought against sleep for as long as I could, but eventually, I gave in, letting myself close my eyes for just a minute.

I woke in the middle of the floor with a hand over my mouth and a pair of dark eyes staring down at me. I screamed, the hand muting my cries.

Madoc pressed a finger to his lips. "I'm going to remove my hand, but I need you to keep quiet. Understand?"

I nodded.

He removed his hand, and I scrambled to siting. Madoc was crouched next to me. "My brothers captured one of your friends alive. A shifter called Patrick."

I swallowed hard.

"I see you know him." He frowned. "That's not going to help your case."

"What case?" I hissed.

"If Patrick names you as a conspirator, you're as good as dead," Madoc says.

"Why are you telling me this?" I asked.

"As much as I wish it wasn't true, you're my mate, so I don't really want you to die," he said.

"You sound real torn up about it," I said sardonically.

"I could have my brothers kill you if that would make you feel better," he said.

I narrowed my eyes, studying his expression. He was trying to threaten me, but there was something hollow in his words. It was different than the last time we'd talked. What if this whole mating bond thing was true, and he really didn't want me to die?

That complicated things. "You haven't told your brother."

"None of them know," he said. "And I intend to keep it that way."

"Why are you even down here?" I asked. "You're not helping me and you don't want this bond."

"Do you?" he asked.

"Of course not," I said. "But I don't understand why you're not just letting your brothers do your dirty work. If they kill me, the bond is gone."

"Death doesn't eliminate mating bonds," he said.

"Sure, it would," I said. "Besides, we haven't completed the bond."

"You have no sense of self-preservation, do you?" he asked.

"I don't see a way I'm going to get out of here," I said.

"That's what I came to tell you. Tomorrow, when Cavan returns, you need to turn in Patrick. They don't know you know he's been captured. Give his name as your leader."

"No," I said.

"It's your only option," he said.

"I don't know how things are in your pack, but we don't turn on each other where I'm from," I said.

"You sure about that?" he said. "Because from my point of view, it looks exactly like your pack used you as a decoy with the intention of throwing your life away."

I wanted to tell him he was lying, but how well did I know the group I'd come here with? Surely, Dax wouldn't agree, but what if they'd acted without him knowing? The elders had more power than I realized. What if they bypassed the alpha?

None of that mattered, though. Cavan already told me that breaking into their estate was enough to end my life. If I'm already dead, why would I take someone else with me? "I'm not a snitch."

"Is your life worth less than his?" Madoc asked.

"Life can't be ranked like that," I said. "What is wrong with you? I don't want to die, but I don't want someone else to die, either. It's not a one or the other kind of thing."

"You'd get eaten alive here," he said.

"Then I'm grateful I wasn't abandoned at the Umbra foundling house," I said darkly.

His brows furrowed. "You were dropped at the foundling house in the Fringes?"

"I've already told you I was a foundling. That's what a foundling is. Go ahead, discredit me just like everyone else," I said.

"When were you born?" he asked.

"Why do you care?" This conversation was getting very weird.

"You know what, it doesn't matter." He stood. "I can't save you if you're not willing to save yourself."

I rose and grabbed his arm. My fingers felt like they'd touched something with an electric charge. I dropped my hand and sucked in a breath. I was never going to get used to the way I felt when I touched him.

"What?" he demanded.

"What do you mean, you can't save me? You have all the power here. You could leave the door open and then not chase me down. Or you could talk to your family. I can't do shit to save myself," I said.

"How the fuck did the fates mate me with someone like you?" He shook his head. "You have the power to fight for your life, Ivy. You just lack the tenacity."

"Condemning another shifter to death isn't tenacity. It's cowardice. If that's how things run in your pack, then I'm grateful I grew up somewhere where we learned otherwise," I snapped.

"You can't be my mate," he said.

"I didn't ask for it, asshole," I said.

"Well, let's just hope there's a way to reverse it before my brothers end your life," he said.

"Aren't I the luckiest girl in the world," I deadpanned.

"You have the tools to save yourself. You just have to decide if you want to use them." He left the cell and locked the door behind him.

I wish I could say I was thrilled he was gone. Instead, my whole body ached for him so fiercely I had to hold myself back from running to the bars to call after him. *Fuck you, mating bond. You suck so hard.*

CHAPTER
THIRTY-TWO

"Good news, little wolf," Cavan said as he jingled the keys in front of the lock. "We caught one of your friends alive."

This was it. Madoc wanted me to turn Patrick in and say he was the one who was responsible for whatever it was the Umbras thought we did. I was still fuzzy on the details, or maybe that was the lack of food and water.

"I'm not sure how that's good news. And I'm also not sure how it's possible considering I have one friend and I know she's safely at home in the Fringes," I said.

"Aw, the noble outcast," Cavan said. "Will it help to know that two of your co-conspirators weren't as lucky? They didn't make it long enough to be captured."

"What?" I wasn't able to mask my surprise. Madoc hadn't mentioned that bit of news.

"They split up and ran after their attack failed, but we caught three of them holed up outside the city. They almost made it to your territory. Thankfully, the Umbra Pack has eyes everywhere. It's only a matter of time before we catch the last of your crew," he said.

"I don't understand. You captured one but killed two and you're looking for others? Why? I was the one who broke in here and you already got me."

Cavan shook his head. "I'm getting really tired of you playing dumb. Madoc thinks you honestly didn't know. I think you're just good at lying. I mean, look at that face of yours. You were built to lie to men. I bet you bat your eyelashes at home and get any shifter you want. That doesn't work here, sweetheart."

"You don't know anything about me," I said.

"I know you're sleeping with the new alpha," he said.

I had no poker face. None. The shock of his comment was completely obvious in my expression. "How did you know that?"

"We have eyes everywhere. Even in the Fringes," he said as he opened the door.

"Does everyone know about that?" I was suddenly terrified Madoc knew I was with Dax. I shouldn't care, but fear gripped me as if it was my own life on the line.

"Why do you think you're still alive? I had my doubts when Madoc said we couldn't kill you, but holding the alpha's bitch hostage will come in handy for us," he said.

"If you think he cares that I'm here, you're wasting your time," I said, again against my own fucking self-perseveration. What was wrong with me?

Cavan stepped inside the cell and closed the door

behind him. "I think I wasn't specific enough with my questions last time."

"I told you, I have no idea what you're talking about," I said. "I was sent in to find some documents. That's it. If there's anything else you're hoping to gain from me, you're going to be disappointed."

"I want to believe you, but I don't. So let's stop wasting time. Tell me the names of your crew and where I can find them. Easy. That's it," he said. "You know what? I'll make it even easier. Simply name the shifter who led your crew. Just one name."

They already had him, but it felt like signing his execution order myself if I were to name him. It wasn't like Patrick and I got along, but I couldn't bring myself to turn him in. "And if I don't?"

"You'll join the others in death," he said.

"Why do I get the feeling that I'm dead either way?" I asked.

"Because my reputation precedes me," he said.

"I thought you were the nice cop," I said.

"I am. If Madoc pays a visit, I won't be getting any more information," he said.

"So, Madoc is more dangerous?" I asked, intrigued.

"Usually," Cavan admitted.

"So send him down," I said.

"You don't know what you're asking," he replied.

"Well, I don't have anything more to say to you." Madoc was my ticket out of here. He didn't want his family to know about our mating bond, but he didn't seem to want me to die to eliminate it. I wasn't sure what that meant, but I had a sense that it was worth talking to him again now that I was a little more alert.

"Madoc is the one who ripped the throats out of your friends. His temper doesn't let him take prisoners." Cavan stepped toward the door.

My jaw clenched, and I tried to keep my expression hard. He wanted to intimidate me, but it wasn't going to work. I grew up hearing how ruthless the Umbra wolves were. It wasn't a surprise that they'd kill first. It was more of a surprise that I was still alive.

Cavan left the cell and locked it behind him. "In case you were wondering, neither of the dead were in wolf form and they were both females. I couldn't tell how pretty they were with all the blood, but I doubt your looks are going to get you out of this."

"How shallow are you, Cavan?" I shouted. "That's all you've got in your arsenal, isn't it? How sad that you can't see any depth. No wonder you're the weaker brother."

I don't think I'd ever seen anyone unlock a door as quickly as Cavan. He was in the cell, fists flying before I had a chance to do anything. I was pulled to the ground, and I covered my face and head, trying to prevent the bulk of the blows. Kicks landed in my stomach and chest, knocking the air from my lungs.

Cavan grabbed my hair, pulling me up. I screamed, clawing at his arms. "Let me go, asshole!"

I kicked him behind his knee, making him falter, but not bringing him down. Trying to twist without having all my hair ripped out was a challenge, but I managed another kick, this time going for the front of his knee. I pushed with my foot, using all my strength.

Cavan let go of me as he fell with an anguished cry. "You crazy bitch."

I took a step back and put my fists up, prepared to fight him again. My nose was gushing blood and my eye was swelling. I really needed to get that shifter healing to kick in to prevent this kind of thing. Or maybe that wasn't how this worked.

"What the fuck is going on here?" Madoc shouted as he stormed into the cell. He grabbed his brother, hauling him up like he was a child, then threw him against the wall. "Is this what I asked you to do? I told you to get a name. To get a confession. I didn't tell you to hit her."

"She was asking for it," Cavan said. He spat blood on the ground, then glared at me.

"Oh yes, the poor defenseless Cavan who couldn't handle himself against a woman who can't even shift?" Madoc tugged on his brother's shirt and pulled him away from the wall. He shoved him toward the door. "Out."

"Madoc, I had it under control," Cavan said.

"No, you didn't. Go clean yourself up before Dad sees you." Madoc's voice was laced with authority and Cavan looked like he wanted to resist, but he left all the same.

"You're the oldest, aren't you?" I asked.

"I am," he said.

"You already have some of the alpha tone when you give orders," I said.

"Only with my brothers," he admitted.

"I didn't know it worked that way," I said.

"That's because your boyfriend is an only child," he said.

"He's not my boyfriend." The words came out defensively and without thinking. Sure, Dax and I didn't have labels, and we were new, but I knew my reactive statement wasn't because of that. It was because I didn't want to hurt Madoc. I hated that I cared. Despite the stupid bond, Madoc wasn't who I wanted to be with.

He might not have harmed me, but he was a murderer. He'd killed part of my team and he had a hand in Darleen's death. I should be doing everything possible to get away from him.

"I heard otherwise," he said. "He misses you enough that he's willing to pay dearly for your safe return."

I swallowed. Really? Dax was going to get me out of here? While I'd been trapped with the Umbras, the one thing I never considered was that someone from my pack would save me.

"What? No comment?" He moved closer to me, and my heart pounded faster with each step. "I thought you'd be in a rush to get back to him."

"What are you doing, Madoc?" Everything inside me was begging me to close the distance between us. I hated how much I wanted him.

All our lives, we'd heard about how rare and precious mating bonds were. They were sacred, unbreakable gifts from the gods. It was forbidden to reject your mate, yet Madoc and I had been dancing around it since we met.

"Nobody knows the truth," he said. "And I think we both want it gone."

Part of me wanted to fight back, to demand we accept the bond, but I knew that would cause nothing but trouble for both of us. I didn't even want to be with him, but the pull was undeniable. "I don't want you."

We couldn't be together. It would ruin everything I'd worked for and probably be even worse for him. I was nothing, nobody. In the Shadows, we had rules about being with members of other packs, but the Umbras were off limits. I had a feeling the same went for his pack.

Shadows and Umbras were not compatible. We were sworn enemies, despite the strange situation of him coming to our territory for fight nights. Which made a little more sense now that I knew he'd been working with Holden. How Dax let it slide was an entirely different issue that I couldn't let myself wonder about right now. There was already too much in my head.

"We need to fix this thing between us before anyone finds out," he said.

"What are you suggesting?" I asked.

"There's a way to break the bond."

"That's impossible," I said.

"It's illegal, but it's not impossible," he assured me.

"Okay, so do it," I said.

"It's not that simple," he said.

"Of course it isn't." I sighed. "What do you want from me, Madoc?"

"First, I need you to stop saying my name," he hissed.

"Why?" My brow furrowed.

"Because it makes me want to do things to you," he admitted.

"Oh." I couldn't argue with that. I felt the same way when he'd used my name. "So what now?"

"I've put in a few calls. But in the meantime, we need distance. And we're going to have to trust one another. Nobody can ever know about this," he said.

"Not a problem," I agreed. "But I can't really keep distance from you when I'm being kept in your house."

"I'm giving you back to your pack," he said.

"What's the deal?"

"You, for Holden. I think your pack is getting the better deal on both counts," he grumbled.

I smirked. "Cause you'll miss me or because you'll have to deal with Holden?"

"Doesn't matter. You won't be my problem as soon as we make the trade," he said.

"What was going on between you and Holden?" I asked.

"That's pack business," he said.

"You might as well keep me here, then," I said. "If I go back empty-handed, none of this is going to matter."

Madoc stared at me, his brows pulled together as if he was thinking hard. I held my ground, looking back into his dark eyes. It made my stomach flip and sent a rush of desire coursing through my veins. I wanted to look away, to end the undeniable pull I felt for him, but I continued to stare him down.

"Holden and I were working on a plan to assassinate Preston, but someone from your pack beat us to it," he said.

My jaw dropped open. I hadn't expected to actually get information, and I hadn't expected it to be that juicy. In all the chaos following Preston's death, I hadn't even spent time wondering who had killed him. I guess we'd all assumed it had been someone from the Umbra pack, but if Madoc was telling the truth, they weren't involved.

"You're certain it wasn't someone from your pack?" I asked.

"Absolutely," he said.

"How do you know it was someone from my pack?" I asked.

"Because Holden knows, and he hid the information with someone else. If they kill him, the name will be revealed."

"That's a hell of a contingency plan," I said.

"Holden's been playing both sides for a long time," Madoc said. "That's why the Umbras kicked him out thirty years ago."

"What?" I couldn't believe it. Holden had been an Umbra wolf? I guess it explained his contacts for fight nights and his ability to get in touch with the alpha's son.

"Wait, I was told Holden was planning an attack with one of the alpha's sons," I said. "That's you. All the fights, all the visits to the Howler, you were trying to overthrow my pack."

"I'm done talking now." Madoc walked to the door. "The prisoner exchange happens tonight."

My mind whirled as I took in everything Madoc had said. Why did he tell me all of that? Was it because Holden was leaving the Shadows and they couldn't follow up on their plan? Or was it an elaborate way to get into my head?

If he was telling the truth, someone in my pack had killed our alpha. Why would he tell me that? And what had my pack been after when we came here?

Clearly, it wasn't just about evidence to put Holden away. The truth of what I'd been sent for hit me like a ton of bricks. They wanted the name of Preston's killer, but they hadn't wanted me to know that was what I was after.

I ran to the door and gripped the bars, instantly regretting it as I pulled my burned hands away. Hissing in pain, I shook my hands out and leaned as close to the bars as I dared. There was nobody in sight. "Madoc! Madoc!" My words echoed in the abandoned hallway.

Frantic, I ran back to the pile of papers on the floor and started sorting through them. It seemed ridiculous that the information we were after would have been so obvious. Why would it be out in plain sight? I'd been instructed to find anything that related to our pack. Anything that might implicate Holden.

I skimmed through the papers, looking at receipts and invoices. There was a flyer for lawn care and an invitation to a party. I'd grabbed the Umbra family mail and nobody seemed to care that I still had it. Junk, junk, junk... there was nothing of use in here.

Feeling defeated, I slumped against the wall and leaned my head back. I closed my eyes. Maybe I'd fall asleep and it would be time to leave when I woke up.

Footsteps sent my pulse racing. I jumped to my feet and moved to the door. Willow approached with a paper plate and a bottle of water. "Thought you might be hungry."

"Thanks." I stepped back, knowing she'd want to set it in front of the door. I was too hungry to risk not getting the meal.

"Everyone's talking about you," she said.

"That's not really a surprise. Unless you often have prisoners in your dungeon," I said.

"We do from time to time," she said. "But they always crack. We've never had someone who didn't give up their friends. My cousins can be very intimidating."

"You're the alpha's niece?" I asked.

She nodded. "My parents were killed when I was a baby. They raised me."

I'd never heard of a shifter family raising someone else's child. Where I lived, even if there was family, all orphans went to the foundling house. I wondered if this was how things were for the Umbra pack or if she was lucky since she was in the alpha's family.

"You can imagine how crazy it was with four boys and me," she said with a grin.

I eyed her suspiciously. Was she being nice to me? "I wouldn't know. I don't have any siblings."

"Right," she said. "Foundling. I heard."

"I don't need your pity," I snapped.

"It wasn't pity," she said. "You should eat. They'll be down to get you in a couple of hours."

I kept my eyes on her until she was out of sight. Willow was an anomaly. She seemed different than the others, but I couldn't trust her any more than I could trust any of them.

Glancing down at the plate made my stomach rumble. I knelt and folded the plate to get it through. This time, I had a cheese quesadilla and a pile of mini red peppers. It was another simple meal, but I wasn't in a position to complain. I wondered if Willow was the one making this for me. Nobody else seemed to care if I survived down here. Even Madoc would probably be fine with me simply fading away.

I carried the plate and bottle of water to the middle of the room and sat on the ground. As I ate, I looked around at the mess I'd made as I sorted through the papers. They were scattered into disorganized piles of random crap. All of it useless.

I frowned at the waste. I'd come here for nothing and I had to hope that the information Madoc gave me was enough to impress the elders so they'd follow through with the bargain. The only thing that might make this worth it was if I was able to gain the status I was after.

Out of the corner of my eye, I noticed an envelope

under the cot. How had I missed that? I set down the quesadilla and crawled over to the cot, sliding my hand underneath.

It was an unopened envelope. The paper was thick and expensive. Probably another party invitation. I turned it over to see who it was addressed to, and my eyes widened in surprise.

This wasn't for the Umbra family. This was addressed to the Shadow Elders. I turned the envelope over again, looking at the seal. My hands were shaking as I tore it open. Inside the envelope was a flat card with a name scrawled across it in Holden's handwriting.

My heart felt like it stopped when I read the words written on the card. I slipped it back inside the envelope and then folded it and tucked it in my bra. This was the exact evidence that I needed to prove that I'd done my job here, but it was completely useless.

There was no way I could hand over a note that claimed that Preston's killer was his own son.

CHAPTER
THIRTY-THREE

THE WEIGHT of the note in my bra kept me from sleeping. I was exhausted, but the restlessness kept me alert. The longer I sat in the cell, the more I started to question everything.

I wondered if the note was the information Holden was going to send or if it was something else. What if Madoc was playing me, and none of it was true? Just because I could feel the mating bond pulling me to him didn't mean I had to trust him.

On the flip side, I no longer felt like I could trust Dax. Sure, I'd gotten close with him. I figured I could let go of the past, but now that I was alone, I knew the one thing I'd never be able to do was trust him. Forgiveness wasn't the same thing as trust.

I pulled the card out and stared at it again. It wasn't stamped, which meant it wasn't ready to be sent. Unless someone was going to hand deliver it.

The address scrawled on the envelope matched the Hall of Records and would likely find its way to the council of elders, bypassing the alpha. What would the elders do if they got this note? It didn't even have any context.

What if it wasn't even what I thought it was? This note could be anything. I wasn't sure why I was letting myself get so worked up.

I held it up in front of me and considered tearing it in half, but stopped myself. It was making me crazy, and I didn't know what to believe.

When I heard footsteps, relief washed over me. I wasn't sure I could spend more time in here alone wondering about this document.

I stood and walked to the door, half expecting to see Cavan. Instead, Madoc greeted me with a tiny nod of his chin.

"What is this note?" I demanded, holding the envelope up. I hadn't planned on asking him, but now it was too late.

He reached through the bars and grabbed it from me. After a glance at the address, he pulled out the card. "So that's who did it."

"You're saying Dax killed his own father?" I asked.

"That's what Holden is saying," he said.

"You didn't know?"

"Holden asked us to take the letter for him in case anything happened. I never opened it and I'm not sure how you got it," he said.

"Your brother dropped off all the things I tried to steal." I felt like an idiot saying that, though now I actually did find something of value. The only problem was I couldn't use it.

Madoc held the card out to me. "Take it back home. Show it to your boyfriend. Watch him stumble over his words as he tries to make excuses."

"You know I can't do that." Shit. Why did I say so much in front of him? It was like I couldn't keep my thoughts to myself around him.

I snatched the card from him. "Is it time to go?'

"It is," Madoc said.

"Did you figure out what we're going to do about our other problem?" I asked.

"I'll contact you when I have a solution. In the meantime, try to stay on your turf."

I rolled my eyes. "Not a problem." The sooner I could get away from Umbra territory, the better.

He unlocked the door. "Don't try anything stupid. You know I can outrun you and even if you got lucky, I could find you."

"As long as you're getting me home, I'll play nice," I said.

"I'm getting you to your pack. What they do with you is their business," he said.

"Nice. Glad to see you care," I said.

He narrowed his eyes. "Don't do that."

"Do what?" I asked.

"Don't let me get in your head. That's the bond. It

makes us care about each other, but it won't be here much longer," he said.

"Well, if you were hoping to make me even less interested in you, you're succeeding," I said.

"Good. And remember, nobody can know or they won't let us break it," he said.

"You really think your dad would have you keep me?" I didn't buy it. Maybe it was the bond that was causing Madoc to look for another way out. Based on what I'd heard about the Umbras, I wouldn't be surprised if they killed me to prevent their future alpha from being with someone like me.

My stomach churned at the reminder that Madoc was the next alpha of the Umbra pack. He would be one of the most powerful shifters in the world as soon as he took over. He already probably held more power than Dax based on the fear and authority the Umbra pack claimed.

"Do you want to take the chance that they start planning our wedding?" he asked.

"No, thank you," I said.

"Then let's keep it quiet," he said. "Now, walk. We've got to get you to the exchange."

I was silent the rest of the trip. Madoc sat in the front of the dark SUV and a pair of shifters I didn't know sat on either side of me in the back seat. They weren't taking any chances, even though I'd been unsuccessful in my escape attempts. I wondered if I should be flattered or if it was all for show.

The streets were mostly empty, but the towering

buildings were lit up as if they were all open and ready for business. We sped past trees lit with colorful lights for the holidays, and down a charming street lined with cookie cutter shops decorated with painted windows. It was a completely different look than the rest of the city. I wanted to take it all in, but we moved quickly until we left all the buildings behind.

Just as the digital clock on the car dashboard turned to one o'clock, we pulled off the highway onto a dirt road. I tensed and a nervous shiver ran down my spine.

I'd been so excited about the idea of an exchange that I never thought to question it. I really, really hoped I hadn't read the whole situation wrong. I shouldn't trust Madoc, but that was all I'd done since meeting him.

I believed he was my mate; I believed he wasn't going to harm me, and I believed we were going to meet my pack.

What if I had put my trust in the wrong person? Hadn't I learned anything?

The car came to a stop. My heart pounded against my ribs and I had to work to keep my expression impassive.

Between Madoc, the driver, and the guards on either side of me, I was fucked if I needed to fight my way out of this.

"Wait here," Madoc said.

"Did I have another option?" I asked.

"Want me to shut her up, boss?" The male on my right asked.

"I'd like to see you try." I glared at him.

"Leave her be. She'll be their problem in a few minutes." Madoc opened the door and stepped out. I couldn't see anything from the view I had and wondered where he was going. Then, light illuminated the inside of the car for a moment and another vehicle approached. It parked nearby and I could see the glowing headlights.

Someone got out of the other car, but with the sharp contrast created by the lights, I couldn't see any details. A second figure joined, and I caught sight of Madoc walking over to them.

Was it really my pack? Had they really come for me?

Madoc walked to the car, then opened the back door. "It's time."

The beast of a shifter next to me got out and stood next to the car, presumably waiting for me. I scooted to the edge of the seat and climbed out. Looking toward the headlights, I tried to make out the figures, but they were still masked by the bright light.

I stopped near Madoc and he closed the distance between us, grabbing my upper arm with his hand. That familiar rush of pleasure and electricity came from his touch. I had to fight the urge to pull away or to act on the impulse to give in to desire. We walked slowly toward the waiting figures.

He leaned closer to me and spoke quietly. "Remember what I said." To my surprise, his breathing was shallow, as if he was struggling with the contact between us. It helped that it wasn't just me feeling this way.

"I don't have a death wish," I said.

"You think your pack would kill you if they knew?" He sounded concerned.

"Possibly," I said.

"Well, it won't matter because you're not going to share," he said.

"I already told you I won't," I hissed.

I felt his hand on my ass and I tried to pull away. "Hey!"

"Calm down, sugar. I'm just putting the card in your pocket." His hand seemed to linger on my ass as he slid the card into my back pocket. My own breathing was shallow now, reacting to the almost intimate touch.

I glared at him as the nickname took me right back to the first time we met.

"Would you rather I put it in your bra?" he asked.

Images of his hands caressing my breasts flooded my mind. I had to fight to push the thoughts away. "Is this how it's going to be until you break the bond?"

"Afraid so," he said, halting our progress. "Feel free to think about me when you're with your murderous boyfriend."

"As opposed to my murderous mate?" I snapped.

"You don't know anything about me," he replied.

My heart pounded, a mixture of lust and fear overwhelming my thoughts. He probably meant the words as a dig against me, but it was what I was dealing with. Was I going to be fantasizing about him until the bond was broken? And what the fuck was I supposed to do about

Dax? He was willing to kill his own father. There was nothing to keep me safe.

Before my capture, I thought I'd had some say in our relationship. Now, I wasn't sure I ever had a choice. Dax was going to take what he wanted. For some reason, his sights were set on me. If he found out about the mating bond I shared with Madoc, I got the sense it would make him want me even more. He wanted power and taking the mate of the future Umbra alpha would likely give him a sick rush.

The figures in front of me moved closer to us, and I could make out the details now. Dax was with Xander and another figure that wasn't yet in view. I should feel relief, but there was a part of me that wondered if I should beg Madoc to take me with him. Leaving him was painful, despite the fact that I didn't want this bond between us.

"Madoc." I glanced up at him, pleading with my eyes. I knew if I asked, he'd let me stay. We had a bond. He couldn't fight it either.

My mate looked like he was holding his breath, as if he was daring me to ask to stay.

"Ivy?" The unmistakable sound of Kate's voice cut through the cold air.

My heart leapt and I turned away from Madoc to see my best friend standing next to Dax. Her face was streaked with tears.

"Kate!" I nearly forgot about her. How could I have considered leaving the Fringes and running away with an Umbra wolf? What the fuck was wrong with me?

Kate was my constant. The one person in my life I could count on to be there for me through it all. She was my only friend; my only family. The man standing next to me was my mate, but not because I chose him. Kate was by my side when it could have cost her everything, but she never turned on me.

Madoc can barely stand the sight of me.

I tugged my arm free of his grip, but he grabbed me again, and pulled me closer. I gasped at the sudden feel of his body against mine. I hated that I felt warm and safe by being close to him when he was the opposite of all of that.

"Where's Holden?" Madoc demanded.

"Release Ivy," Dax demanded.

"I don't think so," Madoc said.

"Take your hands off her so I see she's free, then you can have your traitorous friend back," Dax said.

Madoc tightened his fingers on my arm.

"You're hurting me," I whispered.

Madoc released me suddenly, dropping his hands to his side. "Fine. Happy? Now, give me Holden."

"Ivy, are you okay?" Kate said through tears.

"I'm okay," I said.

Dax nodded to someone in the car, and a door opened. A large figure emerged and limped forward. Once Holden was visible in the light, I could see his injured face and torn clothes. He had not been treated well while he'd been in captivity.

Then again, I probably looked similarly. I hadn't showered and the injuries from Cavan were likely still healing.

"Send Ivy over or I'll shoot the bastard in the back, like he deserves," Dax said.

Holden took a few steps forward, then stopped.

I looked up at Madoc, a sense of dread making my chest feel heavy. I had to leave. The two of us shouldn't be together. We would never work. Us together was a mistake.

But that didn't mean the pain I felt was any less.

"Go," Madoc said through gritted teeth.

His expression was indifferent, and I was surprised how much that hurt. I leaned into that, reminding myself I wasn't wanted and that I didn't want him. Leaning into the pain of Madoc's rejection, I took a few steps forward.

Kate walked ahead, her hands clasped together near her chin. She looked like she was trying to keep herself from running forward.

I focused on her. Things with Dax were complicated before I left, and now they were impossible. Thank the gods for the constant of Kate.

She charged forward, and I picked up speed, the two of us meeting in an embrace. Her tears made me cry and the two of us hugged and cried for a good minute before she wrapped her arm over my shoulder and walked me back to the others.

"Ivy." Dax ran to me, sweeping me up in his arms and lifting me off the ground. He set me down and buried his head in my hair. "I thought I'd never see you again." He pulled away, his hands cupping my cheeks. "What did they do to you?"

I set my hands on top of his, aware of how wrong our contact now felt. "I'm okay."

"I'm going to make them pay for this. I swear it to you," he said.

"Can we go home?" I asked.

He kissed me on the forehead. "Of course. You must be exhausted."

Dax slid his arm around my waist and walked me to the car. I turned back and glanced at my captors. Holden was already in the car with the others. Only Madoc stood outside, his eyes fixed on me. I could feel the intensity of his gaze.

My heart ached with every step I took away from him, but aside from running back to him, there was nothing I could do.

Once the bond was broken, I wouldn't have to worry about this anymore. I'd be free from him. Free from the monsters that were the Umbra pack.

"Go ahead, Ivy," Dax said as he held the car door open for me. "It's time to get you home where you belong."

I returned my gaze to Dax and fixed a smile on my face.

As I climbed into the car, I realized, I was trading one monster for another.

CHAPTER
THIRTY-FOUR

To my great relief, Dax sat in the passenger seat while Xander drove and Kate took the spot next to me in the back.

"We should get you to the hospital," Kate said, as Xander pulled the car onto the road.

"I don't need a hospital," I said.

"You look awful," she said.

"It's really not so bad," I said.

"I bet she gave them hell. Right, sweetheart?" Dax said.

I bristled at the term of endearment, but pushed it aside. "You should have seen the other guy."

"That's my girl," Dax said.

It seemed Dax was picking up right where we left off. I couldn't process everything about Dax right now. That was going to take some time and space. You'd think after my time alone, I'd want some company, but my body wasn't craving Dax. Besides, I wasn't sure what to think about Dax. Was the note in my pocket telling the truth? It was too much.

"You sure you're okay?" Kate asked.

"I'm sure. I really need a shower. And a good meal," I said.

Kate grabbed my hand. "I'm so grateful you're alive."

"How long was I gone?" I asked.

"Four days," Kate said.

"No wonder I'm hungry," I said.

"They didn't feed you?" Dax said with a growl.

"I slept a lot," I said. "One of the shifters was kind, and she brought me food." For some reason, I felt the need to defend them a little. Cavan was terrible, but Willow had shown some kindness. Then there was Madoc. Though it was likely Madoc would have killed me if not for the bond.

"That doesn't make up for what they did to you," Dax said.

"I broke into their house," I said. "What would you have done?"

"You were set up. Patrick told them about our plan. You never had a chance," he said. "Turns out we found out who was helping Holden."

"What?" The Umbras had mentioned that someone from my crew turned on me, but I thought they were trying to get me to talk. "They told me they captured Patrick and wanted me to turn against him. I refused."

"Not everyone is as loyal as you," Dax said.

"They said they killed two of my team. Is that true?" I said.

"Farrah and Marsha are dead," Dax confirmed.

"None of you even had a chance, and we didn't know until it was too late," Xander added.

"The Umbras told me something while I was locked up." I licked my lips and wondered if I should continue.

"They are known for twisting the truth or outright lying," Xander said.

"What did they tell you?" Dax asked, his voice laced with concern.

"They said I was a decoy, and the others were after their alpha. But I thought we were only after information," I said.

"We wouldn't risk a war with the Umbras," Dax said quickly. "We just needed that evidence against Holden."

"Did you find anything?" Xander asked.

"Xander," Dax hissed, then he turned around to look at me. "Ignore him. None of that matters. We're just glad you're safe."

Dax was saying all the right things, but the card in my pocket felt like I was sitting on a bomb, ready to explode. I had done this for a reason. I wanted my debt paid, and I wanted to be full Shadow pack. If I gave them nothing, the risks I took were wasted.

While Dax had essentially given me a way out of saying anything, I knew I had to provide something if I was going to ask the elders to keep their end of the bargain. Simply surviving capture wasn't going to be enough. Especially since my life had cost them a prisoner.

I knew I had to say something, but I wasn't sure what to share. The only thing I knew I couldn't do was give the information in my pocket. There had to be something else of value.

We were quiet for a while and I considered my options. Finally, a thought struck me. Holden was safe, but I wasn't. My gut twisted uncomfortably as I considered what I was about to do, but what choice did I have?

"Dax, I did find out something, but I don't have proof."

He turned to look at me. "What?"

"We were right. The Umbra wolves were trying to take out your dad," I said. "Holden was in on it."

Dax looked disappointed. "We already knew that, Ivy."

"I found out that Holden is the one who did it," I lied. "He wanted to defect to the Umbra wolves, and that was his offering to re-join."

If Dax killed his father, he would know I was lying, but I was offering a perfect out for him. The villain responsible was gone and couldn't stand up for himself, and Dax wouldn't ever be a suspect. He could use my lie as cover for his misdeed.

"He came from the Umbra pack, didn't he?" Xander asked.

"He did," Dax said. "Before my dad was even alpha."

"That explains his connections there and why he hosted those fight nights. He was trying to get into their good graces. Probably held those fights to meet important people," Xander said.

I recalled Dax and Madoc in the ring. Dax knew who Madoc was. Why had he allowed him to fight in our territory?

"I wanted to be more open than my father," Dax said. "But now I see why he was so strict on keeping the borders closed. We can't allow this to happen again. We have to keep our pack safe. The Umbra wolves have declared war with this act."

Dax was going to run with this. I felt a little guilty throwing Holden under the bus, but he wasn't here and if he was friends with Madoc, I got the feeling he'd be protected.

"I can't believe Holden would kill the alpha," Kate said. "Though, I suppose he's done some super shady shit."

The sympathy I'd felt seconds ago drained away as I recalled that Holden *was* a killer. He might not have killed Preston, but he'd killed Darleen and her boyfriend. There wouldn't be any repercussions for killing a shifter who didn't matter. Darleen had a higher status than me, yet nobody even mourned her death. Perhaps this was the only way Holden could be punished for his actions.

"Ivy, do you think you'd be up for sharing this information with the council?" Dax asked.

"Of course," I said.

"I'll set up a meeting after you get some time to rest." He reached back and set his hand on mine. I pulled away reflexively.

A dark look crossed his face.

"Sorry, I'm still a little jumpy from my ordeal," I said.

His expression softened. "Of course."

The rush of cold passed through me without warning and I realized we were crossing back into Shadow territory. "We're home."

"Welcome back, Ivy," Kate said.

"Do you want to stay at my place?" Dax offered. "I have extra security."

"Thank you for the offer, but I'd like to have my own clothes and shower and bed," I said.

"I'll send some guards over to keep watch," Dax said.

"Thank you, Dax," Kate said.

"Yeah, thanks," I added. The gesture sounded nice on the surface, but I couldn't help but feel like I was still a prisoner.

Dax walked me to my front door, lingering outside with me after Kate had gone in. "You sure you don't want to stay at my place?"

"I'm sure. I could use the familiar space tonight," I said.

"Do you want me to stay with you?" he asked.

That was the absolute last thing I wanted. We'd just barely started a relationship that wasn't antagonistic, yet he was acting as if we were already an official couple. I shouldn't be surprised. He'd made his intentions with me clear from the beginning. Though I wasn't sure why. If Madoc was telling the truth, had the plan always been for me to be sacrificed? If that was the case, did Dax know?

Was it a matter of time before he would do something to eliminate me?

The thought sent a shudder through me.

Dax rubbed his hands up and down my arms, probably thinking I was cold. "Why don't you get some rest."

I nodded. "Thanks."

"Call me when you're up," he said. "The elders need to hear what you discovered."

"I will," I said. "Thank you for getting me out of there."

"Of course I got you out of there." His brow furrowed. "Did you think I wouldn't come for you?"

"I wasn't sure," I admitted.

He lifted my chin with his index finger and locked his eyes on mine. "I will always come for you. You stole my heart, there's nobody else."

"What if you find your true mate?" I asked.

"I'm not sure I believe in that," he said.

"But your parents and Stacey... it happens, then it changes everything." My stomach tightened with guilt.

"I've met every shifter in the Fringes over the years. There's been no spark with anyone but you," he said.

What if your mate is outside the Fringes? I thought about Madoc and how intense the attraction was between us. There was nothing close to that between me and Dax. But Dax was the Shadow Alpha. Unless his mate happened to get sent here, it was possible he'd never meet his mate. Not everyone found theirs.

"You went through a lot," he said, a touch of hurt in his tone. "We can talk about this more later."

No matter what I thought about Dax, I needed to stay on his good side. It was going to take time to work everything out. I'd already told one lie. What harm was it to play along with him while I waited for Madoc to break our bond? I needed to gain my full pack status, at the very least. If I was going to end things with Dax, I needed to make him feel like it was his choice. That would take a little time, but I was confident I could pull it off.

I stood on my tiptoes and kissed his cheek. "Thank you for being my hero."

Dax smiled, then captured my jaw and turned my face to his. He pressed his lips to mine gently. The kiss was sweet and quick, but everything about it felt like a lie.

"Sleep well, my Ivy," he said.

My name on his lips sounded wrong. "You, too." I stepped into my apartment and closed the door behind me. When I turned, I saw Kate waiting for me in the living room.

"Do you want to talk now or do you need some time?" she asked.

I wanted to tell her everything, but there was too much to work out. The lines between fiction and reality were blurred, and I wasn't sure who I should trust.

My pack wasn't known for playing by the rules, but then again, neither were the Umbras.

The only thing I knew was that I was stuck in the middle of something more complicated than I realized. Before I shared with Kate, I had to be certain the information I was giving her was accurate. And it had to be done in a way that wouldn't put her at risk.

"I kind of just want to shower and sleep," I said. "But I wouldn't turn down a snack."

"No tea?" she teased.

"I don't think that's going to fix me right now," I said.

"Grilled cheese and tomato soup coming up," she said. "You shower. I'll make food."

I pulled her in for a tight hug, then released her. Nothing in my life made sense anymore, but at least I had Kate.

CHAPTER
THIRTY-FIVE

Kate had managed to cover most of my injuries with makeup while I sipped her grandmother's tea. It was disgusting, but it made her happy. Plus, she was so much better at makeup than I was.

Despite the fact that I knew I looked a lot better than I felt, I was more nervous than I had been the whole time I was locked up.

In the Umbra estate, I figured I was as good as dead anyway, so none of my actions felt like they mattered much. That wasn't the case here at the Hall of Records for my meeting with the elders.

Maybe it was the formal setting that was getting to me. I'd met most of the elders in Dax's house before my failed heist. I wasn't sure why they'd insisted I come here, but at least it was neutral territory for me and Dax.

"You haven't spoken much," Dax said. "How are you feeling?"

I glanced over at him. We were sitting on a bench outside a conference room, waiting our turn. "I guess I'm just nervous about this."

He took my hand and squeezed. "You're going to be fine. The elders loved you when they met you before and they're pissed about what the Umbras did to you."

"Right." I was still struggling with the fact that I had violated the treaty. I crossed into Umbra territory and broke into their home. Dax kept acting like the Umbras were in the wrong, but the guilt I felt at my part in it continued to gnaw at me. Add in the fact that I was flat out lying about Holden, and I was in a very murky space morally.

All these years, I saw myself as the one who stayed on the right side of the law. I took what I thought was a legit job and kept to myself. My pack was known for its back alley deals and gray areas. I had done all I could to keep my nose clean. This whole thing was really messing with my sense of self. There wasn't even a job waiting for me at the Howler when this was over.

And it wasn't actually over. Not when I had a mating bond I couldn't tell anyone about. Madoc flooded into my thoughts and I wondered what he was doing right now. Did he find himself thinking about my eyes or the curve of my smile?

Because I couldn't get him out of my head. It was enough to make someone feel a little crazy.

The door opened, and I nearly jumped off the bench.

"Hey, it's alright. Nobody here is going to hurt you. I'll be with you the whole time." Dax said soothingly.

He was being so sweet and supportive, which added another layer to my constant confusion.

"Ivy, we'll see you now." Benjamin, the council leader, was standing in front of the open door.

I stood and let out a slow breath. This shouldn't be a big deal. I just had to tell them the same thing I told Dax, and they'd rule on what came next.

Dax kept hold of my hand as the two of us walked into the room. He released my hand and took a seat in a row of chairs behind a podium.

I walked up to the podium and looked up at the bench along the back wall. The elders were seated in a row facing me. Each one had a microphone and a little plaque with their name displayed.

Benjamin took his seat in the center of the group. Three elders sat on either side of him. All the elders were middle-aged males and while I knew all of them by reputation, I had no idea what they were really like.

"Welcome back, Ivy," Benjamin said.

"Thank you," I said.

"We are glad that you survived your captivity, though we are curious to see what your safe return bought us."

I blinked a few times. They were expecting something good, and I wasn't sure I could deliver.

"You were traded for a valuable prisoner as a favor to our alpha, who seems to have a soft spot for you," Benjamin said.

My cheeks burned. I didn't realize Dax may have had to pull rank to work this deal. "Thank you for bringing me home safely."

Benjamin nodded once. "Dax says your adventure wasn't fruitless. What do you have to share?"

"I learned that the Umbra pack was working with Holden and that they agreed to accept him back into their pack if he killed our alpha," I said.

The elders leaned into each other and I heard whispers. My pulse raced, and I wondered what they were discussing. If my story was to be believed, they'd released the alpha's killer to rescue me. Suddenly, I wasn't sure my lie was going to help me much. Who was I? Some foundling nobody cared about. Surely, they didn't think I was worth losing the chance to punish the shifter who murdered their alpha.

"You're certain?" Benjamin asked.

I nodded, hoping they couldn't feel the nervous energy rolling off me in waves.

"Holden worked alone?" Benjamin confirmed.

I nodded. Internally, I was screaming. The note was safely hidden in my closet and even if anyone found it, they wouldn't know what it meant.

Holden wasn't here. I was. If I turned in Dax, my life was over and I knew it. This was the only way.

"Where did you get this information?" Benjamin asked.

"Madoc Umbra," I said. "He told me when he informed me there had been a trade made for my safe return."

The elders conferred with each other again, rushed whispers and glances my way. I was terrified one of them was going to call me out or that they were going to punish me for losing Holden.

Finally, they turned to look at me again. I lifted my chin and forced myself to keep my expression calm. There was no place for fear in the Shadows.

"Ivy Shadow, you have done a great service to your pack," Benjamin said. "We have agreed to honor the alpha's request and will eliminate your debt."

I couldn't hold back my emotion. Tears welled in my eyes, and I bit down on my lip to keep from screaming in joy.

Benjamin smiled. "Congratulations, Ivy. You are officially a full member of the Shadow Pack."

"Thank you," I said, my voice thick with emotion.

I might not have gone about it in the way I planned, but this was my dream. No more foundling status for me. No more restrictions or rules to keep me from going after bigger dreams. Sure, I had no idea what those dreams were, but now I could start to plan.

"I'm sure this goes without saying, but the events of your capture and the information you learned are confidential," Benjamin said.

I nodded. "Of course."

"The Elders or the alpha may call on your services again," Benjamin said.

I tensed. What did that mean? "I got caught. I'm lucky I survived."

"You're the only one who has ever escaped capture by the Umbras. From our perspective, you weren't just lucky, you were good," Benjamin said.

I forced a smile onto my face and nodded. "Of course." My head was spinning as I accepted Dax's hand and exited the council chambers.

A deep, sinking sense of dread hung over me. Would they really make me do something like this again? I only signed on to get my debt wiped, and I'd achieved that goal.

"I'm so proud of you," Dax said.

"Thank you," I said. "For everything."

"I told you, I'll always come for you," he said.

Before my capture, those words might have sounded sweet. Now, they felt more like a threat. I was in way over my head.

"What are you going to do now that you're a full pack member?" he asked.

"I have no idea. I've worked so long to reach that goal, but it always felt like it was just out of reach," I said.

"You've got time to figure it out," he said. "And don't worry, I told the council you needed at least two weeks before they sent you back out on a job."

I stopped walking. We were standing on the stairs outside the Hall of Records. "I don't want to go work for the council. I nearly died. That kind of work really isn't for me."

"I'll see what I can do," Dax said. "But they think you

got solid intel out of the Umbra pack. That's not something they're going to give up easily."

"Look at what happened to the others. Most of them didn't make it home," I said.

"That's because they had different orders than you," he said.

"What do you mean?" I asked.

"You already know, don't you?" he asked.

"What do I know?"

"That Holden didn't kill my dad," he said. "I have to admit, I had my doubts about you, but after what you just did, I know I can trust you."

"Oh, that," I said, feeling breathless.

"I'm sorry I used you as a decoy," he said. "I wouldn't have done it if I didn't think you'd survive."

"You really did send me in to distract them. You tried to take out their alpha," I said.

"The elders would never approve, but it has to be done. They've gotten too bold. It's time for us to rise from the Shadows, Ivy. And you're going to help me," he said.

"You sent me in to get captured," I pulled my hand from his. "They wanted to kill me."

"But they didn't," he said. "I had my suspicions, but your survival confirms it."

Did he know about Madoc? That was impossible. How could he know that? He'd seen us interact once at a fight, but that wasn't enough to know about our bond, was it? If he knew, I had to hear it from him. "What are you even talking about?"

"There was something interesting in your folder," Dax said. "I went and got it the night after our fight. You were too strong for someone who'd never shifted."

"Dax, explain." Anger was making my chest feel hot.

"You're not a full shifter, Ivy," he said.

"What are you talking about?" I demanded. "You saw me shift."

He reached for my face, and I batted his hand away. He grinned. "That fight in you, that's more than just wolf shifter blood. Your father was something else. Something ancient and powerful. It's why your mother abandoned you. She was afraid of what you'd grow into. But I'm not. I want you by my side. Together, we'll make the other packs pay for what they've done to us. The Shadow Pack will be something to be proud of instead of a place where they send their rejects. It's time for us to take that power."

Dax's eyes shined with excitement, and I could feel the energy radiating from him. He was serious about this. Serious about me being part *something else* and about taking over the other packs.

"Dax, you're wrong. There's nothing special about me." He seemed to think I'd survived due to some unique skill, when in reality it was a mating bond that had saved me.

"Your parents gave you a gift, Ivy," he said.

"My parents abandoned me. I don't want anything to do with them."

"You'll change your mind after you train," he assured me.

"There has never been anything different or special about me. What makes you think it would suddenly show now?" I demanded.

"It wasn't awake before. Why do you think I wanted you to shift?" he asked. "It's the first step in waking your power. Don't worry, I'll be here to help you every step of the way. Once you're able to master it, there will be no stopping you. Nothing stopping *us*."

This was far worse than anything I could have imagined. It felt like I was still a prisoner, trapped by something beyond my control. He didn't want me for anything other than the blood running in my veins. How had I not seen this before? Dax was insistent on us being a couple, even without a mating bond. That wasn't normal. Especially not for him.

I'd been blinded by my need to fit in; to be a part of the Shadow Pack. Now that I was, though, it all felt wrong. I never fit in here and I wasn't sure I even wanted to.

"What do you think, Ivy? You and me, we're going to burn it all down and build everything back up. With the Shadow Wolves at the very top. With *us* at the top." Dax's greedy expression was too calculated to be a farse. He was serious about this. He really believed that something inside me was strong enough to overthrow the other packs.

If Dax was right, and there was something powerful inside of me, I needed to learn how to use it. My parents might have left me to fend for myself, but if they gave me something that would make me stronger, I needed to use it.

But I wasn't going to master it for his sake, or even for the pack. All I'd ever wanted was my freedom, and even now as a full member of the Shadow pack, I wasn't free. Dax wanted me for something I wasn't even sure existed, and the elders wanted to use me to help their causes.

If I had a power I didn't know about, I had to find it. And then I could free myself from everyone once and for all.

I opened my mouth to speak, but a surge of heat and pain more intense than anything I'd ever felt ripped through me. It cut deeper than the fangs in my leg and I felt as if I might be split in two. An agonized scream filled my ears, the sound making my head feel like it was going to explode.

I fell to my knees and covered my ears, desperate to make the pain stop. It was endless and pulled me deeper, dragging me toward something. Then I felt a tug deep in my gut, a connection I hadn't felt since I'd left the Umbras. Madoc's face flashed before my eyes, then the pain faded.

Panting and shaking, I moved to my knees, trying to grasp what had just happened. I'd felt Madoc. I knew the moment of sheer agony was his pain, not mine. It didn't matter if Madoc and I wanted the bond broken, we were still connected. And he was in big trouble.

Thank you for reading *Darkest Mate*!

Find out what happens next for Ivy and Madoc!
Book Two, Forbidden Sin, is available on Amazon

Want a scene from Madoc's Point of View?
Sign up for my Newsletter to get a bonus scene!

About the Author

Alexis Calder writes sassy heroines and sexy heroes with a sprinkle of sarcasm. She lives in the Rockies and drinks far too much coffee and just the right amount of wine.

Printed in Great Britain
by Amazon